D1562523

CHAOS THEORY

the sanguine crown series

BOOK 1

BY: SUSAN HARRIS

CHAOS THEORY
Copyright ©2020 Susan Harris
All rights reserved.
Printed in the United States of America
First Edition: May 2020

CLEAN TEEN PUBLISHING
WWW.CLEANTEENPUBLISHING.COM

Summary: The vampire race is on the brink of extinction, and their fate now rests on the shoulders of an unlikely pair. When Ryan Callan is sent to the human world to protect her former best friend—the Crowned Prince Nickolai—she has to put her differences with him aside when a rogue vampire threatens to reveal the existence of vampires to the world.

ISBN: 978-1-63422-389-8 (paperback)
ISBN: 978-1-63422-388-1 (e-book)
Cover Design by: Marya Heidel
Typography by: Courtney Spencer
Editing by: Chelsea Brimmer

Young Adult Fiction / Vampires
Young Adult Fiction / Paranormal / Romance
Young Adult Fiction / Paranormal, Occult & Supernatural
Young Adult Fiction / Royalty

For more information about our content disclosure, please utilize the QR code above with your smart phone or visit us at www.CleanTeenPublishing.com

Anita Blake, Rose Hathaway, Cat Crawfield, Merit, Elena Deveraux, Darian, Celaena Sardothien, Charley Davidson, Mercy Thompson, Faythe Saunders and Kate Daniels.
This book is a labour of love for me and is dedicated to the fierce females of fiction who came before Ryan and the authors who created them.
Because, without them, I would never have found such amazing inspiration for Ryan Callan.
Chaos Theory pays homage to the books that came before me.

Prologue

SCREAMS RANG OUT FROM BELOW STAIRS, STOPPING ME MID-pounce as I lunged toward Prince Nickolai, who was pre-pared to parry with his own wooden bokken, ready to block my advancement. Even at seven years old, I knew how to wield a sword, all too aware I would wield one for my future king someday, the princeling who now glared at me with fear in his eyes.

Dropping the bokken, I raced over to the door of the prince's playroom and, finding it slightly ajar, peered into the hall. It was chaos. Vampires raced about, pulling axes and swords—whatever they could find—from the walls of the royal quarters before rushing off.

The scent of blood permeated the air, forcing my fangs to slip free of my gums and a hiss to whistle through my lips. Nickolai came up behind me, just as eager to see what had sent the older vampires into such a state. My eyes darted over to where Prince Kristoph lay, fast asleep and oblivious to what was occurring right under his nose.

"Let me out, Ryan. I want to see what is going on!"

I ignored the prince's order; even though he was older than me, I was the better fighter. Everyone was afraid of hurting the heir to the sanguine throne, but not me. I had no issue punching him square in the jaw if the circumstances called for it.

I growled in response, turning and shoving him back into the room. "Someday, your nose will get you in trouble," I said, glaring with my hands on my hips.

Nickolai made to retort, no doubt ready to lord his elder two years over me as he tended to do, but my mother slipped into the room, her beautiful cheeks streaked with blood. Dropping to her knees, she cradled my face in her hands and pressed her lips to my forehead.

"What is it, Momma? Where is Father?"

Brushing back the errant strands of my long blonde hair, Mother held my gaze for a moment before answering. In her eyes, I saw such sorrow, as if a sadness had been ingrained in her soul.

"Your father is exactly where he is meant to be, protecting the king."

"What is happening?" Prince Nickolai asked in a small voice. "Are my parents okay?"

My mother smiled over at the worried prince as if to reassure him. "We are doing all we can, Nickolai. Some very bad vampires want to hurt your parents, but I will not allow it."

My mother was a warrior, yet I had never seen her more afraid than she was in that moment. She ordered Nickolai to wake his brother and take him to one of the hiding places built into the walls—the ones to which, should the worst happen, we were trained to run. It seemed that time was now.

Even as she placed a finger on my chin and lifted my gaze to hers, tears began to cascade down her cheeks.

"Ryan, my beautiful, smart, headstrong daughter, know we love you, your father and I." Reaching down to her waist, she handed me one of her sai, keeping the other one close to her. "Take this and protect the princes. You do not hesitate, my girl. This is what you were born to do. You are destined to protect them."

My mother placed the sai into my palm and curled my fingers around the hilt. I wanted to say something, I wanted to beg her to stay, to protect us and not the king but I would never voice the words; my parents were born to protect the royal family from those who meant them harm. One day I would do the same.

My heart raced faster as a bloodcurdling scream came from just outside the door and my mother shooed us into the small cupboard hidden within the walls. She ordered me to not come out until someone came for us, someone we knew. And to kill any who tried to harm the princes. With a final glance, she told me she loved me one more time and then slid the door back into place. Darkness flooded the cramped space.

I wasn't sure how much time passed as Nickolai muttered comforting words to his brother while the screams and the scent of blood intensified even in our hiding place. We stayed there for what felt like an eternity, with me crouched in front of the princes, my lone sai a comforting weight in my palm, my fangs extended as I snarled and waited for my parents to come back, take me in their arms, and tell me everything was okay.

Some hours later, Queen Katerina came to let us out of the darkness, nodding as I finally lowered my sai, the muscles in my young arms burning, adrenaline suddenly wearing off.

As we stepped out into the playroom once again, my eyes darted around in search of my parents. When I looked back *at the queen, my mother's best friend, I knew. I knew no one was coming back for me.*

I ran from the room, searching for their bodies, ignoring the sound of Nickolai calling my name.

Chapter 1

"BITCH, PLEASE. WAS THAT SUPPOSED TO HURT?"

It had indeed hurt.

The pain from Zayn's punch rattled the common sense in my head and knocked me to my knees. Shockwaves of fiery agony travelled down the underside of my jaw and along the nerves in my face until my ears rang and my vision blurred. Spitting blood onto the mat, I marked movement in the corner of my vision, an animalistic snarl snapping me back to attention as I dropped and rolled out of his grasp and crouched before him, beckoning him forward with the flick of my fingers.

The rumble in his chest gave away his irritation, but I was used to being considered an irritation by most of the Royal Guard. I was the only female in the training group, and the only one who would not bend to the social restrictions my species put upon me. The human world may have evolved and changed to treat women as equal to their men, but that could not be said of the vampires.

Zayn and I were almost the same age, him recently

turning eighteen and me having just had my seventeenth. He had a good foot in height over me, his shoulders were strong and broad, and his fists felt like shovels hitting me; yet I had made it through most of my life faced with people who underestimated me because I, according to some, looked like a Nordic princess: petite and pretty, with ice-blonde hair and eyes of lavender. Of course, most usually followed it with a comment about keeping my mouth shut.

In all my years of working my ass off to be within a sliver of a chance of becoming one of the Royal Guard—the soldiers who guarded the royal family—and fulfil my life's mission, I'd learned one thing that gave me an advantage: During their later teen years, all males' tempers were frayed easily. And frayed tempers led to costly mistakes.

With eyes narrowed and fangs in full view as Zayn's lips curled into a snarl, he launched forward, his hand reaching for me. Ducking under his arm, I elbowed him in the gut and used his momentum against him, tucking my leg around his and taking us both to the ground. Zayn hit the ground face-first as I landed with my knee pressed into the small of his back, his arm twisted back, using my vampiric strength to keep rotating his arm until he slapped the mat in defeat.

I let go of his arm, rose, and held out my hand to help Zayn off the ground as he rolled onto his back. With a sneer, he knocked away my hand and clambered to his feet unaided as I sighed and rolled my eyes. A giggle sounded behind me, and it took all my willpower not to turn and glare at the area from which the sound had come. The female vampires always came by on Fridays to watch the men train and spar, hoping to see me get my ass kicked.

Swallowing down the bite of loneliness threatening to wash over me, I walked off the mat, flicking my tongue out and tasting the blood on my lips. My jaw would no doubt swell, but at least I'd managed to hold onto my teeth this time. We may heal from most wounds by drinking blood, but growing back a tooth still hurt almost as much as healing a broken bone.

I pulled a bottle of water from the cooler and gulped it down, stealing a glance over at my class as they huddled together, clapping each other on the back while laughing and joking. I'd felt separated from them since my entire world shattered when I was seven years old and my parents were murdered.

My breath caught in my chest as I remembered the aftermath of the coup that had stolen both my parents from me, leaving me alone in the world, an orphan to be pitied. Even now, people still speak of the image of me, lying between my parents, covered in their blood and refusing to move for hours, snarling at anyone who tried to pry my little hands from theirs.

My parents had sacrificed their lives protecting the king and queen as was their solemn vow, a vow that had both brought them together and torn them from me. Everyone had loved my parents. My father, Tristan, was the king's right-hand man; my mother, Imogen, was lifelong friends with the queen. Neither had a bad word to say about another person; they smiled easily and laughed even more so. I remembered the way my father looked at my mother with complete devotion, and my mother obviously felt the same.

Shoving down my melancholy, I tensed as my class-mates strode past me, Zayn Nasir muttering under his breath as Kingsley Day sneered and knocked into my shoulder, calling me "Frosty" as he did. The gaggle of admirers laughed as they followed the boys out, and I hissed, flashing my fangs as I started forward, ready to retaliate.

"Ryan, enough."

I spun to glare at Idris Nasir, the vampire who had replaced my father as head of the Royal Guard. His brow arched as he held my gaze and I tried to reign in my tem-per. I opened my mouth to argue but quickly snapped it shut when I realized whining to Zayn's father was use-less. I'd be the one left polishing their weapons because I had dared to stomp all over the boys' club.

My fists clenched and unclenched by my sides, and I sank my teeth into my tongue to stop from unleashing a scathing comment. I stood there, seething with rage as the training room cleared out, leaving me alone—a place where I was entirely at home. The moment the door swung shut, I flung the empty water bottle across the room and growled, the sound rumbling in my chest as I closed my eyes and tried to calm myself.

It took a little bit of time, calming myself, the dawn a long time away. But it was always around the time of my parents' anniversary that I fought hardest against the tide of my emotions. Every year was another stab in the chest, reopening the never fully healed wound. Ev-ery year I had to stand beside the royal family, in front of people who despised me, and acknowledge how my fierce warrior parents had died so they could live. Every year it broke me even more.

Pulling out my phone, I untangled my headphones, popping them into my ears as I lay down on the ground, needing the peace and tranquility to drown out the overwhelming silence of my life. I set my legs on the bench in front of me, my back flat against the ground, heavy bass in my ear as I began to lift my upper body in time with the beat, the burn in my muscles my only friend.

The human world had changed over the years—advances in technology, medicine, human rights, climate—however, us vampires had yet to emerge from the shadows, rebelling against changes in the human world that set us on a path toward the eventual extinction of our species.

Everything you thought you knew about vampires is wrong. The movies and TV shows – Vampires are born not created, carried within their mothers just like humans. So yes, before you ask, technically it is possible to have a child with a human, creating a dhampir, but those children are often quite sickly, their physiology unable to cope with the vampire gene. Some clans, like ours under the reign of the Royal House of Romanov, believe that for survival of true vampires, one must only breed with one's own kind, and I guess it kind of makes sense.

Anyway, back to the truth about vampires. Yes, we drank blood to survive; yes, we could compel someone to forget if we needed to; and yes, sunlight burned like a mother; but no, we weren't soulless creatures who crept from graves after death to suck life from the living. The changing times made it harder and harder for us to feed. Humans were less easily compelled, less likely to believe a falsehood these days, and therefore not good for us to snack on. And while we had some human families who worked for the crown, and had done so since the Romanov line came into power, they weren't enough to sustain us all.

We used to live among the humans before the attempt to overthrow the monarchs, leaving the royal families of the sanguine crown now confined to the royal compound, shutting out the human world as much as possible. We still had to hunt—that was a given—but with humans being so much more clued in with their technology implants and skeptical natures, the murmurs around the compound hinted that if we could not find a solution, vampires could be extinct within twenty years. After all, there were only so many blood bags a girl could drink before she started to lose her strength.

The Romanovs had been in power since the time of the Grand Duchess Anastasia Romanov, the famed Russian princess who disappeared. In fact, Anastasia was a vampire, though how she became one was the stuff of myths and legends. Our current queen, Katerina Romanov, was a direct descendant of hers and sat on the throne alongside her husband, King Anatoly, ruling over the eight families of the Sanguine Sovereignty Council. The court of Romanov was the responsible for the governance of the European vampires, and while we weren't the only court in the world, we held the most territory.

Seven... There were only seven now. House Callan did not have enough members to form a family. I was not enough by myself. Unless I conceded and stepped away from the Royal Guard to procreate, House Callan would remain forever dormant.

Another arcane rule brought in after the deaths of my parents.

So now the council was made up of seven families—think high society but with fangs—Nasir, Day, Reeser, Johnson, Hamilton, St. Clair, and Smyrnoi. Vampire families from around the world. Every half-century, the court was moved to a different country because if we stayed in one place for too long, people became suspicious.

My father had been delighted when the court decided to convene in Ireland, his home country, but we had been here for only three years when they were killed. Lots of vampires had died that day, the day we were betrayed by those within our confidence. Entire families had been wiped out. Our numbers were now less than a hundred true-born vampires.

Not as glamourous as the books and movies made it out to be, was it?

Our aging process also differed from what humans portrayed in books and movies. We weren't frozen at the age we became vampires; rather, we aged until around our mid-twenties, depending on the individual. Our bodies then slowed, a decade of human life the equivalent to one year in vampire time. Up until then, we aged just like humans—other than that, we were nothing like them.

Vampires were preternaturally stronger and faster, with sharper senses. A vamp toddler could manage to lift a car just a tad. At full strength, a male vampire could stop a train in its tracks. I was stronger than the average female vampire, but only because I made it so. I wasn't content to sit around and paint my nails, hoping to catch the eye of a suitable male—especially one whose family was of notability.

The only reason I was indulged was because my mother and Queen Katerina had been as close as sisters.

My mother had defied social conventions to become the first woman in the Royal Guard. All our histories tell the story of Imogen Callan, the soldier who petitioned the crown to marry *and* remain an active member of the Royal Guard. Every single vampire knew that once my mother set her mind to something, she was stubborn in her pursuit and would not relent until she achieved her goal.

I guess you could say I got my stubbornness from her.

We began training in childhood. Both my parents trained me, but in different ways. My mother trained me in the art of swordplay, Imogen Callan favoring a twin set of sai—a present from my father. Tristan, my father, trained me not only to defend myself and use misconceptions against my opponent, but also to still my mind.

My heart clenched again as I stretched out on the mat, closing my eyes to see my mother and father smiling with such an abundance of love. I had always felt safe with them, never alone—not like this—but this was now my reality and had been since I was seven.

When I lost them, when they were taken from me, I decided I couldn't go through that kind of pain again. The queen had tried to take me under her wing at first; however, after many a time where I refused to stay in the royal quarters, sneaking back to the attic area where my family had once lived, she let me be. Even my friendship with Nickolai, the crown prince, turned to ash as I pushed him away for fear I would one day lose him, too.

So, I spent my days trying to live up to my parents' legacy, trying to ignore the name-calling, the women who regarded me with both pity and contempt, the continuous attempts to beat me into submission. My peers called me Frosty the Ice Queen. I heard them whisper about me when they thought I was not listening, wondering if I were so broken, I had no feelings.

It wasn't that I had no feelings. In fact, I had too many. I'd just perfected how to wear the mask of a girl who was indifferent to it all. I made sure I spurned any attempts they made to befriend me. I had hundreds of years ahead of me, and I intended to spend them alone.

Assuming, of course, I didn't die in a pool of blood like my parents.

Yanking the buds from my ears, I lay there for an age, staring at the ceiling and trying to still my mind. I could almost hear my father's lilting tone as we sat perched in the gardens, surrounded by night blooms under a twinkling night sky. Our legs were crossed, and as I huffed out a breath, my father ruffled my hair and cupped my cheek.

"Réalta beag, *my little star, you are fire and fury, shining brighter than any star in the sky. In order for you to be strong, just like your mother, you must learn to be strong in your mind and your body. One day, when you are grown, and your mother and me are old and gray, you will be the absolute best of us.*"

Beating my fists against the mat, I choked back a sob as hot tears slipped past my defenses. I longed to scream, yearned to shout out my pain so I could be rid of it.

My senses prickled as I felt eyes watching me from the royal viewing balcony. Lurching upright, I gulped in a breath and wiped tears from my face. My gaze snapped upward, clashing with eyes the color of the night sky. Scrambling to my feet, I dragged my gaze away from the crown prince, my cheeks heating in embarrassment. I was usually so careful, but with tomorrow looming, I was ready to fall into the abyss.

Gathering up my belongings, I stormed off down the hall, fleeing the prince's scrutiny. The halls were full of bustling vampires finishing preparations for tomorrow's memorial, but they quickly moved out of my way when they saw me coming. I needed to escape to my rooms, lock myself away until the morning. I needed to cry and scream and rage against the night in order to function tomorrow.

Rounding the corner, I ran straight into two people I would have rather avoided, my most ardent tormentor and her royal squeeze.

"You need to watch where you are going, Ryan." Natalia Smyrnoi snapped, snaking her arm around the waist of Prince Kristoph.

"Leave her be, Nattie," chided Kristoph, giving me a small smile. When I tried to return the smile, I earned a click of the tongue from Nattie.

Kristoph was a year younger than me, three years younger than his brother. Kris had always been kind to me, but Nattie... I refused to attend one of her lavish birthday parties when we were teens, choosing instead to spend the time training, and she and her cronies have done everything they could since then to make me feel inadequate.

Nattie threw Kristoph a look before casting her gaze back at me, hatred in her eyes. She sneered, pulling Kristoph away from me before he could say any more. I could have caused a fuss and pointed out Nattie was only with Kristoph because Nickolai had cast her aside, but that would have led to even more drama, and I just wanted—needed—to be alone.

Taking in a breath, I rested my head against the wall, listening to the steady rhythm of my heart. As I worked to calm myself, the throne room door opened ahead of me and Queen Katerina strode out. The queen was beautiful, with long blonde hair and a smile that never wavered. There was a warmth in her bright blue eyes that infected everyone around her; Katerina truly was a monarch whom everyone loved and adored.

When her eyes landed on me, her smile deepened, even as panic flared in my chest. She took a step toward me as I flattened myself against the wall, unable to move from my spot as my mother's best friend pursed her lips. Every year, the queen tried to get me to speak about my parents, and every year I politely declined. I had my own pain to carry; I could not endure hers as well.

A figure stepped in front of my line of sight, blocking the queen from me. I heard the hushed tone of his voice, telling his mother to leave me be, and I took the opportunity to dart up the stairs and away from the prospect of having to once again be The Girl Who Had Lost Her Parents.

I did not spare them a second glance as I rushed to the safety of my room, but I could feel the weight of Nickolai's gaze upon me as I fled.

Chapter 2

Staring at my reflection in the mirror, I fastened the lapel of my uniform and smoothed down the edges, trying to get rid of creases that were not there. Though I wasn't a sworn member of the Royal Guard yet, we still had uniforms to wear on formal occasions: a deep black material stitched with a rich crimson trim, long sleeved, with black pants that echoed the top half. It was the same uniform that the sworn guards wore; what they'd always worn. The only indication I was not yet a full soldier was the yellow armband fastened to my jacket announcing me a *Trainee*.

Slipping my feet into my black combat boots, I glanced once more into the mirror and tried to ignore my tired eyes with the dark circles under them. Sleep had evaded me for most of the day, dreams of my parents haunting me even ten years on. When I'd finally given up on any chance of rest, I lay staring at the ceiling until the faint chime of dusk rang through the compound and the shutters lifted for the day.

Looping my belt around my waist, I reached out and

grazed my fingers over my sai where they lay on my bed, wishing I could sheath them and have their comforting weight to anchor me, as if my mother's spirit came with the weapons she had favored. Glancing up, my eyes settled on my father's katana, resting on the wall above my bed for the last ten years, only to be taken down when it needed cleaning or I needed to unwind. Instead, knowing full well I had little need of weapons at a memorial service, I sighed, peering back into the mirror and trying to decide what to do with my stick-straight hair.

I'd spent my life training to become a member of the Royal Guard under intense rules and regulations; most of which had to be tailored to suit the lone female in the class. The boys in my class were asked to keep their hair neat and off their faces when training. I was never asked to do that but once, when Zayn had grabbed hold of my hair and yanked me off my feet in training, his father, Idris, had remarked that if I'd not had such long hair, then it might not hinder me.

Only a cry of anguish from Queen Katerina herself had halted my attempts to shave my head. She'd chided Idris for his behavior, remarking that neither Tristan nor Imogen would have stood for his words, and said any attempt to cut my hair would be dealt with by her.

I'd been so angry with her for that—for the queen coming to my rescue when I hadn't needed saving. I'd flinched when she cupped my cheek, a monstrous rage swelling in my chest as I recoiled from her grasp and retreated to my room. I had seethed and boiled for hours until I decided to take back control.

The very next day I walked into class with the ends of my ice-blonde hair dipped in lime green. My teachers were appalled, but their gazes turned silently to the queen, waiting for her to intervene. Katerina had not, and, from that day on, my hair had been a rainbow of colors. Even today, my hair was sprayed a dark red that glittered toward the ends.

For the occasion, I pulled the stands back off my face, wrapping a hair tie around and fixing the mass into a sort of messy bun, leaving the strands of color visible. The audible ticking of the clock grated on my already frayed nerves as I glanced around my tiny kingdom.

The attic room ran from one side of the building to the other, nestled firmly on the roof of the residential wing. With high ceilings and an open-plan layout, it felt small but also somewhat grand. I'd used my family trust to outfit the whole place, and it wanted for nothing. The simple layout and windowed roof were everything I ever dreamed off. Special tinted glass that prevented sunlight from searing through was the biggest luxury I had splurged on—well, apart from an antique record player.

A small kitchen unit had been installed, as had steps leading up to a bed so close to the overhead windows that it sometimes felt like I could reach out and dance my fingers across the sky. Obviously, over time, my taste in décor had changed somewhat, but not much. As my mother once said, I'd been born with an old soul and unicorns and fluffiness were never my things.

The chime of the downstairs-lobby clock alerted me to the time. Inhaling a breath and watching as the Ryan my peers called the Ice Queen fell into place, I steeled my resolve and left behind the comfort of my sanctuary, heading down to the last place I ever wanted to be.

But on the bright side, there would be food…

As I made to leave my room, my eyes fell on my mother's wedding ring, a blood-red ruby my father had had mounted in a setting especially for her. It had been given to me shortly after their deaths, but I never wore it. My hands needed to be free every single day as I fought my way to be where I wanted to be.

Chewing my bottom lip, I snatched the ring up, slid it over a thick chain, and then, before I could change my mind, fastened it around my neck, tucking it inside the collar of my uniform and out of sight.

Tears welled in my eyes and I swallowed hard, putting one foot in front of the other as I made my way down the small staircase that led to the main residential area and then down the master staircase. This area was empty, but I knew it would be; most of the vampires were already out in the gardens, ready for the memorial service to which I knew I was late... but hell, I hadn't wanted to go in the first place.

I quickly strode across the lobby and through the conservatory, pushing open the double doors and stepping out into the crisp night air. On most days, spending time in this garden would be a treat—the silence and serenity made it one of my favorite places, plus it was a space in which I'd spent time with my father. But now...

Now, the tranquility was broken by the gathering of maybe a hundred vampires, some who had come from outpost missions for this yearly event. The murmur of voices cracked the peacefulness of the night. I stood rooted to the spot, my feet digging into the grass as I turned my head to look out at the lake, wanting to dive headfirst into the water just to get out of this fucking painful loop of misery.

It was the exact same thing every year—rows and rows of seated vampires on either side of a pathway leading down to the lake. An entire congregation of vamps who'd lost loved ones in the event, all wanting to wallow in the sorrow they felt linked us all together. I may have been the only child who had lost everything that night— someone they felt they should pity, whose sorrow was greater, somehow, than theirs—but what none had ever understood when they remarked on my quiet, brash, and sometimes insolent demeanor was that under the layer of expected sorrow, under the sadness etched in my walled-up heart, burned a rage so hot it would explode if I did not control myself so. Blood would be spilled.

Chairs to my right and chairs to my left. Lanterns illuminated the path to the dais where the royal family would preside, where the queen would give her yearly speech, her own sadness so painfully visible that the little girl in me wanted to reach out this woman who shared in my grief and cling to her as if a simple embrace could erase the weight in my chest.

Gulping in a breath of air, I rolled my shoulders and strode forward, used to the pointed stares and whispers by now. I kept marching, one foot in front of the other, my eyes fixed forward until I found my chair, the solitary family seat two rows back from the royals. When I reached my spot, I sank down, tucking one ankle behind the other, hands folded neatly in my lap.

One of the caretakers struck a match and ignited the firepit sitting in front of the lake. Orange flames roared to life, casting shadows against the water, and I felt the blazing heat rippling against my skin. My heart began to thunder in my ears as the side doors opened and we all stood in one fluid motion as the royal family stepped into the garden.

Escorted by her husband, King Anatoly, Queen Katerina wore a skirt of crimson and a tailored jacket of the same color. If not for the crown of glistening, blood-red diamonds on her head, she would have looked like any other well-dressed businesswoman. Her hair hung loose around her shoulders and she lifted her eyes to scan the crowd, smiling softly when they landed on me.

I didn't return her smile.

Where Katerina was soft and inviting, Anatoly was all hard angles. I had memories of him smiling and laughing with my father, but it was hard to imagine the man before me doing that. Lean and tall, with eyes that watched you like a hawk, the moment Kristoph strode into view, it was easy to see who he resembled in the family. The youngest son followed his parents out, no crown on his head, wearing a suit matching his father's and a shirt of the same color as his mother's.

Did I mention before that the royals like to match?

I felt his energy before I saw him, my nails digging into my palms as Crown Prince Nickolai came through the doors, his face impassive, his entire being so utterly calm I wanted to throw something at him just to see if he would react. When we were children, it had been so easy to incite a reaction from Nickolai. I knew every tick of his jaw, every flinch, every arch of his brow. I'd studied him thoroughly, because I knew one day I'd stand by his side, ready to take a bullet for him.

We used to be best friends... until I fucking shut that door with a resounding slam.

There was no denying Nickolai looked like he'd

stepped off a magazine cover for the most handsome, eligible bachelors. Long strands of blond hair fell over eyes of darkest blue. Nickolai was all broad shoulders and muscle. He worked out as much as we did, claiming he would not stand by and not be able to defend himself against an attack. At nineteen, he had a smile that made girls go weak in the knees.

Dressed in a suit similar to his father and brother, the material clung to his muscles, exuding power as he walked. And he knew it. A constant gaggle of girls, especially the Heathers—oh, we'll get to them later—followed him everywhere, all vying for the chance to parade around on Nickolai's arm and someday, hopefully, become queen when he ascended to the throne.

The king had already taken his seat facing us, which left Nickolai rushing forward to help his mother to hers before taking his own seat beside her. Once settled, he lifted his gaze, staring directly at me.

Those goddamn heartthrob eyes.

I ducked my head so I could avoid the intensity of his gaze, then felt more eyes on me. Daring a glance to the side, I spied Nattie shooting laser beams from her eyes at me. She snarled, flashing her fangs at me, halting only when her father, Boris, tsked at her. Nattie spared me one last glance, and I flipped her off, smothering a grin as she hissed like a duck at me.

It was the little things in life that made people happy, right?

A hush descended over the assembled vampires, and I blew out a breath, lifting my eyes slightly so I could see Katerina rise ever so regally and lift her hands to gesture before her.

"Gathered friends," she began, her voice soft and melodic, calm but full of power. "Tonight, we honor those who died ten years ago defending the palace and the lives of those who survived that night. Every year, we remember their bravery, their sacrifice, and we also come together as those who are left behind, to help each other with our grief."

Katerina roamed her eyes over the crowd, and I suddenly found my hands remarkably interesting.

"In death, I have no doubt those who made great sacrifices to preserve the lives of many are now reborn in Eden with Eve, where their battle is over and they can bask in the happiness of the forever garden."

Breathe, Ryan. Breathe.

"May we remember them this evening and rejoice in the parts they played in our lives, for death is not the end. Our memories will keep them alive in our hearts for eternity."

Breathe, Ryan, breathe. Just breathe.

"And now we will cast roses into the lake in remembrance of the dead. Step forward, those who grieve, and remember your dead."

I stayed planted to my seat as everyone who was meant to throw roses into the water got to their feet and formed a line. I waited until I had no other choice but to steady my legs, stand up, and walk forward. I could feel everyone studying me, waiting to see if I would lose my mind and freak out.

I kept going until the procession had moved enough that I was the last to reach into the basket containing roses. Only two remained—one for each of my parents. Cursing my trembling hands, I took the stems in my fingers and closed my eyes as the queen stepped forward, a hand from her son the only reason she stopped and I did not crack.

I knew she'd lost her best friend. They were as close as sisters. I should've clung to the person who knew my parents even better than me. But I knew when the queen looked at me, she saw a pale imitation of my mother, that my strange lavender eyes were my inheritance from Imogen. That when I smiled, on the rarest of days, I looked just like my father.

I was the perfect combination of the two people who created me out of love, and I hated myself for it.

Spinning away from the queen, I found myself alone as I came to the water's edge, thankful my hesitation had left me in the only company I felt comfortable in—my own. Already, people had begun to gather in groups behind me to mingle, ignoring me as the mild inconvenience I was to most—as if they could no longer bear to witness my grief. After ten years, they'd spent enough time watching me wallow.

Copper scented the air, and I glanced down to see I'd pricked my finger on a thorn. I snorted out a bark of laughter, startling some vampires standing nearby. Pressing my finger to the petals on the roses, I closed my eyes and tossed the blooms into the water, watching as they drifted away with the current, taking a little piece of me with them.

As they did every year.

A moment later, the queen clapped her hands and trays upon trays of food were brought out, the scents of delicious cakes, pastries, and other mouth-watering delicacies dragging a growl from my stomach. Sucking the blood from my finger, I made my way back up the embankment, my eyes roaming over the crowd as everyone seemed to gravitate toward their cliques.

If this was an American high school movie, you could pick out the cliques right away. My classmates were the jocks, the debutante like girls were the mean girls, the parents were like members of the PTA and then you had me...the loner...the teenage dirtbag.

I ambled my way toward the food and found an empty stretch of wall to lean against while studying the crowd like the weirdo I was. I picked up a piece of cake with a fork and shoveled it into my mouth, standing in the cover of shadows, hoping if no one realized I was still here after I horsed down some food, I could manage to slip away.

Washing down my cake with a blood-infused cola, I almost choked on my drink as one of my fellow classmates broke away from his pack and walked toward me. Instantly tense, I set the drink down, my body prepping itself for a fight. Everything with them was a fight, but tonight... Tonight, I was tired.

Edison St. Clair grinned, flashing me the megawatt grin that had already worked its way through most of the Heathers. Six feet of muscle, Edison was attractive if you liked men who looked like they were in a boyband and had more charm in their little finger than I had in my entire body.

"Ryan."

"Edison." I shoved my hands into my pockets so I wouldn't clench them into fists as Edison ran a hand over the back of his neck.

"Listen, Ryan," he began, his voice lowering to a

hushed whisper as if we were buddies sharing a special secret.

Please spare me.

"A few of us were planning on sneaking out to a human club Friday night, and we wanted to know if you wanted to come."

"Why?"

"I'm sorry?" Edison stumbled, and I could hear his friends laughing.

I felt my cheeks heat. "Why do you want me to go?"

"Because we're classmates, and we only have a year left before we graduate and have to work together."

Edison didn't sound convinced by his answer, and neither was I.

Chapter 3

"Bullshit."

"Pardon me?"

I took a step closer to Edison, revelling in the sudden spike of fear I smelled as I slipped my fingers along the collar of his uniform and flashed him a toothy grin.

"I said *bullshit*. None of you want to be my friend—don't make me laugh. Why would I go to a human club with any of you when you despise me so? What did you plan to do, leave me miles from home just before dawn and force me to seek shelter in the human world?"

Edison swallowed hard, and I laughed, a cold harsh sound as I reached up and patted him once on his cheek. A growl rumbled in his chest as he slapped my hand away, which made me laugh even harder.

"You really are a crazy bitch," Edison snarled, but he'd already lost any edge he'd had. His knuckleheaded buddies were beside themselves with laughter.

"Oh, Eddy," I sighed and roll my eyes. "Did you really think you would be the one to thaw the Ice Queen? Oh, you did, didn't you? So, what's the bet up to now? Couple of grand? I'm sorry, Eddy, but you won't be collecting any money, *friend*. I mean, it's not really attractive when I can kick your ass, is it? I mean, be a man..."

I'd gone too far; I knew it and yet I couldn't help myself. Edison raised his hand, poised to strike me, and I prepared to take it, wanting to feel the sting of his blow, wondering if it would match the pain in my chest. He hesitated, and I smiled smugly, inciting him again. But the blow never came.

Atticus St. Clair, Edison's older brother and current member of the Royal Guard, had latched onto Edison's hand. "Enough," Atticus growled at his brother.

Edison yanked his arm free and stalked away from me in a blaze of fury, bypassing his friends and walking away from the gathering until I could only see his silhouette at the far end of the garden.

Atticus rolled his eyes at me, an expression I seemed to draw from most people. "You walk a dangerous line, Ryan Callan."

I shrugged my shoulders and popped a strawberry into my mouth. "I'm just here to cause trouble."

Atticus shook his head, unable to hide his own smile. He continued shaking his head as he wandered away, glancing over his shoulder after a few paces. I gave him a wave before his attention was dragged elsewhere.

It wasn't strange I got on with most of my teachers and current members of the Royal Guard but not with my peers—I respected the hell out of most of them. They'd fought side by side with my parents, many of them under my father's command, and they saw something in me that warranted extra lessons and instruction.

It was Atticus who'd stumbled upon me one night,

long after classes had ended, trying to work on my upper body strength. I was hanging from the salmon ladder, trying to drag myself up and failing miserably. Atticus had chuckled, but then he spent time with me, building the strength in my core so that, three years on, I had won the challenge day, scaling the bars quicker than any of the boys. After that win, everyone started looking at me differently, acknowledging me as the competition I was.

Leaning my head against the concrete wall once again, I let my eyes wander to the mean girls. Remember when I said they were called the Heathers? It was their self-proclaimed girl-gang name because they loved the movie. When I pointed out no one was named Heather, so their title didn't make sense, I was met with more than just nasty looks. No, that hadn't gone down well at all. I mean... I did make some spectacular suggestions for names of their snobby mean-girls-wannabees group. Some people just couldn't appreciate creativity. These girls really did have brain tumors for breakfast.

The Heathers acted like princesses because they were raised to think of themselves that way. Female vampires were rare, far less common than males. So, in a society where boys always outnumbered girls, it made sense some families raised their girls to consider themselves special.

I suppose I was lucky with my parents. They never expected me to be anyone but me. When I picked up a toy sword instead of a doll, my mother's eyes had watered with pride. When I learned the words to my father's favorite song so we could rock out to it together, my father had tossed me into the air, the two of us laughing ourselves breathless.

Maybe that was why I'd never made friends with the Heathers—we had nothing in common. With only Natalia Smyrnoi, Farrah Nasir, Kayla Johnson, Victoria Day, and myself in our age range, it was entirely likely one of the Heathers would be our future queen... unless Katerina decided to ship in a princess from another court.

We were not the only vampire court; however, we were the largest.

In order to increase our numbers, arrangements would be made soon for alliances through marriage. I had to admit I was petrified a decree would come from above demanding, due to the survival of the species, that I drop out of training and offer my hand in marriage to the highest bidder. As my legal guardian until I turned twenty-one, Queen Katerina had the power to do that.

Yeah, I know. I should be nicer to the woman who held my future in her hands.

Rubbing the ache in my chest, I grabbed another plateful of treats and pushed off the wall, slipping inside the foyer and away from the rest of the crowd. Apart from a few employees who milled about with more food and drinks, the entire compound felt empty.

Our compound was nestled deep in the Irish countryside, outside the overcrowded city of Cork. As technology advanced over the past few decades, the need for additional centers to work on more advances led to farms being bought and clinical buildings replacing the lush countryside around the city. Having thus rid itself of everything that had made it such a charming, vibrant place to live, Cork was now considered a technological hub.

Our home, our court, stood on a couple of acres far

enough from the city so as not to arouse suspicion, a newer suburb created at Katerina's request. To those on the outside looking in, we were foreign diplomats, choosing to live a cultish life. We even had large security fences and people manning them.

Appearances were everything when the survival of your species was involved.

Taken as a whole, the compound was a mixture of centuries, featuring high-tech, modern training facilities scattered throughout a maze of grand hallways and ornate antique furniture that looked like the set of *Downton Abbey*. It was easy to get lost if you weren't paying attention to where you were going.

For example, if I veered off to the right, I would find myself entering the royal wing—a place I had not stepped inside without cause for over a decade. To the front of me was the throne room and the conference hall, where not only were royal events held but also meetings of the Royal Guard.

The stairs beside the oak doors to the throne room would lead to the second and third floors, where the council families resided. Another staircase by the edge of the third stairs led to my own rooms.

To the left was a door leading to the main dining hall, where we celebrated events like Samhain and sometimes Christmas. We hadn't done that, though, not since the last time children roamed the halls.

Beyond the dining hall were classrooms, a library, gymnasiums, practice rooms, and armories. While it was most important to study weapons and martial arts, the queen wanted us to learn about life, languages, and history as well.

She also implemented compulsory movies on Sunday nights in the theater room for all trainees. It was to help us relax before we began another week of schooling and training. Sunday was our only day off, and I was loathe to spend it with any of those idiots, especially when the Heathers happened to join us—with the queen's permission, of course. Our queen was quite fond of "bonding experiences." I usually spent the time by myself, up the back, feet on the headrest in front of me, counting down the seconds until I could leave.

I made my way to a side door, situated right next to the throne room. Pushing down the handle, I slipped inside, using the dimmer switch to illuminate the room so I could find what I was looking for. Not that I didn't know exactly where I was going. I could walk into that room blindfolded and still stride right on up to the pictures of my parents.

The room in which I now stood was called the "Hall of the Fallen". As was our custom, vampires burned the bodies of their dead, so there were no cemeteries to visit like the humans did. Instead, the queen commissioned this gallery of portraits for us to visit when we wanted to lay our gaze upon those no longer with us.

There was no sound in the room apart from the pounding of my own heart in my ears. My eyes glanced over the royal portraits, starting with Anastasia Romanov and following down through her bloodline. I ignored them all and kept walking until I came to a corner, stepped around it, and then tears welled in my eyes.

A portrait of my parents smiled back at me. Both posed with their weapons, depicting the fierce warriors they were. I'd always wondered how someone could paint a portrait so lifelike of my parents when they weren't sitting in front of them. I only learned later, once the queen had given me a photograph of this exact image, that the picture had been used to paint the likeness.

My father wasn't looking at the camera. Instead, his Irish-green eyes—as my mother used to call them—gazed lovingly at his wife. My mother stared straight at me, a warmth in her eyes I missed like an aching limb. Her smile was wide, a sense of happiness written all over her face. I didn't remember what it felt like to know that kind of happiness anymore. I wasn't even sure if I was capable.

"That photo was taken moments after your mother told your father she was carrying you."

I startled, cursing myself for not hearing the queen sweep into the room. I was to be a Royal Guard, dammit.

"Imogen waited until the camera was poised, and then she leaned casually into Tristan and asked him how he felt about becoming a father. Tristan was overjoyed, of course, as we all were."

Powerless to do anything but stand there staring at the picture, my heart breaking at this new piece of information Katerina revealed, I couldn't help but look at the picture with new eyes. For the first time, I notice the palm of my father's hand resting on my mother's stomach. The realization I was in the picture with them formed a lump in my throat.

"Tristan spent the next few months treating Imogen as if she were made of glass, which both irritated and bemused your mother. She would curse Tristan's very name with the biggest smile on her face."

"Please stop."

my blood.

"Tristan said, 'Well, feck it, let's just call her Ryan. If she's as badass as her mother, she can hand them their arses if they so much as try and mock her.'"

I was bleeding into my chest, my fragile hold on sanity sending a wave of dizziness through my head as I tried to piece the words together. I felt as if I were floating, and I struggled with all my might to re-cage my feelings.

Then, I realized the queen has sworn while trying to impersonate my father's Irish accent, and I laughed. I laughed like I was crazy, doubling over until tears ran down my face. When the laughter had died, I straightened, but the tears, they still cascaded down my face. Bleary-eyed, I hiccupped, my chest burning as I stumbled backward.

"Oh, Ryan."

And then I was undone. Unable to stand anymore and listen to how much my parents loved me. How much they wanted me. How much they expected of me. Stories meant to bring me peace simply added fuel to the rage simmering under the surface, waiting for its chance to be unleashed.

I was struck by a memory of my father reading poetry to me before bed, as he often did—especially poets he admired. Curled up in my father's strong arms, I listened as he recited Dylan Thomas, telling me to rage against the dying light. I understood those words more now than I ever did back then.

My entire body trembled as I fought against the anger I had for the woman in front of me. It was unwarranted—ludicrous, in fact, considering I had made it my sworn mission to protect everything she stood for. Yet the little orphan girl in me wanted to rage against the woman in front of me for being the reason my parents were dead. If she hadn't needed protecting, if her husband had been a warrior like my father, then maybe they wouldn't be dead and I wouldn't be a shell of the person I could have been; the person my parents expected me to be.

As if she sensed a charge in the air, Katerina slipped her feet back into her heels, preparing to leave me to my rage. Before leaving she paused, hesitating as if she were going to rest a hand upon my shoulder.

I'm grateful she didn't but surprised when she speaks to me again.

"There is a meeting of the Sovereignty Council at six tomorrow evening. I would like you to be there."

"Why?" The word fell from my lips.

"Because I have asked it of you. Because you cannot continue to live as if you died too. Because I made a promise to my friend that I would always look out for you. Six o'clock, Ryan. Do not be late."

The queen left in a flurry of movement, and as the door closed with a bang all I could think was, *Well, shit.*

Chapter 4

I was beginning to think I would never sleep again.

After another fitful day of tossing and turning, wondering why the hell the queen requested I—neither a member of the council nor a fully-fledged Royal Guard—attend this meeting. I had no place sitting in on the Sovereignty Council meeting, no matter what the queen said.

"Because you cannot continue to live as if you died too."

It was true; I wasn't living. Those words played through my mind again and again, the weight of their truth punching me in the gut each time. I wasn't so stupid I'd thought anything different, but I had no idea how to get out of my own way. I'd conditioned myself to this. It was a learned habit.

I'd changed my clothes six times in the last hour, wondering what to wear to this thing. It wasn't a formal meeting, so my dress uniform would be overkill. However, I felt underdressed in jeans or leggings. Finally, I decided to just wear a pair of black training pants and a black, long-sleeved T-shirt. I refrained from adding extra spray to my hair because I knew I would stand out enough by just being there.

As the clock reached ten minutes to six, I huffed out a breath and made my way downstairs to the foyer. I stood at the base of the stairs, watching as members of the Royal Guard made their way into the meeting.

"Well, if it isn't Ryan Callan, looking just as much trouble as the last time I saw her!"

A genuine smile lit up my features as I came down the remaining step and embraced the man who'd just sauntered in the door. Jack O'Reilly was an old friend of my father's, an Irish vampire with hair the color of carrots and cheeks adorned with freckles. He was the most quintessential Irishman I'd ever laid eyes on and every bit the lovable rogue my father had once called him.

"Hey, Jack."

The soldier wrapped me into a warm hug, and I let him because I had not seen him in an awfully long time. Plus, he was one of the few people I could stand to be around.

"Hello, kiddo," he said with a grin, releasing me to get a better look. "Now, are you gonna tell an old man you heard I was coming and just had to see me? C'mon now, don't break an ole man's heart."

I laughed before I could stop myself, alerting other people in the foyer of my presence and earning a few looks. "You are terrible," I said with a smile.

"But you still love me, though?"

Atticus interrupted our reunion and beckoned Jack in, holding the door open for his fellow guard.

"Will I see you after?" Jack asked.

"Actually," I said with a sly grin, "I'm to attend this shindig at the behest of the queen."

That stopped both men in their tracks, their mouths dropping open so much I could see a hint of fang. Jack recovered first, holding out his elbow to escort me into the room, and I took it, even if it was just to have someone to anchor me.

Entering the room, I ducked my eyes as everyone turned to see what had Jack chuckling to himself. I'd never been in this room before on official business. Seated around the oval table were the male heads of the seven remaining families. First came Everett Hamilton, then Idris Nasir beside Cornelius Day, followed by Grant Reeser, Alistair Johnson, Theodore St. Clair, and finally Boris Smyrnoi.

The members of the Royal Guard stood to attention behind them. Reece Hamilton stood by his father, as did Keegan Johnson, Atticus St. Clair, and Carter Reeser. Jack remained stoic by my side.

I was fairly sure the council members were wondering why I was here, and, soon enough, one questioned me as Jack held out the last chair for me.

"Child..." Everett Hamilton said, sneering as if I were something he'd scraped off his shoe. "Why are you here?"

"Ryan."

"Excuse me?"

"Did I stutter?"

A bubble of laughter rippled through the room at my audacity, and heat flared up Everett's neck.

I sighed, leaning forward to rest my chin in my hands. "If you want to ask me a question, please use my name. It's *Ryan* by the way, not *child* or *girl* or any other way you think you can address me. Just Ryan. It's not hard to say."

"You insolent girl."

I rolled my eyes and sat back in my chair, then felt a reassuring pat on the back from Jack as I folded my arms across my chest.

Leaning in to whisper in my ear, Jack's tone was teasing as he chortled, "Damn, I forgot how much fun you were to be around, Ryan."

I made to answer when a voice cut across us.

"Can someone tell me why one who is neither a council member nor a Royal Guard is sitting in on our very confidential meeting?"

I was on a roll already, so I grinned, ready to unleash more sarcasm on them when a voice sounds from behind me.

"I asked Ryan to be here."

The men bristled at the sound of the queen's voice, and I felt my lips twitch but refrained from flashing another grin at the shocked vampires. I didn't glance up but did make to stand, hesitating when Katerina motioned for me to remain seated.

I noticed Anatoly was missing, but in his place stood Nickolai, who was studying me with such intensity I felt my face heat. Looking down at my hands, I glanced back up at the scrape of a chair as Nickolai set a chair at the top for his mother.

Once the queen was settled, she tapped a nail on the table, and everyone jerked to attention. Katerina inclined her head toward Boris, whose eyes darted to me before he addressed the queen.

"My Liege," he began, his Russian accent making the words sound shorter, "what we are to discuss is a matter of grave importance. Confidentiality is key. We cannot have information like this passed around as girlish gossip."

I snorted, then remembered where I was, quickly sobering and letting my mask fall back into place.

The queen simply gave Boris a friendly smile. "Ryan will be model of discretion, won't you, Ryan?"

"Of course, My Liege."

"Then continue, Boris."

I sat and listened as Boris read from a report about the impact of blood shortages, the inability to find willing donors, and the prediction that, if trends in technology continued as they were, vampires would have no food sources for survival within a decade.

Nothing he said was news to me. Movies and TV had killed the allure of vampires years ago. We were no longer seductive creatures who played on a human's lust for the supernatural. No longer revered as we once were, we'd been reduced to being mocked and ridiculed as sparkly, broody messes.

"Perhaps it is time to reintroduce the breeding farms our ancestors used to enforce." The suggestion came from Idris, a vampire with skin that looked sun-kissed even if he'd never walked underneath its rays.

"That is not an option," Katerina replied. "We are more civilized than our ancestors, and we will not resort to taking them by force. At our last meeting, we discussed integration with the humans. Has anyone ideas on ways to do so?"

"The humans may be less skeptical in this dawn of technological advancement, more willing to accept a new species into their midst," Boris said, "but we all remember the Salem witch trials and how well they went. What's to stop a budding Van Helsing from taking up arms against us?"

"We need to build their trust," I replied, then blinked at the sound of my own voice. Surely, I hadn't said it out loud.

When the entire council turned toward me, I cursed myself silently for not having the good graces to keep my thoughts to myself. I held up a hand in apology as the heads of the families glared at me, wishing I could shrink back into the shadows.

"Please explain what it is you meant, Ryan," Katerina said.

When I hesitated, the queen offered me a warm smile of encouragement. Glancing down at my hands, I explained, "Well, you can't just come right out and say, 'Hi, here be vampires.'" That earned a chortle from the room, and I relaxed a bit. "Shoving vampires in their faces will do none of us any good. The older generations are hardened by war and by life. You need to slowly introduce a person into society who can appeal to, say, college-age humans, who are hungry for knowledge and experiences."

I took a breath, checking to see if I still had everyone's attention. I was surprised to find I did, so I carried on while I had the chance. "Let this Chosen One make friends with the humans, let them immerse themselves in human society and then, if they determine it's possible for us to be part of that world, we can make ourselves and our plight known to mankind."

Not a soul said a word in response. They all stared as if I'd said the most bizarre and outlandish thing known to vampires, as if I had no right to be here let alone speak. Perhaps I didn't, but I couldn't take back my words or go back in time.

"I'll do it."

My head snapped in the direction of the voice, and I blurted out, "Say what?"

Nickolai ignored me, peering down at his mother. "I will do it."

"My Liege," Theodore St. Clair interjected, "you cannot expect us to endorse sending our future monarch into the human world by himself. What if you are discovered and, Eve forbid, killed?"

"Then you would be lucky my mother has another son to take my place, and I would no longer feel insulted you have so little faith in me."

Score one for the crown prince.

Reaching up, Katerina clasped her son's elbow, and I flinched at the tenderness in her gaze—a mother's gaze. "Explain to me why I should let you."

"Ryan is right; subtlety is key. Who would think anything of a rich college kid attending classes by night, mixing with the locals as his parents go off on a diplomatic mission and leave their son, who has a sun allergy—"

"Photosensitivity is what it's called." Again, I needed to learn to think before I spoke.

Nickolai smiled before he continued. "A son who suffers from severe photosensitivity and can only attend classes by night on a generous donation from his wealthy parents. I've been around politics my entire life; I can mix with humans."

I had a sneaking suspicion the queen and her son had already made this decision and it was a done deal, even if we liked to paint ourselves as living in a vampocracy. And if I had the brains to figure that out then so did the rest of the council... although I couldn't be sure.

"My Lieges," Cornelius Day said, "when we discussed the possibility of this plan, I should have been clearer I was suggesting we send one of the trainees. They are of the right age." Cornelius looked appalled at the thought of his plan putting the crown prince in danger.

"So am I," replied Nickolai.

I could tell, just by the tone of his voice, that Nickolai was set on being the guinea pig, the knight who'd ride in and save the vampire race by leading the charge into the human world. I'd heard that tone many times as a girl, when Nickolai was convinced he could do what no other vampire could do. It usually resulted in a broken arm and a telling-off from our parents.

This, however, was bigger than any of those reckless adventures.

When no one else spoke up, Nickolai's lips curved into a grin. "Good. Then it's settled. Cornelius, I will leave the finer points to you. Don't sign me up for any boring classes if you can avoid it."

Nickolai swiveled on the spot and began heading for the door, but Idris beckoned him back. I inhaled a breath of surprise at the smugness in Idris's smile to our future king and the utmost lack of respect in his tone.

"Pardon me, My Liege, but there is one matter than needs to be discussed before the council can sign off on this... shall we call it, *humanitarian trip* of yours."

Nickolai folded his arms across his broad chest and glared at Idris. "And what is that?"

"The matter of your ascension, My Prince. You are two years from ascending the throne and taking a queen. If this mission of yours takes time, do you plan to not ascend and take a bride? Are we just to forget our traditions and laws?"

A ripple of aggression thickened the air in the room to near suffocating, and I sucked in another breath, wondering what might happen next. My eyes drifted to the queen, who looked unaffected by all the men tossing around testosterone. She greeted my gaze with an arched brow and a smile, and I smothered a laugh, wishing I had some popcorn to enjoy while watching all this unfold.

"What is the point of being king, dear Idris, if I have no vampires left to rule over? What would be the point in taking a wife for our children to die of starvation before our eyes? If you are so desperate to keep up with tradition, then perhaps I should, as I have offered before, step aside and let Kristoph be your king when he comes of age."

Katerina held up her hand, and instantly the brewing storm in the room calmed. She paused, letting time further defuse the ticking time bomb before she spoke.

"There is no law as to when a new reign begins. It is a courtesy as to when one monarch steps down and another takes their place. Have I been such a bad queen that you wish to replace me as soon as possible? That you would stifle the progress of our entire species because you wish to have me deposed?"

"I meant no offense, My Liege. I merely feel that now, in a time where panic and chaos may reign supreme, that our traditions, our *values*, will see us forward during this crisis."

"As my son said, Idris, there will be no traditions or values to keep you warm during the day if we are wiped from existence."

Ding, ding, ding. Bonus point to our queen.

"Mother, you and I have discussed this, and we agreed. Do you still have faith in me to do this?"

"Absolutely," she said, her utter pride, love, and faith in her son audible to all.

"And my stipulation?"

"It will be granted."

"Then I have no more to say on the matter." With that, Nickolai swept from the room, taking all air with him.

I sat quietly, still wondering why the hell I'd been compelled to attend this meeting, but now also curious as to what Nickolai would have asked of his mother in order to wander out into the world by himself.

"My Liege, are you seriously sending our crown prince into the human world all by himself with no support from those who've sworn to protect him?"

The queen beamed at his words, as if she'd been waiting for just this moment to unveil the last twist in her tale. With a gleam in her eyes, she uttered a sentence that splintered my world in two.

"Of course not, gentlemen. Ryan will be there to watch over him."

Every single goddamned eye turned on me, causing me to squirm in my seat under the scrutiny. I had the good graces to remain silent, ignoring the chuckle from Jack as the heads of the council threw questions at the queen, who simply reclined in her chair and, like me, said not a single word.

My heart began to beat a drum against my chest. Katerina was looking at me, really *looking* at me, and I knew this was what she must have planned all along. Last night, when she'd spoken to me, she must have known she was about to throw me under the bus and cause ructions within the council.

I wasn't entirely certain what her game plan was, just that I was not happy being a piece on her chessboard.

"You mean to send this *girl* as your son's only protection against the outside world?"

The queen lifted her head, her eyes finding Atticus St. Clair. "Atticus, please tell the council who is top of their class in multiple disciplines?"

"Ryan Callan, My Liege."

"Which student completed most of her normal studies last year—a year ahead of her classmates—and could already have taken college classes like some of the current Royal Guard do online?"

"Ryan, My Liege."

"Atticus, you were top of your own class and served under Tristan Callan yourself. You could have your pick of the new trainees to be your protégée. When the time comes, as it will do soon, who is it you'd want to work alongside you during their first year as a junior member of the guard?"

Atticus tore his gaze from the queen's and turned to me, holding my own gaze with such a fierce solidarity it made my chest hurt.

"I'd have asked for Ryan," he said. "I was fortunate enough to learn from both Tristan *and* Imogen, and Ryan is the best parts of her parents in one body. There is no better person to watch my back."

I was speechless. The air had been sucked from my lungs. I couldn't say a word to acknowledge what Atticus had said, but I heard Jack agree with Atticus's statement with a resounding, "Hear, Hear!"

The blood was still pounding in my ears as Katerina rose from the table, followed by everyone else. I was still glued to my seat, unable to move. Jack set his hand on my shoulder as the queen gave instructions that Nickolai was not to know someone was guarding him. That I was to remain in the shadows and be the epitome of discretion.

I still couldn't catch my breath as the queen announced this was my final test, that on successful completion of this mission, I would be appointed to the Royal Guard.

I still sat there like an idiot as the council filed out of the room, even as Jack clasped me firmly by the shoulders in a kind of embrace.

With a grin the size of Texas, he said, "Welcome to the big leagues, kid."

Chapter 5

I'd dreamed of joining the Royal Guard because I wanted the sense of achievement that came with it.

I joined the Royal Guard because it was what sang in my blood every time I wielded my mother's sai.

I fought and clawed my way through the minefield of being a woman in the guard to continue my mother's and father's legacies.

However, I had not achieved all that I had just to become a glorified babysitter.

For six weeks now, I'd been lurking in the shadows, watching Nickolai to ensure his safety. For about a week, I'd been on tenterhooks, waiting for the prince to out himself, but it never happened. Nickolai was like a chameleon, fitting right in with the humans, making friends instantly with some of his fellow classmates. His carefully crafted alias provided him the appeal of a foreign student with heaps of money.

Nickolai had spent an incredible amount of time learning his backstory and making sure he was ready to blend in. Human-style clothing was purchased, human mannerisms mimicked. The day before Nickolai—and I, of course—left for the exclusive private night school on the fringes of Cork, he was summoned before his parents, the council and members of the Royal Guard to answer questions about the human world.

Like everything else with Nickolai, he excelled and was able to answer questions regarding pop culture, Irish history, and sports. He looked pretty pleased with himself, standing like a proud peacock, arms folded across his chest and the smuggest smile on his kisser. Dressed in dark denim jeans, a faded, slate-gray T-shirt layered with a black button-down shirt left open, and the latest sneakers on his feet, Nickolai looked ever the frat boy.

I'd had my own training to complete—spending as much time as I could watching Nickolai and not getting caught. Everyone knew he was embarking on this mission, but none of the other trainees knew I was going with him. The story we'd concocted was that Jack wanted to take me to see the little village in the west of Ireland where my father had been born.

The instant Nickolai arrived at St. Patrick's Institute of Education, he'd been made welcome; staff and teachers were waiting for him as he sauntered through the front door. If they could have rolled out a red carpet for him, they would have. Then again, if every student's parents donated an undisclosed, but undoubtedly obscene, amount of money for their son or daughter to attend a unique night college, they too would have received a fancy assistant walking around after them.

Nickolai quickly made friends with a group of male students all attending the college for various reasons involving sporting commitments. They did the jock thing, clapping each other on the back and grinning like idiots. Most were envious as Nickolai explained he lived just off campus in a penthouse apartment normally reserved for visiting dignitaries and the like.

So, I settled into the mundanity of following Nickolai around like a shadowy puppy. I studied my former best friend as he expertly steered his way through the human world, and I hated him a little for it.

I'd never told a soul—not that I had anyone to tell, really—that I had dreamed of going to college like a normal person. Spending so much time alone, I'd watched as many old TV shows as possible. I remembered watching episodes of *Saved by the Bell: The College Years* and imaging myself there. I loved being a vampire and all, but when I was younger, watching those TV shows or movies where even the loner could be a hero, they made me long for a cure for the world into which I'd been born.

Unfortunately, cures for vampirism only happened in *The Vampire Diaries*. No, wait—those zompires in Van Helsing had magic cures, too!

Today, I studied Nickolai from the end of the corridor as he fist-bumped one of his new buddies and smiled at a girl who blushed a vivid shade of pink the moment Nickolai glanced in her direction. The human females seemed explicitly drawn to Nickolai, smiling, chatting, and giving little touches to his arm during break periods or between classes.

Thank Eve they didn't know Nickolai was royal— nothing good would come of any dalliance with a human female who thought she'd found her Disney prince. The mere thought of having to watch Nickolai make out with a girl made my stomach turn.

When the door to the lecture room swung shut, I was left alone in the corridor. This was the last class on the prince's schedule tonight, and I usually followed him home afterward, making sure he was safely inside before I snuck into the large ventilation shaft above his apartment and dozed.

In the six weeks since we'd left the compound, I'd only slept a few hours, most of which had been on one of the nights Atticus had shown up and he and Nickolai spent the majority of the night playing cards.

Now, coupled with the fact I was well overdue for a feeding, I found my awareness fraying and my nerve endings aching with the need for blood. I was exhausted, but I was solely here to watch over Nickolai, nothing more, nothing less.

Failure was not an option. While the queen was willing to send me to watch over her son, it would seem her husband did not share in his wife's confidence. Anatoly had cornered me one day after training, telling me that, should I fail in my duties, I would never become part of the Royal Guard and he would make sure I was married off as soon as possible.

I must have had an expression of pure horror on my face because the king smiled, flashing his fangs and leaning in closer to tell me that he hoped I failed. I had made to retort with a snappy tone, but Kristoph cleared his throat in warning, stopping me from saying something that would only solidify Anatoly's plan.

A chortle of laughter brought be back to the present and pricked my curiosity. I couldn't help but wonder what the harm would be in sitting in on this one class. I crept along the wall and quietly opened the door, sliding in and closing it without so much as a sound. I ducked my head around the corner, my heart almost bursting. I was actually standing in a college classroom!

It was a typical lecture hall—we had similar ones back on the compound, but this one... this was so much better than I could ever imagine. Seats covered in bright blue followed the path of steps running down until the ground met them, a whiteboard covered the wall behind where the professor was perched on the edge of his desk, his glasses set on his crooked nose, framing eager eyes.

Humans now could pay almost nothing for image enhancers, lenses that fit on one's eyes and corrected vison. This man was obviously in the rare minority of humans who were authentically themselves, and it instantly endeared him to me.

I spotted Nickolai leaning back in his seat, listening intently to the man, surprised he was taking this so seriously. Most of the girls kept looking at him, and I rolled my eyes. A long strand of hair fell into his eyes, and Nickolai swept it away automatically, utterly oblivious to the drool forming on their heavily painted lips.

Edging my way into the back row, I lay down on the seats, hidden from view, my heart racing as I became engrossed in the debate going on below me.

"As part of your assignment over the break at Halloween, I want you to take one of the theories we discussed regarding monsters in literature and either support or oppose it. You must provide detailed reasoning as to your position. And writing 'because I said so' is not a valid answer, Mr. Sullivan."

The class laughed once again, and I felt ever so jealous I was not a participant in this. Everything we'd done while training had been geared toward how best to serve the crown; our own interests never came into play.

"Tell me, class, of some of the alternative mythologies from TV or movies we've discussed where monsters are concerned."

"Fairies are evil," a voice called out.

"Yes," the professor replied. "It is widely known the fair folk are notorious tricksters and masters of word manipulation as they cannot lie. Even in Irish literature, fairies and leprechauns are quite different from how they're painted in many films."

"Mermaids," a female voice said. "I mean, in *The Little Mermaid*, Ariel is just a girl who wants to be where the humans are."

Same, Ariel. Same.

"But in the original story," the student continued, "the mermaid endures tremendous pain to become human and is unable to make the prince love her. The suffering she endured was for nothing. In the end, she dies."

Well, this got dark very quickly...

"Good, good. Anyone else?"

"There are always lots of theories on vampires. I mean, girls have been lusting after vampires for years."

It was a different girl's voice this time, quiet and unsure, as if she rarely spoke out in class.

"Tell me more, Krista."

"Vampires will always hold more appeal than other supernatural creatures. Their mythology is endless because each variation is so believable."

"Except *Twilight*!" someone shouted, earning a laugh from the class.

"*Twilight* was believable in its own way because it

made vampires accessible to teens. Parents preferred they read or watch *Twilight* over, say, *Lost Boys* or *The Forsaken*, where vampires were bad to the bone and the stuff of nightmares." The girl Krista knew her stuff...I liked her.

"What about shows like *The Vampire Diaries*?" The professor asked.

Krista was excited now, I could hear it in her voice and the sharp inhalation of breath she took before launching into another statement. "*The Vampire Diaries* created complex characters with possibly good intentions, but who had to make a conscious decision to switch off their humanity so as not to feel the enormity of human emotion. If you compare those vampires with, say, *Buffy* vampires, the soul plays a huge part in what makes a vampire evil. Both Angel and Spike were murderous fiends until they got their souls back, albeit in different ways."

"They were then," continued Krista, "plagued by the weight of their actions, and it even made Spike crazy for a time."

"Excellent, Krista. Now, as we've delved into vampires, what of their origins? In *The Vampire Diaries*, vampires were created by a witch's spell, creating an original vampire and thus introducing lines of sires. In *Buffy*, you had The First. In modern literature, Stoker's *Dracula* is considered the first vampire novel; however, Jeaniene Frost tells a different story of Vlad the Impaler than Stoker did."

Damn, I was really starting to fall in love with this teacher. I loved Jeaniene Frost's books. And yes, I was a vampire reading vampire novels. You can stop smiling now.

"In *Supernatural*," the professor continued, "all vampires are descended from an Alpha vampire. These vampires are grotesque, evil monsters. Who here would prefer to watch or read about those types of vampires than, say, the inhumanly handsome ones?"

Laughter erupted from around the room, and I longed to see for myself what was going on. A smile curled up my lips as someone commented on Ian Somerhalder's hotness as the bad boy of Mystic Falls.

"Let's get back to Jeaniene Frost's novels. Her vampires consider themselves descended from Cain, so what about the theory Cain was the first vampire? I know we try to leave religion at the door; however, it's important to consider this idea as well. Mr. Sullivan, care to remind your fellow students of the legend of Cain?"

The boy groaned, taking his time before replying, and I found myself fascinated by the ways his answer differed from the histories we'd been taught as young vampires.

"Cain committed the first murder, killing his own brother out of jealously. God then expelled him from Eden and punished him by making him the first vampire."

I snorted—I couldn't help it. It was ludicrous to think Cain was the first of my kind. Of course, it just *had* to be a man.

Just then, I realized all conversation had halted and the classroom was silent. My heartrate kicked up a notch and panic flared in my chest; I should have just stayed outside. Or learned to keep my mouth shut.

"No point in hiding, my dear. Let us see you."

The teacher's voice was kind, so I only lay still for a couple of heartbeats before sitting up with a sheepish grin on my face. I noticed, but tried to ignore, the white-hot glare Nickolai was sending in my direction.

One of the boys sitting in front of Nickolai whistled, leering at me, and I restrained a chuckle as Nickolai smacked his friend upside his head.

"Welcome to my media class, Miss...?"

It took me a minute to realize he was waiting for my name. I cleared my throat, sitting up straighter. "Ryan... just Ryan."

"Well, Miss Ryan, tell me what was wrong with Mr. Sullivan's interpretation of the story of Cain."

Oh yeah, like I could just spill the secrets of vampire origins to a group of humans and not look insane. Although... I'd rather look insane than stupid...

"It's always a man," I said finally. "I mean, God, Jesus, Cain—all men. No one considers it may have been a woman who started it all."

The teacher smiled warmly as Nickolai stood, shaking his head at me. I shrugged as the teacher told him to take a seat before motioning for me to continue.

"Where I come from, according to the lore—"

"All right, Sam Winchester." The boy Sullivan joked.

Well... I walked face-first into that one.

The group laughed, causing my cheeks to heat and my fingers to curl into fists in my lap. The teacher clapped his hands to hush the room.

Mustering my courage—or maybe my stubbornness—I ran my tongue over my lips and continued before I could chicken out. "Cain was not the first vampire, he was the first vampire to be *born*, and his hormones and bloodlust resulted in the death of his brother Abel, who was, as Adam's only legitimate child, human. Cain was actually the son of Eve and Lucifer."

The class regarded me as if I had lost my goddamn mind, apart from Nickolai, who looked like he wanted to strangle me. I'd fucked up royally, but if I was going down, then I might as well go down for something noteworthy.

"Lucifer fed Eve blood apples from his own garden," I continued, "and this gave Eve a thirst for blood. She grew fangs and drank from both Lucifer and Adam, who still loved his wife. Cain was cast out of Eden for draining Abel of his blood in a fit of rage. Cain spent an eternity wandering the world, sleeping with humans until enough born vampires were alive to create trueborn vampires."

Sullivan's eyebrows furrowed. "So basically, you're saying Eve was a slut and Cain even more so, and that's why vampires exist? *Puh-lease.*"

I was beginning to hate this Sullivan guy more and more.

"Miss Ryan, this is not a mythology I've ever heard before. Where did you hear it?"

Biting my bottom lip, I decided to answer as truthfully as I could. "It's an old tale passed down from my mother's people. She was born in a small village in Iceland."

The professor nodded. "Interesting. Now how did you happen upon my class? You are not a student in my class."

My eyes darted to Nickolai's and back to the teacher, and then I flicked my hair like I'd seen the Heathers do and smiled. "I came to surprise Nickolai. I was travelling through to visit some people and said I'd drop in to say hi. I was waiting outside to surprise him, but the lecture sounded so interesting I couldn't help but sit in on your class. I'm sorry. I just wanted to see my friend."

The word *friend* tasted like sandpaper in my mouth.

The boys were looking at Nickolai with envious eyes, and I knew what they were thinking. They assumed I was an ex of his who'd stopped by in hopes of a hookup. Nickolai, at least, had the good graces to look disgusted as lewd suggestions were thrown about under their breaths as they assumed I couldn't hear them.

A chime sounded as class ended, and I was up and out of my seat, fleeing the room and frantically wondering how I could talk my way out of this. Maybe if I begged hard enough, Nickolai would neglect to tell his mother I'd given away my presence and the entirety of our species' origin story because of a snort.

Once outside, I waited on the opposite wall as students began to pile out and gawk at me. I could feel Nickolai's rage as he stormed out the door, his eyes darting left and right until his gaze landed on me. Striding toward me, I expected him to grab my arm and drag me off somewhere so his dad could force me back to court and up the aisle, but he didn't.

Stopping inches from me, I swallowed hard and said, "Hi."

"My mother sent you, didn't she?"

I said nothing, but he read the truth in my reluctance to rat out the queen.

"For the love of Eve, Ry, how long have you been stalking me?"

Ry… He hadn't called me Ry in so long. My heart constricted.

"Since day one."

Nickolai swore, and I giggled, clasping a hand over my mouth as I did.

"I'm going to call my mother and have you sent back. I don't need a babysitter, especially not one who isn't even a member of my guard yet. Pack whatever bags you have because you are leaving right now."

Rage filled my stomach, spreading like fire into my veins as I jerked back from him. "Sure, send me back," I hissed, "and take away the last thing I have in my life. Take away any free will I have and force me to… force me to…"

I couldn't get the words out. Rage had stolen the last of my composure as I lifted my gaze to clash with eyes of cerulean blue.

"Go on, send me fucking back. I'll be married before the sun rises."

Chapter 6

"WHO?"

There's a growl in his voice that sends shivers down my spine, the authority in his tone making me want to comply.

"Your father said so far, Idris is the highest bidder. I'd rather be dead than forced to marry someone I don't love."

A crowd had begun to gather to watch our heated display, the tension between us so palpable even those standing in close proximity could feel it. I dared to lift my gaze again to meet Nickolai's eyes and found myself swallowing hard. Those cerulean eyes watched me with an intensity that made me crave things from the prince I shouldn't be considering.

"Hey Nico, you gonna introduce us to your gorgeous friend or not?"

Nickolai peered over his shoulder and gave the gaggle of guys a sly smile. "Not tonight, fellas. I'll see you all for class tomorrow."

The guys whooped and guffawed as Nickolai grabbed

my arm and all but dragged me along the corridor and out into the night air. A chill had set in while we were inside, and even though vampires didn't really feel the cold as much as humans did, I shivered against the frigid breeze blowing strands of my hair into my face.

As soon as we were a suitable distance away from anyone, Nickolai dropped the hand on my arm, and I was ashamed to say I immediately missed the warmth. I hadn't realized I was so touch-starved, though I supposed it made sense. The only physical contact I was used to was when my fists connected with someone else's face... or, of course, if theirs connected with mine.

Standing in the middle of the courtyard, Nickolai whirled on me once more, and I dug my heels into the ground, ready to bear the brunt of his anger toward his mother. He studied me for an age as the wind gathered, whistling through the empty courtyard, an eerie sound that reminded me of my attic at home.

Finally, Nickolai let loose a sigh and ran his fingers through his now-windswept hair. A smile tugged on my lips as the longer strands in the front fell back over his eyes. As children, Nickolai had bucked against tradition to cut his blond locks, and because he would one day be king, not a single vampire would disagree with the princeling.

I had teased him relentlessly for it, my own hair a bone of contention between my own parents. Imogen wanted it cut short so as not to impede me in battle. However, Tristan, as he braided my hair, simply said it would be a shame to hack off such beautiful hair, and if a few extra strands of hair could impede me in battle then I shouldn't be there in the first place.

"What are you thinking?"

Nickolai's voice dragged me back to the present, and even though I wasn't willing to share memories of my parents with him, I could share my initial musings.

"Zack Morris called—he'd like his hairstyle back." My hand lifted of its own accord, and I stopped myself just short of tugging on the strands like I'd done when we were children. Snatching my hand back, I managed a small smile as Nickolai continue to stare at me.

"All right, weirdo. Stop staring and tell me whether I need to do a runner. Because I have no intention of marrying Zayn and being a meek little housewife for him to use as a punching bag."

Nickolai chuckled, his laughter low and husky as I folded my arms over my chest.

"I'm glad my future suffering amuses you."

"I'm laughing at the thought of anyone thinking you are meek. Fools, the lot of them."

As I opened my mouth to say something in retort, a scream rent the air, the sound a cry of terror and pain. I exchanged a brief glance with Nickolai before taking off, the prince needing no instruction to keep pace with me. We ducked down a narrow alleyway leading to a sports field, one Nickolai and the rest of his gang often used to kick around a soccer ball.

The floodlights illuminated the field, but I ground to a halt just shy of where the lights began and hissed. A gym bag and sports equipment lay strewn across the tarmac, giving the impression the kid had been surprised with an attack from behind. A young man was lying face-down in a pool of his own blood, the coppery scent rousing my hunger. My fangs sprang from my gums as a growl rumbled in my throat, and I cursed myself for not having fed long ago.

Closing my eyes, I worked to control my breathing and center my mind, trying to convince myself that snacking on a dead guy would be in bad taste—no pun intended. Cracking my peepers open again, I found Nickolai frowning at me. With a shrug, I turned my gaze down to the dead man before us.

I knew he was dead because I could hear no heartbeat, sense no blood coursing through his veins. I strode around to the front of the victim and sucked in a breath as the light revealed his face. Sullivan, the smartass kid from Nickolai's class, stared at me with glassy terror in his lifeless eyes. Nickolai snarled as he came to stand beside me, his hands clenching into fists at his side. We stood silently for a few heartbeats to calm our inner monsters before I set about to see where the blood had come from.

For there to be such a large pool of blood already, a major artery or vein must have been involved, but apart from the still-spreading pool beneath his upper body, he looked completely unharmed. I didn't know what made me consider it, but I crouched down by his head, grabbed a stick, and used it to push his blood-soaked hair from his neck.

Swearing, I glanced up at Nickolai. His own eyes were focused on the two very visible, very messy puncture wounds on the side of the boy's neck. I leaned in and inhaled, trying to see if I could pick up the scent of the vampire who'd stolen life from this young man.

"Did you tell any of your new friends you're a vampire?" The question slipped from my lips before I could stop it, even though Nickolai hadn't been far from my sight or hearing over the last six weeks.

The prince did not answer my question directly, but his snarl and glare were enough of one for me.

I let Sullivan's hair fall back over the wounds and stepped away from the body. Was there a rogue on campus? Surely if an unaligned vampire was wandering around campus, I'd have sensed him... or her?

"Ryan, we need to go. We can't be seen near the body. There are only so many people who'll believe I have an allergy to sunlight. You won't be afforded the same if we have to answer questions to human police."

I slowly stood up straight, turning my attention to the prince when the hairs on the back of my neck stood to attention. On reflex, I all but shoved Nickolai backward, the prince landing on his ass but now far enough away to keep him out of the fray as a figure charged at me, brandishing what looked to be a meat cleaver.

Taking the hit as the attacker's shoulder hit mine, I grabbed the attacker by the arms as I fell and used the flat of my feet, once we hit the ground, to shove him off me. He—and it was definitely a *he*—landed in a crouch as I rolled to my feet and yanked my sai free of the custom strap at my back. Twirling the weapons in my hands, the siren call of the fight sang in my veins as I took a step forward.

Our attacker was covered head to toe in black, his eyes barely visible in the darkness. As I inched closer, I let a sadistic smile spread across my features. When the vampire saw my face he stepped back, and I knew I had won this little battle of wits.

The sound of voices snapped the attacker's attention, and he darted off—but not before flinging a rusty blade the rogue had plucked from somewhere in Nickolai's direction. I leapt in front of the blade, my sole purpose being to protect Nickolai, although somewhere inside I was torn between my desire to chase after the vampire and my duty to the prince.

Sirens wailed in the distance as I jogged forward, sliding my sai back into the sheath at my back as I neared Nickolai. The prince had gotten to his feet while I was fighting, and his expression was murderous.

"How dare you shove me out of the way! What possessed you to face off against a rogue like that and cast me—"

Stopping midsentence, Nickolai blinked, his eyes fixed on my shoulder. I craned my neck to see what he was staring at, discovering what had happened to the assailant's rusty knife—it was lodged solidly in my flesh, right by my collarbone. Adrenaline must have stopped me from feeling the impact, but the moment I knew it was there, I hissed in pain and made to yank it out.

Nickolai put his hand over mine, preventing me from doing so. "Are you mad?" he exclaimed. "You can't just pull the blade out."

"Wouldn't be the first time," I retorted with a shrug, my skin stinging at the movement.

The prince rolled his eyes and slid his arms out of his varsity jacket, draping the coat over my shoulders. The front panel blocked the knife from view should we happen by anyone.

Nickolai nudged me forward, pausing for a second to look at his friend one last time before we strode in the opposite direction. I heard footsteps behind us, and my body flinched as screams carried with the wind as we walked. Neither of us uttered a sound, the burn in my shoulder intensifying with every step I took.

Using another alleyway, we made our way to the front of the college, crossing the bridge to the exclusive apartment complex where Nickolai had the penthouse all to himself. Nickolai nodded in greeting to the doorman, who ran his eyes over me and grinned at Nickolai, even as I rolled my eyes.

Nickolai placed a hand on the small of my back to guide me inside, and the heat of his skin on mine burned more than the knife. I repeated to myself over and over it was only because I was touch starved. The only people I'd allowed to touch me in a familiar way in over a decade were Jack and a drunken kiss with a vampire I couldn't remember at a Halloween party a couple of years ago.

Nickolai called the elevator, and the moment we stepped inside and the doors clanged shut, I leaned against the cold glass and closed my eyes.

"I can't believe you've been here all this time and I never knew."

With my eyes closed I couldn't see his face, and his voice was so calm, so even toned, I couldn't discern his emotions from it. I decided staying quiet might be my saving grace.

"Then again, you were always good at playing hide and seek. I could never find you. I only knew where you'd hidden when you leapt out and frightened me half to death."

I said nothing, trying to ignore the lump in my throat as Nickolai reminded me of the carefree, mischievous little girl I had been. But that was before. Before the blood and death and rage I was now wholly made up of.

Just then, the elevator stopped and the doors opened, giving me a reprieve from having to respond. I pushed away from the wall and strode into the glorious luxury of Nickolai's penthouse apartment, leaving the prince to follow after me.

Lush burgundy carpet against a backdrop of cream, the open-plan kitchen and living room were every bit as spectacular as the view from the wall-to-wall glass windows suggested. I made my way over to stand in front of the windows and gaze out. They'd been treated with a special tint that allowed Nickolai to leave them uncovered even when the sun was at its brightest. It was the closest any vampire could get to the sun, and I was more than a little jealous.

Flickering lights like fireflies cut though the darkened night, the sky a darker shade of blue as Nickolai's eyes. The city seemed to span out for an eternity, and I lifted my fingers to touch the cold glass as if I could touch the humanity below.

"Hey, come on, let's get the knife out of you and get you cleaned up."

I peered over my shoulder, ignoring the splinter of pain as I narrowed my gaze. "Thanks, but I have my own stuff where I've been sleeping. I can do it myself."

"And just where have you been sleeping?" Nickolai asked in a tone that demanded I answer him.

But my lips remained sealed... for now.

"And if I said it was an order?" His voice held no such order, but I still bristled.

"Whatever My Liege asks of me, I shall do."

A muscle ticked in Nickolai's jaw, and I smiled on

the inside as I shrugged off his jacket and tossed it onto the armchair. I slipped off my own jacket as well before walking into the bathroom in just my leggings and a tank top.

The bathroom was just as glorious as the rest of the apartment, bigger than the cramped vent I'd called home the last few weeks. Marble countertops that housed various grooming products faced a bath so big three people could fit in it, a seating area circling the tub. A standing shower stood in the center of the bathroom, a toilet off to the side.

Sitting in the immaculate bathroom, I felt instantly grubby. I'd stolen a quick wash in one of the campus locker rooms every few days while Nickolai was safely in class, but that hardly felt like enough when surrounded by such pristine accommodations.

Hoisting myself onto the marble countertop, I settled my fingers over the hilt of the knife and made to yank it out as Nickolai came in and sighed.

"Didn't we just have this argument?"

"Yes, My Liege, we did."

There was that muscle ticking in his jaw again. I suppressed a grin as I dropped my hand, taking in the first-aid box and bottle of blood dangling from Nickolai's other hand. My stomach rumbled at the sight of it, causing him to grin.

"Be a good girl and I might share with you."

I flipped him off—a gesture I shouldn't have used against my future king, but I liked living dangerously. Nickolai simply smiled even deeper, showing off his dimples. I rested my palms on my thighs as Nickolai set down the blood and the kit, taking out disinfectant and bandages. We vampires had long life spans, but we could still get sick; and while infected wounds weren't often lethal, they still hurt like hell.

Fingers grasping the handle of the knife, his free hand braced against my shoulder as he said, "Ready?"

"Just get it over with and stop bloody dancing 'round it, for fu—"

The air left my lungs as Nickolai did as I'd asked, my vision blurring as bile threatened to spill from my lips. I swallowed hard and sucked in a breath, then grimaced at the sting of disinfectant. Once I felt the press of the bandage against my skin, my eyes sprang open and I caught the prince watching me with curious eyes.

He was standing awfully close to me; I felt my blood heat and my body start to react. Suddenly uncomfortable in my own skin, I slid across the counter and pushed slowly off it, my legs needing a minute before I could walk away with any dignity.

Reaching around Nickolai as I bypassed him, I snatched the bottle of blood, making my way to the armchair and dropping into it with a sigh. I uncorked the bottle, and the delicious scent coupled with the wound sent my hunger into overdrive. Resting my feet on the antique oak coffee table before me, I lifted the bottle to my lips and tipped the chilled blood into my mouth.

I didn't even try to suppress the groan in my throat as I drained the bottle, the synthetic beverage doing little to sate my hunger. I set the bottle down on the table in front of me and leaned back in the chair.

Nickolai came out of the bathroom and, following my earlier actions, sank down in the armchair opposite me, so he faced me. He leaned forward in his chair, resting his elbows on his knees and wearing a rather impressive princely frown.

"When was the last time you fed?"

I didn't bother using words to answer him, I simply waved my hand in the direction of the bottle and smirked.

His frown deepened and his lips curled into a snarl. "Answer the goddamn question, Ryan."

Again with the fucking orders.

Sitting up straight, I met his gaze. "Apologies, My Liege, I forgot myself. I haven't fed from a vein since the night before you left to come here."

"Stop with the *liege* bit, Ryan."

"In what way should I address my future king?" I asked solemnly. I knew I was being an asshole, but hey, so what?

Nickolai ignored my question and countered with one of his own. "Why would you be so careless? The last thing we need when trying to convince humans we're harmless is for you to be overwhelmed with bloodlust."

"Oh, I'm so sorry," I began, my tone as sharp as any katana. "If it pleases My Liege to consider me careless for using the one night he was protected in the last six weeks to get some sleep instead of feeding, then by all means, Sire, call me careless. You're probably right; I should have abandoned my mission, wandered off to a bar, and picked up some random dude for some fun. It's not like my life, my *future*, depends on making sure you succeed."

I got to my feet, and Nickolai did the same.

"Now, if you'll excuse me, dawn is approaching and I need to get back to work. That is, if you haven't decided to put an end to my mission and are happy to be a guest at my wedding?"

Chapter 7

An expression that could only be described as bewilderment fell over his features as Nickolai swallowed hard. "Why haven't you been sleeping?"

Folding my arms across my chest, I shrugged. "It wasn't in the job description."

"Cut the snark, Ryan. Just answer my question."

I curtsied low, holding it longer than necessary before I rose and said, "Again, forgive me, My Liege. It has been some time since I've been in such company. My queen was quite clear in my objectives: watch the prince and ensure his safety at all costs. Never take my eyes off him. And sleeping meant I would have to do just that, so I haven't slept."

His eyes widened for a brief second before his expression darkened once more. "So, what, you've spent six weeks watching me? Not sleeping?"

"To be fair, I did sleep for a solid six hours when Atticus came by for a visit."

Nickolai threw his hands in the air. "That's ridiculous. Not even you can function on six hours' sleep. It defeats the purpose."

I cleared my throat. "I think I proved I *can* function on little or no sleep considering I saved your ass tonight."

"And got a knife in the shoulder."

I dismissed his comment with the wave of my hand. "Technicality." Standing, I added, "Now, if you'll excuse me, I have a nice sleeping bag waiting for me and, as you implied, I could do with a few hours' of kip. So be a good little princeling, Nicky, and stay inside this apartment until at least sundown."

I only realized I'd called him by my childhood nickname for him when he froze. It was far too late for me to take it back, so I pretended it hadn't happened at all. Gathering up my jacket, a faded black one that had once been my mother's, I made my way toward the elevator.

Nickolai stopped me with a hand on my elbow. "Tell me where you've been sleeping, Ryan. Please."

It was the please that stuck my snappy retort in my throat. All I did was lift my eyes to look at the vent over his head. His eyes snapped upward and then snapped back to clash with mine, pity and remorse in them.

Unable to handle that expression, especially from him, I snatched back my arm and stalked to the elevator, pushing the call button so hard I almost broke it. When the door opened with a ping, I strode inside and pressed the down button. The door began to close, but then Nickolai put a halt to that with his hand.

"Don't go, Ryan. No one should be forced to sleep in a vent."

"It's quite homey, actually. I can't have guests, but I'm an antisocial prick anyway, so it doesn't really matter."

"I'd feel more protected if you stayed here. I mean, the rogue could come back."

I snorted, arching my eyebrows.

"It's not like you can go back to hiding, is it? I know you're here now."

With a sigh, I stepped back out of the elevator. "I might as well take advantage of the cozy-looking couch," I said. "Might be my last night of peaceful sleep."

I tossed my jacket to the side and flopped down on the couch, ignoring the dull ache in my shoulder. The wound would be healed by morning, probably just in time to haul my ass back to the compound. I crossed my legs over one another and folded my arms in my lap.

"I'm not sending you back."

I blinked at the hushed words and sat upright with a hiss at the burn in my shoulder. "Say what?"

Nickolai sank back down into the armchair and scratched the stubble on his chin. "I don't see the point. You're here now, and it seems pointless to stop my own mission. I'm sure we can come up with a cover story for you."

"But why?"

Nickolai's eyes dropped to look at the floor. "It would be remiss of me to send you back to a fate I myself ran away from."

It took a few minutes for me to realize he was taking about marriage. It was written in the clan charter at the age of twenty-one, the new monarch should be crowned and the reigning sovereign should stand down. Nickolai turned twenty-one in twelve months, but he'd delayed taking over as king until his mission was complete. Did that mean he was not going to marry until then, either?

I made to question him, but the prince looked so forlorn I just couldn't do it. Instead, I resorted to old tactics, wondering if I could drag him from his sadness like I had when were children.

"Well, since you're being all hospitable and shit, any chance of a pillow and a blanket? And since I saved your ass tonight, you can make breakfast in the evening. And Nicky, I swear, if you don't have bacon in that monstrosity of a fridge, then how are you even a royal?"

His lips twitched with a hint of a smile. "Are you naturally this much of a pain in the ass, or do you just try really hard?"

"What can I say? It's one of my better qualities."

Nickolai barked out a laugh, glancing toward the bedroom and then back to me. "Take the bed."

Heat flushed my skin. "Excuse you?"

"You can sleep in the bed."

"I am not sleeping in the bed with you."

Nickolai jerked backward, his eyes widening. "I didn't mean that, and you know it. You take the bed, and I'll sleep on the couch. And by the way, there's no need to look so horrified at the thought of sleeping in bed with me. It's not like we haven't done so before."

I wasn't horrified at the thought of sleeping in the same bed as him; I was horrified I *wasn't* horrified at the thought of it. "We were kids back then. We aren't kids anymore."

"I noticed. Just take the bed, Ryan."

I shook my head from side to side. "No chance. I'm fine right here."

"Not everything has to be an argument, you know," Nickolai growled, his hands shoved into the pockets of his jeans in a very human gesture.

Unstrapping my sai sheath, I set it down on the carpet within reach and folded my arms behind my head as I lay back on the couch. "Yeah, I know. But I can tell you you're wrong in almost seven languages, which definitely gives me an advantage."

Nickolai was still staring at me, his eyes wandering to the sai before he smiled smugly. That smile made me super uncomfortable, so I closed my eyes and slowed my breathing, trying to convince the prince I was falling asleep. I tried not to flinch—but failed—as I felt a blanket being draped over me, and even though I heard him walk away afterward, I could still feel his eyes on me from across the room.

"Goodnight, Ryan."

"Goodnight, Nicky."

That earned me a chuckle. The room plunged into darkness a second later, the only remaining light coming from Nickolai's bedroom door being slightly ajar. Sleep weighed me down, and I let myself relax enough to doze, praying that, even just for tonight, I was not haunted by dreams of blood and dead parents.

A knock sounded at the door to my room, and I stared at it, hoping whoever was knocking would get the hint and buzz off. The knock sounded again and again, and I longed to scream, to demand, they leave me in peace. When the knock sounded again, I slid off my bed and marched over to the door, ready to fling it open, when a voice called out from the other side.

"Ryan, it's only me. Please open the door."

My hand froze on the handle, my heart racing in my chest. I couldn't see him; I couldn't face him his sadness and pity. Everyone already me treated like a broken girl who would never be whole. But it hurt more when I caught Nicky's expression conveying those sentiments.

"Come on, Ry. I know you're in there."

"Leave me alone, My Liege. I don't want any company."

"Ryan, open this door right now, or I'll kick it down."

He wouldn't—Prince Nickolai Romanov was always the epitome of calm and poise until I dragged him out of it. I began to smile and then caught myself, letting tears slip down my cheeks.

"Come on, Ry. It's your birthday. Can we just pretend for today we're still friends?"

My heart clenched at his words because we would always be friends. For his eighteenth birthday, I'd had Jack source a replica of a sword from a TV show I knew he'd loved. Jack gave it to him with no note or anything—none was needed. Only I knew Nickolai would love that gift, and I knew the prince would understand whom it had come from.

My sixteenth birthday was today. I felt no cause to celebrate, the memories of birthdays surrounded by love and laughter too much for me to bear. I slowly took my hand away from the handle and slid my back down the door.

"Don't make me sing thought the door, Ry. We both know I don't have a note in my head. Come outside and we can take a walk—we don't even have to talk. Please, Ryan. I'm going to sit here until you answer me, dammit."

I sat on my side of the door as Nickolai talked about anything and everything to entice a response from me. I let my eyes fall shut, listening to him ramble on and on as night seeped into day. Soon enough, my birthday was over.

"Please, Ryan," he said after a pause.

My resolve worn through, I reached up to drag down the

handle when I heard a voice and stopped.

"Come away now, My Liege. You tried your best."

I opened my mouth to ask him not to leave, willed my hand to fling open the door and let him embrace me in the hug I'd denied him for almost a decade, but nothing happened. My voice and body were frozen, rusted.

Nickolai sighed, muttered his goodbye through the door, and then he was gone.

"The prince is gone, kiddo," Jack quietly said, "but he did leave you a gift. It would be rude not to accept it."

I said nothing in response, the sound of Jack's Irish lilt reminding me so much of my dad I could not stand to hear it.

"Let me know you're okay in there, Ryan, or so help me Eve, I'll do what the prince threatened earlier."

Clearing my throat, I managed to free my voice. "I'm fine, Uncle Jack," I answered. "I'm fine."

"Open the door and take in the prince's gift before someone runs off with it," he said. "I'm tempted to, myself." And with that, he turned and walked away.

I listened to the sound of Jack's boots as they descended the stairs, and once again, I was alone. Cautiously, I opened my bedroom door and scooped up the small parcel. Nickolai had wrapped the gift in Teenage Mutant Ninja Turtles wrapping paper, a joke we'd shared as kids whenever I trained with my practice sai. I smiled fondly as I remembered how Nicky would jest with me about the fact I couldn't be a turtle because I didn't like cheese. Written on the label in elegant calligraphy was just my name: Ryan Skye Callan.

I carefully unwrapped the box so as not to tear the paper, my eyes widening at the sheath sitting inside. I had been trying for ages to find a way to carry my sai other than at my waist. This was a crisscross sheath that fastened around my waist and hooked over my arms, settling the sai against my shoulder blades for easy access.

Setting the box on my bed, I quickly fastened the sheath over my back, delighting in the lightweight material—I barely noticed it was there. How had he known? How did he find such a perfect fit?

Before I could stop myself, I launched out the door and down the stairs so loudly I could've woken the entire house. Without so much as another thought, I ran through the halls of the royal family's residence, looking for Nickolai. Rounding a corner, I ground to a halt.

Nicky had indeed made it back to his room, where he now stood tucking a stray curl behind Nattie's ear, and I flushed with embarrassment as they both turned to look in my direction.

What had I been thinking?

My heart clenched in twisted agony as I backed away, spun back around the corner, and darted back the way I'd come. I made it to the top of the stairs before Nickolai called my name. I stopped.

"It's not what it looks like," he said.

I shook my head. "You don't have to explain anything to me, My Liege. You don't owe me anything."

"Ryan—" he began, but I held up a hand to stop him.

"I simply wanted to thank you for your gift. I'm sorry to have interrupted."

"Ryan, wait."

Ignoring him, I bounded back up the stairs, not daring to take a breath until I was safely back in my room. Closing the door, I banged my head against it, thinking how much I hated birthdays.

My eyes darted open, and I sat up in the darkened

room, Nickolai's raised voice snapping me to attention.

"Seriously, Mother, she was living in a vent to watch over me. Had you told me you wanted to send someone with me, I would have agreed."

The queen sighed, and my spine locked ramrod straight. When did she get here?

"You were adamant you wished to see this through alone," Katerina replied. "Had I asked for Ryan to accompany you, I'm sure you would have stubbornly declined."

"I'm not above compromise, Mother."

"Do you wish for someone to replace her?"

There was a pause, and my heart pounded in my chest, waiting for Nickolai's answer.

"No," he finally said. "Had I not been so curious and gone off in search of the screaming, I'd be none the wiser she was even here. The first time I laid eyes on her was when she pushed me out of harm's way. The fault of her discovery lies with me, not Ryan."

I expelled a breath, and the door to Nickolai's bedroom opened. He gave me a small smile and held up the phone, giving me a glimpse of the queen sipping her tea. I ducked down as Nickolai strode barefoot into the kitchen.

"Should I send Atticus to debrief you both?" she asked.

"That won't be necessary, Mother. Although, perhaps if he called with one of the donors, we could discuss the possibility of enrolling Ryan in my classes."

Excitement bubbled in my chest. *I could go to college like a real person!*

"Would Ryan be agreeable to that? Have you even

asked her?"

Nickolai grinned as he turned the phone in my direction and told his mother to ask me herself. I hissed and tried to smooth down my hair.

"Good evening, Ryan."

"Good evening, My Liege."

The queen sipped from her cup before addressing me again. "Would you be agreeable to Nickolai's suggestion of enrolling you in his classes?"

I nodded a little too eagerly. "I would be able to keep a better eye on him if I were in class with him."

"Then it is settled. You will live and go to class with Nickolai. I will send Atticus to follow up on the rogue. Come up with a viable story as to why you two are living together. The easiest solution would be to act as if you are a couple." With that, the queen hung up.

I didn't dare look at Nickolai as I struggled to change the subject. "Is... is that an iPhone? That must be ancient. I haven't seen one in ages. How the hell does it still work?"

Nickolai ignored my babbling, turning his back to me as he took some bacon from the fridge and set about cooking breakfast just like I'd asked. Smiling.

I pulled out the bread and set four slices into the toaster.

"It's not such a bad idea, pretending we are together," he said. "We already argue like an old married couple."

Leaning against the fridge, I glared at him. "What, has the Russian bridegroom been getting some indecent proposals? Aww... poor baby."

"I do not look like a Russian bridegroom," Nickolai muttered as he flipped the bacon.

"Sure you do," I said with a smirk.

"If I look like a Russian bridegroom, then you must look like an ice queen. What is it they call you? Frosty?"

I snarled and snatched a piece of bacon from the pan, narrowly missing being swatted with the utensil Nickolai was holding. "The last person who called me Frosty ended up with a broken nose, though I've heard some women like a man with flaws. Shall we test the theory, Nicky?"

"Sure thing, Frosty, if you promise to kiss it better after."

I punched him on the arm, earning a growl in response as the toast popped. I grabbed the toast, set the slices on two plates, and then slid the plates over to Nickolai to fill with bacon. Grabbing two bottles of blood from the fridge, I returned and leaned on the counter, waiting for Nickolai to finish cooking.

When he placed more bacon on my plate, I hungrily devoured it as he watched me.

"When did you become so uncivilized?"

I snagged a piece of bacon from his plate and shrugged. "I'm not sure I was ever civilized."

Nickolai chuckled, and the sound heated my veins.

"So, why don't you want to pretend to be my girl-friend?"

"I'm sorry, but Russian bridegrooms who look like Zack Morris circa 1990 don't do it for me."

"And what does, Frosty?"

I told myself the heat in his gaze was merely us teasing one another, that this taut electricity simmering between us was just Nickolai wondering if I was still his best friend. But *she* was dead, and I wasn't certain who I was right now.

You cannot continue to live as if you died, too.

The queen's words sounded in my head as I winked and flashed Nickolai a mischievous grin. "You'll never find out."

Nickolai met my grin with one of his own. "Sure, Frosty. Whatever you say."

Without another word, the git nicked my toast and bit into it, then walked away humming "Do You Want to Build a Snowman?"

Fairy tales were dead wrong—not all princes were fucking charming.

Chapter 8

AFTER WHAT COULD ONLY BE DESCRIBED AS THE MOST GLO-rious shower of my entire life, I dressed quickly in a simple pair of black leggings and a longline black T-shirt, slipping my feet into a pair of Chuck Taylor IVs and hurried out to find Nickolai lounging on the couch where I'd left him.

His nose was stuck in a textbook as he chewed the end of his pencil, deep in thought. I studied him for a minute, wondering when the boy I'd easily dragged into mischief, who'd hated his lessons, had changed so much. But I guess we both changed over the last decade, and Nickolai looked more at ease here than I'd seen him look in a long time.

"When you've stopped staring at me, we should get going."

"I was simply wondering how much you'd fetch on the black market. I mean, I'm sure some aging socialite would love you on her arm at some charity event."

Nickolai arched his brow, and I rolled my eyes, striding forward to grab my discarded sai sheath by his feet. I slung the sheath on with expert precision like I'd done many a time, mindful I could feel Nickolai's eyes on me.

His sudden movement dragged my gaze in his direction. The prince had slung a backpack over his shoulder and was angling toward the door. I folded my arms across my chest and sighed.

"You don't have classes until after seven. Where are you going?" It was only a little after five-thirty; the sun had barely set.

"We don't have classes today," Nickolai replied, shifting the bag as if it was heavy, mirroring human action with admirable ease. "With the murder on campus, classes have been called off for the rest of the week. They are offering the students counselling. A few of the guys wanted to meet at the restaurant on campus, so I said I'd go. Matt was my friend."

I wanted to argue with him, persuade him to remain at the apartment so I could stalk the campus in search of the rogue. I could only do that if Nickolai was safely locked in this apartment. But how could I stop him from going to be with those he called his friends? Maybe the rogue would see us hanging around campus and I'd get the chance to kill him.

"Fine," I said. "Let's go."

"You don't have to come. I'm perfectly capable of crossing the campus by myself. Stay here and rest up."

"Like hell I will. This is not negotiable, Nicky. Where you go, I go. If you want me to go back to hiding in vents so your ego isn't bruised, fine, but I will go with you *everywhere.*"

Nickolai's expression darkened, but I did not so much as flinch.

"My ego has nothing to do with this, Ryan, and you know it. But whatever you need to tell yourself to feel useful."

Nickolai spun on his heel to leave, halting only when I sighed his name. Turning back, he watched as I kicked off my Chucks and stepped onto his couch, stretching my arms up and lifting the cover off the vent. Balancing on my toes, I grabbed my gear bag and the paperback I was currently reading and dropped them on the couch, setting the cover back into place. Stepping down off the couch, I slipped my feet back into my trainers, grabbed my jacket, threw it on, and picked up my book.

Ready for the night, I strode over to Nickolai, who grinned as his eyes fell on the book I was reading.

"All right, Anita, let's go."

I wanted to growl at his mocking of my book, but Nickolai wasn't the only one who considered my love of vampire novels a tad unconventional. What they didn't understand was I grew up with only one role model in my life, and when she died, when she was taken from me, I found the strength to carry on through the characters in books—the badass females who could kick ass and be loved even though they weren't soft. I survived because of Anita, Cat, Merit, and Rose. I learned life lessons from them and so many more. But that was my secret; I would not share it with anyone.

I waved my book at Nickolai. "You should read a book or two, Nicky. I mean, the vampires in these books... damn. A girl could get ideas."

Nickolai flushed, and I grinned. He reached for the book, and I shook my head, hiding the paperback behind my back. Returning my grin, he called for the elevator.

Once inside, we didn't utter a word, remaining silent even as we strode across the quad.

The quad was illuminated by floodlights—more so than it had been the previous night—the college no doubt worried the murder was not an isolated incident. I took in the added security tucked discreetly around the many twists and turns on campus that led off to secluded pathways.

Flags flew at half mast, a very human gesture when someone had passed. I stopped. Looking at the tricolor flag flapping in the wind reminded me of the tattoo on my father's arm. A proud Irish vampire, he'd been extremely proud of his heritage.

I swallowed hard, blowing out a breath, and ignored Nickolai's curious gaze, continuing toward the café ahead. When we reached the door, I turned and pointed a finger at Nickolai. "You do not leave without me. You don't leave this building without telling me. I will stay out of your way and not embarrass you, but in turn, please don't make a mockery of me by dodging out and making me come find you."

I put as much threat and malice in my tone as I could and noticed a muscle ticking in Nickolai's jaw as I held his gaze. Fire burned in his eyes, and he slowly smiled, reaching forward to tuck a strand of hair off my face. I growled low in my throat.

Leaning in close, so close I could smell the minty freshness of his toothpaste, Nickolai whispered, "Very fierce, Frosty. I like the fire. How about we make an agreement? I won't take unnecessary risks, and you'll try and make some friends."

"I don't need friends, My *Liege*. I'm working."

Nickolai jerked back, breaking eye contact as he withdrew his hand and walked away from me. I hurried after him, ducking inside under an arm holding the door open, but stopped in my tracks at the sight of the busy café interior, suddenly unsure what to do next.

My eyes followed Nickolai as he found his friends and greeted them with hugs and claps on the back. The group of guys took their seats and began chatting away with somber expressions on their faces. One seat lay empty, as if left in memory of their slain friend.

One of the guys pointed at me, a grin on his face I wanted to punch. Nickolai glanced over his shoulder and crooked his finger with a grin tugging at his lips. I flipped him off, and the guys chuckled. Spying a free table in the corner, one with a clear view of both the door and my charge, I sank down into the seat and set my book on the table as I tried to relax.

A waitress came by the table and I ordered a coffee, watching as a group of girls stopped by Nickolai's table, offering sympathies. A brunette set her hand gently on Nickolai's shoulder. He patted her hand once, then lifted it from his shoulder and inclined his body toward a ginger-haired man to his left.

The waitress came back with my coffee and I thanked her and took a sip before opening my book and beginning to read, my attention half on the book and half on Nickolai.

When Nickolai and his buddies ordered food and settled in for the evening, I leaned back in my chair and concentrated on the words on the page. Time passed by, and soon I'd blocked out the noisy coffee shop, immersing myself in a word where Anita raised the dead and solved crimes. I didn't know how long I lost myself in the book, captivated until a voice cracked through the magic and broke the spell.

Lifting my gaze, my eyes landed on a familiar, petite girl who smiled as if I were a long-lost friend. Her blonde hair was short and wavy, her features cute in that girl-next-door way. She wore a *Sons of Anarchy* tee, tied up at the waist.

Setting her armful of books down on the table in front of her, the girl's smile widened as she extended her hand and said with a hint of an American twang, "Hi, I'm Krista."

"Ryan," I muttered in reply, staring at her hand until it dawned on me that she meant for me to shake it. Nickolai's words about making friends rang in my head as I grasped her hand in mine.

"Can I join you? There's not a free seat to be had tonight."

Her expression seemed genuine enough, but I was suspicious as to why she wanted to sit with me. Krista didn't wait for my answer, dragging out the spare seat and sitting down in front of me, blocking Nickolai from my line of sight. I shifted my chair slightly so I could easily watch the princeling.

Krista must have been studying me herself as she followed the path of my gaze and grinned. "Are you watching St. Pat's most eligible bachelor? I mean, every single woman on campus has their sights set on him. Though tonight, most are sulking at the fact a mysterious runway model went home with him last night."

Annoyed everyone seemed to be watching us both, especially when I wished to blend in with shadows, I narrowed my gaze. "Is that why you sat with me tonight? For gossip? Don't try and pretend you wanna be my friend if all you want is to find out about us. I spent a great amount of time and energy avoiding girls like that, so if that's all you want, then have at it. Nickolai's a free agent."

Krista blanched, horrified at my words and my disgusted tone, her chair scraping as she stood. She made to leave, then paused, turning back. "I have no designs on Nickolai, Ryan. I have a boyfriend at home in the States. I genuinely wanted to be friends with you because... Do you know how hard it is to find another girl who's intelligent and not afraid to speak her mind like you did in class the other day?"

Guilt and regret washed over me. I wanted to apologize, but Krista kept going.

"I don't know who hurt you and made you think kind words are ploys of deceit, but that's not me."

Krista gathered up her books, and I stood to stop her, knowing I was being fifty shades of an asshole.

"I'm sorry, Krista. Please, let me try this again." This time, I held out my hand and tried to give Krista the most genuine smile I could muster. "Ryan Callan. It's nice to meet you."

Krista shook my hand again. "Krista Meyers Gill."

We sat down again, and I struggled to find something to say. Krista smiled, sensing my discomfort.

"Not very good at small talk I take it?"

"Not really," I admitted. "I... I... I don't have many friends where I live, so I spend most of my time alone or with..."

"With Nickolai?"

"Hell no! I, um... I train in martial arts, so I spend a lot of time with men who think a girl's place is barefoot and pregnant."

Krista rested her chin in her hand as she propped her elbows on the table. "And our world leaders think the world has changed, eh?"

"Definitely not the world I live in."

We shared a smile and I felt eyes on me from across the room, yet I fought against the urge to glance in that direction. The waitress came by again, and Krista ordered more coffee for us both and a plate of fries. I avoided talking for a few minutes by reading the spines of Krista's textbooks. They were all media related, from one about investigative journalism to monsters in literature.

"I want to be a journalist, interview movie and TV stars. I wanted to be a crime journalist at first, but I don't have the stomach for it."

I waited as the waitress returned with our order, and Krista pushed the plate in my direction. I snatched a fry so as not to be rude and nibbled on it.

"Why not study in the States?" I wondered aloud. "Why come all the way to Ireland to study?"

Krista took a sip of her coffee before explaining. "Ireland, and especially St. Pats, is the only place where you can study about all the technical aspects of journalism and have someone like Professor Sykes who will let us debate *Buffy*, *The Vampire Diaries* and *Van Helsing* in the same class as Laurell K. Hamilton and Jeaniene Frost. Conrad, my boyfriend, was transferred to Ireland about a year ago, so I came along. He went home in September, but I stayed."

"That must be hard."

"It is what it is," she said with a shrug.

"I've decided to stay around for a while," I said. "Nickolai's mother is going to try and get me enrolled, so we might have some classes together."

"Oh my God, that's awesome!"

Krista babbled on about classes and assignments, offering to help out where possible to get me up to speed and telling me I'd arrived at the perfect time with Halloween approaching, that all kinds of events and displays would be happening around campus. She mentioned a party at one of the frat houses and how everyone wanted to go because it was one of the events of the year.

I certainly wouldn't be going.

"That's if the party still goes ahead after what happened to Matt," she added.

"Matt?"

"Matt Sullivan. He was murdered last night on campus."

I remembered the professor calling him Mr. Sullivan and Nickolai calling him Matt this morning. I tried to pretend I was saddened by the death, but humans were born and then they died—some tragically, some of old age. For vampires, death was something that happened after a sprawling gap of time. Unless, of course, death came calling for you long before your time, shrouded in blood and despair, masked in honor and duty.

Krista ate a few more fries, washing them down with a gulp of coffee before she leaned in. "Rumors abound on campus as to how he died. The police have been very tight-lipped, but I heard one say his blood was drained and he had two prong-like marks on his neck that looked like he'd been gnawed at."

Shrugging my shoulders, I ran my thumb over the

spine of my book. "Some sort of wild animal must have come upon him after he died." I lifted my mug to my lips, taking another sip of coffee.

"Or a vampire killed him," Krista said simply.

I spluttered, coughing harshly as I tried to regain my composure, her words so blunt and accurate I had no idea how to respond except for absolute denial. "Vampire's aren't real. They're fictious monsters created from the minds of men with overactive imaginations."

"Why don't you seem overly convinced, Ryan? All stories come from some aspect of truth. I would bet you anything that all monsters are real."

Yeah, and she was sitting right across from one.

"You're completely insane," I said with a laugh.

"And by that, you mean we're gonna be best friends."

Despite the situation, I found myself grinning at Krista as she stood and asked me to meet her again for coffee tomorrow. I spared a glance at Nickolai, and Krista grinned, advising me the boys always met here when classes were cancelled. I already knew, but I still bobbed my head in agreement.

Just as Krista inched away from the table, a siren wailed outside, and I had to cover my ears at the loudness of it. Lights flashed in the café, and people screamed, the scent of their fear so strong it roused the predator in me and I had to close my eyes and find my Zen.

"Ladies and Gentlemen, please remain calm. There is an active assailant on campus grounds. For your own safety, please remain inside the grounds until further notice."

Krista peered at me, sinking back down in her chair as I sprang up, adrenaline flooding my veins as I pushed my book at her and said I needed the bathroom. With a quick glance at Nickolai, I begged him to stay put as I marched toward the main doors of the café.

A stout security guard manned the doors, arms folded across his chest, his expression smug. "Go back inside, little lady. No one can leave."

"My boyfriend went out for a smoke about ten minutes ago; I just want to see if he's okay."

"Don't worry your pretty little head about him," he said. "There was nobody in the smoking shelter when I came on shift just before the alarm. Go back inside."

The doors swung open, another security guard coming inside. As the first guard tore his eyes from me, I angled my body sideways, slipping past both guards and out the open door, grinning as they called after me. Bolting around the corner, I set my back to the wall and waited a few heartbeats to see if they were brave enough to follow me.

They weren't.

Lifting my nose in the air, I inhaled deeply, searching for the familiar scent of blood on the wind to lead me in the right direction. Just then the wind shifted, blowing right in my face, and I caught it—the coppery scent of blood mixed with the sicky-sweet scent of death. According to my nose, I needed to cross the quad in order to find the body.

That meant the body was close enough to Nickolai's apartment to cause concern.

Reaching back, I grasped the hilts of my sai, relishing the comforting feel of them. I relinquished my hold, channeled my inner Anita Blake, and rushed forward into danger.

Chapter 9

By the time I reached the scene of the crime, the place was so riddled with police and crime scene investigators I couldn't get close enough to the body to examine it, but I didn't actually need to see matching puncture wounds. I knew in my gut the rogue vampire was responsible for this second death.

I was puzzled as to why the rogue had wasted so much blood—the amount seeping into the concrete could have fed at least three fully grown vampires. No self-respecting vamp would waste blood like that. We were raised to believe those who gave us blood—willingly or unwillingly—were sacred, the blood in their veins keeping us alive. We respected the hell out of the fact that, without humans, our species would become extinct. Wasn't that what the council wanted to prevent?

Knowing I could not be of any use to the dead man, I kept to the shadows, glancing up toward the window of Nickolai's apartment, the proximity of the murder too close for comfort. I felt an overwhelming urge to grab Nickolai and drag him home. Swallowing down the bile in my throat, I stole one more glance at the slain man, noting his similarity to Nickolai. It was not a coincidence; someone knew the crown prince was on campus, and they were not one bit happy about it.

Moving away from the scene, I made my way down a back alleyway, glancing down at the ground and following the bloody footprints that led all the way to the high wall surrounding the outer edge of campus. There was a partial print on the wall, as if the rogue had scaled it and escaped before the humans could so much as get a whiff of him.

Glancing around, I made sure no one was watching before I crouched low and used all of my strength to leap up and grasp the top of the wall. Ignoring the dull ache in my shoulder, I pulled myself up and balanced on the top of the wall, my feet gracefully settling on the flat, narrow surface. I scanned the area in front of me, my eyes peeled for any sign of the rogue.

There was nothing for miles as I peered out into the pitch-black night, scanning the field and looking toward the forested area beyond. If I'd been looking for the perfect place to hide, I'd have been out there with scents and sounds masking my presence, watching, waiting to see if I'd been discovered.

The wind gathered again, whipping strands of my ice-blonde hair into my face but also carrying a scent on the air, one I recognized from the night before. It was strong enough that I knew it was fresh. The rogue was nearby; near enough for me to scent him and for him to have scented me.

We'd always been told rogues were predominantly male, that female rogues were so rare they basically didn't exist. But rogues craved a mate just like all other vampires, and with trueborn females being so rare, that was a recipe for trouble. There were even rumors of court vampires in the past falling for rogues and casting aside title and prestige to join them. As the Romanov dynasty's vampire clan liked their women soft and protected, finding a full-blood female vampire alone in this part of the world was a rarity. Hopefully, that meant the rogue would be just as intrigued with me as I was eager to make his acquaintance—I was counting on it.

My senses prickled, snapping my attention to the right as a shadowy figure stepped out of the tree cover and into the moonlight. He was tall, standing at almost six feet, and lean, but I knew *lean* didn't mean he couldn't overpower me. He had a pinched-looking face, his eyes narrow and snakelike as he tilted his head, observing me.

Lifting a hand, he beckoned me forward. I snorted and mirrored his gesture, telling him to come to me. He took a few hesitant steps, then flashed me a fanged grin, looking over his shoulder as if he were waiting for someone else.

Could the rogue have a partner in crime?

Wanting to lure him out, I dropped down from my perch on the wall, my Chucks squelching in the mud, the wetness soaking through my shoes as I walked toward the forest. Stopping halfway, I held out my hands and shrugged, halting my advance so the rogue would come to me. I saw him consider it, and as I waited my hands snaked behind my back, ready to unleash my sai and rid the world of this stain the moment he drew close.

Adrenaline set fire to my veins, my fangs slipping free of my gums, my muscles tensing at the prospect of unleashing the coiled tension in my body. I was poised to strike, ready for battle, and I would be victorious.

Suddenly, the rogue turned on his heel and darted into the forest. Cursing, I started after him, but a hand fell on my shoulder before I could chase after the murderer.

Quick as lightning, I pulled one of my sai free and spun, pressing the tip of my weapon to the flesh of the person who'd managed to creep up on me.

Nickolai did not so much as flinch as my sai kissed the flesh at his neck, although he did have the good graces to hold up his hands in apology. I snarled at him, the adrenaline in my veins needing an outlet for its aggression, but I knew I would not get it.

Hissing as I yanked my sai away from Nickolai's skin, I sheathed the weapons and stalked away from him, growling low in my throat, trying to appease the monster in me to no avail. My fists clenched and unclenched by my side as I tried to reign in my temper.

"Ryan."

Nickolai's tone was full of authority, demanding obedience, and it only frayed my temper even more. I snarled, my gaze narrowing as I turned back to face him. The crown prince stood smugly before me, and I wanted to punch him for disturbing my hunt. How sweet it would feel to let my fist connect with his face, to feel bone crunching and skin splitting under my knuckles.

He said my name again, and my temper flared, my feet moving of their own accord until I was nearly nose to chest with him. "You fucked up my hunt," I growled low in my throat.

"I'm sorry. I didn't mean to. Hit me if it will make

you feel better."

Oh, by Eve, I wished I could just punch him in his stupid face. But I could just imagine his mother asking why her son had a broken jaw, and me explaining it was because I'd wanted to wipe the smugness off his face. I'd be facing a court martial, a charge of endangering a member of the royal family. In the heat of the moment, no doubt it'd be worth it. But afterward, I knew I'd regret it.

Being the petty little creature I was, I pressed the palms of my hands against Nickolai's chest, shoving hard enough he staggered back a few steps. It felt good, but instead of sating my adrenaline, it only thrilled me even more, made me crave it even more.

Anger flashed in Nickolai's eyes, and his calm expression slipped. I pushed him again and he reached for me, flashing his own fangs as he did. I slipped under his arms, pushing him again as I stayed out of his grasp.

We faced each other, both of us breathing hard, circling each other like lions, ready to unleash our claws and make the other bleed. Nickolai's nostrils flared, his aggression subsiding as I lurched forward only to be grabbed around the waist from behind. Before I even had time to react, Nickolai was snarling at the person who'd dared to stop me.

"Now, now, children. Don't make me put ya in time out."

I stilled at the sound of Jack's teasing Irish lilt. As soon as he loosened his grip on me, I slipped out from his grasp and shot him a look of pure contempt, to which Jack merely chuckled, inciting my anger even more.

I decided it might be worth it to take my anger out

on a seasoned member of the Royal Guard. I knew Jack wouldn't pull his punches, wouldn't give me an inch, and it would quite possibly give me a much-needed release if I bled.

"I can see the ole wheels turning in your head, kiddo, and I'm not for sparing with ye this night. Get your ass back to the apartment. Atticus is waiting there for you with someone for dinner."

I balked at his tone, his chastising of me, and dug my heels in, silently standing my ground.

Jack's expression darkened. "Take a walk, Ryan," he said in a tone I'd never heard from him before—one that said I'd pushed too far and embarrassed myself. "I mean it. Don't make me throw you over my shoulder, girl."

I wanted to rage at him, the closest thing I had to family, but the frosty demeanor I'd spent years building up slowly slipped back into place. I clenched my jaw and glared at Nickolai, putting the blame on him.

Brushing past Jack, I took off at a jog, ignoring the sound of my name on Nickolai's lips. I made it to the wall and use the momentum of my pace to jump up and swing myself over the wall, landing on the opposite side with a feline grace. My emotions a tornado inside me, I jogged the rest of the way to the apartment complex and, once inside, eagerly pressed the button that would take me to the penthouse.

My foot tapped an angry rhythm as I waited, and I all but jumped into the elevator when it arrived. As soon as it reached the penthouse, I stalked forward, kicked off my Chucks, and headed straight into the living area.

Atticus rose to greet me, amusement all over his features as he chortled, "Who had the audacity to piss you off, Ryan?"

"At the moment, it's the entire race of male vampires, so I'd keep the smart remarks to myself if I was you, Atty."

The other vampire only laughed harder, then pointed to the bedroom. I glanced inside to see a young woman sitting on the bed, her head bent and hands clasped in prayer. She lifted her head as I approached, smiling widely as she greeted me.

"Hello, Ryan."

"Hey Simone."

The girl brushed her hair to the side and craned her neck, revealing the side of her neck that bore scars from offering her blood on many an occasion. I always felt guilty when I laid eyes on the scars of the Children of Eve, wishing their lives were not all about keeping us vampires alive. Simone never complained, though; her ancestors before her were Children of Eve, and her own descendants would continue to be. Well... if we managed to prevent our extinction.

"It is my pleasure to serve you," she said quietly.

Hunger punched my gut, and my fangs were already elongated from my aggression. I flopped down on the bed and murmured, "Thank you for your gift."

Wrapping my hand around the curve of her neck, I tilted her head to give me better access. I hovered my mouth over her skin, felt her tense at the feel of my breath on her throat, and waited for Simone to shiver in anticipation. When her scent become mingled with a hint of fear, I struck.

I sank my fangs into her neck, drinking deeply as I tightened my grip. The roar of my pulse and Simone's pulse forced a moan from my lips as I swallowed another mouthful of delicious blood. I could feel the warm liquid work its way down my throat, relishing the slight burn it left at the back of my throat.

I felt Simone tense and the rage in me subside slightly, the beast temporarily sated, so I reluctantly, carefully, pulled my fangs from Simone's neck and licked at the wounds to seal them off. Simone sighed in bliss, and as my fangs ascended, I reached around her, grabbed the glass of juice I'd noticed on the bedside table, and held it out to her. Her hands were a little shaky, so I held the glass to Simone's lips, and she opened her eyes and sipped the juice slowly.

When she could hold the glass herself, I slipped off the bed and allowed her the time to collect herself, exiting the bedroom and ignoring the three vampires who now sat in the living room. Locking myself in the bathroom, I tossed water over my face, snagged a toothbrush—probably Nickolai's—and brushed my teeth so my breath wouldn't smell of blood.

Once I'd composed myself, I walked out of the bathroom to a roomful of silence. Ignoring the three of them, I swirled the coffee that was in the pot on the counter, filling a mug before I grabbed an apple from the fruit bowl and washed it under the tap.

Taking a bite of the apple, I grabbed my mug and went to sit in front of the window, sliding down the wall and stretching my legs out before me, wiggling my toes. Looking out to the night sky, I sipped my coffee, ignoring the boys.

After a few minutes, Jack rose from his seat and joined me, sliding down the opposite wall so our toes almost touched, his legs longer than mine by many an inch. I continued my intense scrutiny of the world outside until Jack sighed.

"By Jaysus, it seems not only have you gotten your mother's stubbornness, but you've also inherited Tristan's bullheadedness."

I remained quiet, his words like a knife in my chest. Draining the last of my coffee, I polished off my apple and placed the core into the cup. Jack nudged my foot with his, and I pulled my knees to my chest.

"What do you want me to say, Jack? You spoke to me like I was a child out there. I don't need you to parent me. I haven't had a parent since I was seven years old, and I don't need one now."

My words were sad as I spoke them, even if they were Eve's honest truth.

Jack frowned. "I didn't mean to chastise you, kiddo. I just didn't want you to bruise the prince's ego. You would have handed him his ass on a plate and then done it again just to prove a point."

I shrugged, glancing out the window again as Jack sighed and got to his feet, muttering about how he'd never understand women. I closed my eyes and rested my forehead against the cold glass, hiding a smile. After another minute or two, I heard Atticus escort Simone out, returning a short time later with delicious-smelling Chinese takeout that made my stomach rumble.

Laughter rang out in the room as the boys settled in to play cards and drink beer. I got up from my self-imposed naughty step, wondering who had dished up the plate of salt-and-pepper chicken for me on the counter, and perched myself on a stool by the counter as I ate.

When Jack got up to grab another beer, I cleared my throat and held out my hand for one. After a brief hesitation and a growl, Jack opened the bottle and handed it to me, shaking his head as I drained half the bottle in one gulp. Finding his seat again, I realized how tired I was—not sleepy, just bone weary.

"Hey, Ryan, come play a hand with us."

"No thanks. I'd hate to take your money from you, St. Clair. The last time I played cards, I made a grown vampire cry."

"My brother deserved it, the twerp, if he thought it advisable to squander his monthly salary on a stupid bet."

I took another sip of my beer and then shrugged. "I mean, he was playing for glory. What he wanted if he'd won would've made him the big man on campus."

"And what"—Nickolai said, his tone low and dangerous— "did he want if you lost?"

I thought about not answering, about shying away from Nickolai's and possibly Jack's reactions. Atticus had been there that night, when I'd taken ten grand off his brother, and now Edison hated me even more than he had before. This had been years ago, one night I'd been forced to interact with both my classmates and the Heathers. I'd never been asked again.

"If I won," I began slowly, resting my hands in my lap, having set my empty plate down, "I got the money. But Edison wanted to up the stakes, and the rest egged him on. So, he bet me his pocket money for one night with the Ice Queen. One night to see if I could be thawed."

Jack let loose a string of curse words as Nickolai's face went deathly still. He turned to face Atticus. "And you let her bet herself for money?"

Atticus held his future king's gaze. "This is Ryan we're talking about—nobody tells her what to do. Plus, Tristan was the biggest card shark in the Royal Guard. I knew the apple wouldn't fall far from the tree. She wasn't going to lose."

Nickolai got to his feet and glared at me. "How could you put yourself on the line like that? How could you treat yourself like you matter less than goddamn Edison St. Clair?"

"Because I don't. I don't matter. You all keep telling me to live, to stop acting like I died with my parents, but I *did* die that day. The only reason I'm still breathing is because I promised my father I'd go on even if they didn't. If not for that promise, I'd have walked into the sun long ago."

The men all stared at me, speechless. My heart hammered in my chest as I clasped a hand over my mouth, wondering what sorcery had made me voice my most secret thoughts.

Pushing off the counter, I slipped my feet into my trainers and rushed to the elevator. Not a single soul moved to stop me, and the last thing I saw as the doors to the elevator closed was a look of pure anguish on Nickolai's face.

Chapter 10

I WALKED AROUND FOREVER, THE GLOOMINESS OF THE night my faithful companion as I methodically put one foot in front of the other, blocking out the sounds around me by blaring music in my ears. Streetlights illuminated the pathway for me after the moon disappeared behind clouds, and I walked a loop of the college to make sure the rogue wasn't wandering around.

As Little Mix's "Salute" ended and a classic-rock song came on, I wondered how long I could keep going, how long I could withhold myself from those around me now that I was forced into the human world. I'd thought being as detached as I felt would make me a perfect asset to the crown. After all, I had nothing to lose and would lay down my life to protect them. Attachments would only make doing that harder... right?

My mind drifted back to a conversation I'd overheard between my parents. They were worried I was too focused on my swordsmanship and not becoming as ladylike as my peers. My mother had scoffed, the sound so melodic, so enticing, that my father had smiled.

"Ryan wasn't born to be soft and quiet," she'd said. *"She was born to make the world shatter and shake at her fingertips. Our daughter will one day change the world."*

But Imogen Callan had been wrong, so utterly wrong. I would not change the world. The world had upended, and I was a shell of a vampire. Despite my earlier statement, I wasn't sure I actually wanted to die; I just wasn't altogether certain I wanted to live, either.

Coming upon a bridge connecting the city to the college, I perched myself on the ledge, watching the waters of the River Lee rage beneath my feet. I envied the waters, free to come and go as they pleased, be as fierce or as unassuming as they wanted. I popped an earbud out and listened to the roar, the water lapping over the edges of the bank as the tide rose, morning no more than an hour or two away.

Sometimes, on the darkest of days, when my emotions were too much for me to bear, I wondered who I would have been if my parents had survived. Would I have been happy? Would I still have been adamant on joining the Royal Guard? Would Nickolai and I still have been best friends? I pictured *that* Ryan, smiling and laughing at family dinners, at royal gatherings, on birthdays and Christmases.

My chest tightened, and a lump in my throat made it hard to swallow. My grip on the railing hardened, the metal groaning under the strain of my strength. I relaxed my grasp, blinking away tears as I blew out a breath.

Upon inhaling, my spine straightened as I caught a scent on the wind. Not making any sudden movements, I glanced toward the end of the bridge to see the rogue standing in a veil of shadows, the red tinge of his eyes visible as he watched me with primal hunger. He was far enough away to get a head start if he ran, his legs much longer than mine, so, I decided to play his game and see if I could unnerve him—enough, anyway, to make a mistake.

"Did they send the pretty girl out here to distract me before they pounce?"

He spoke with a foreign accent, and his voice sounded like gravel, as if his throat had been injured somehow. I searched my memory but could not recall any mention of a rogue with such an affliction.

I shrugged. "Would you believe me if I said I was alone?"

"It is not the nature of male vampires to leave such a prize to venture out by herself."

I laughed loudly, plucking the other bud from my ear as I noted the turn of phrases he used. His speech was proper, almost courtly. He seemed startled by my laughter, which made me smile.

"If you knew anything about me, you'd know there are no vampires who consider me a prize. I'm sarcastic, a little psycho, messy, and I talk back. I snore in my sleep and curse like a sailor. I'm far from a prize."

The rogue angled his head, his shadow casting shapes on the wooden bridge as he considered me. "Then they do not deserve you. They do not see the potential in you. I see it and would treat you like the queen you are. Come with me, and we shall bathe in blood. I will make you a queen among vampires. We will not die out like those who remain chained to past notions."

I shrugged my shoulders again, keeping my heartbeat steady so as not to give myself away to this monster.

Swinging my legs back around, I stood on the bridge opposite him and smiled. "As tempting as that sounds, I have no desire to become queen of anything. I do, however, want to separate your head from your shoulders and present it to *my* queen. Now be a good little rogue and get on your knees so we can do this cleanly. I'd hate to get blood on my clothes."

The rogue hissed, taking a step toward me but halting as he inhaled my scent as if he was suddenly struck by how good I smelled. I reached around my back to grasp the handles of my sai as the rogue inched backward, all bravado seemingly gone as morning began to sneak through the clouds. I knew the rogue would bolt soon, but I'd gained some valuable knowledge during our conversation.

I knew that, the first time we met, he'd been intrigued by me because female vampires were few and far between. Now, I had his full attention; I was fairly confident he'd be focused on me in the near future rather than attacking humans.

"We must reconvene another day, Beauty. I am eager to discover if your skin feels as soft as it looks."

Rooted to the spot, I watched as the rogue fled the incoming sun's rays, ducking once again out of view. I remained standing on the bridge until I felt the heat of the sun on my skin, and then I used my speed to get back to Nickolai's apartment complex just in time.

Once inside the private elevator, I mulled over the reactions of those who no doubt awaited my arrival. The doors pinged as they opened, and the moment I stepped into the penthouse, all three men stood as if they hadn't expected me to appear.

I guessed we were having a slumber party for the day. Awesome.

Jack stepped forward, opening his mouth to speak, but I held up a hand to stop him. Whatever apologies or platitudes he'd planned on saying were not warranted, and we had bigger fish to fry than dealing with my obvious mental health issues.

"The rogue is eastern European and was either part of a court at one point or at the very least was raised by wealthy vampires. His accent sounds Hungarian, but I can't be sure. He knew about the issues we're having with blood and possible extinction. Not sure he knows who I am or who Nickolai is," I said, wrapping up my intel report, "but he did offer to make me his queen after we bathe in blood together."

With a shrug, I turned toward the kitchen, grabbed a bottle of blood from the counter, twisted the cap off, and drank down a few gulps, resting my forehead on the closed fridge door. A moment later, I sensed Nickolai coming up behind me.

"Are you okay?"

Straightening, I turned, leaning against the fridge as Nickolai rested against the counter. The space between the counter and the kitchen area was small, made even more so by Nickolai's bulk. Broad shoulders, a stomach Tom Hardy would have been envious of, tree-trunk legs; when Nickolai became king, he would lead from the front, and his people would adore him for it.

"I'm good," I said. "He didn't get near me. Plus, I can handle myself."

Nickolai smiled, and I tried to ignore the sensation in my stomach as he said, "I wasn't worried about that.

The rogue doesn't know what he's let himself in for. I just hope I get to watch."

I returned his smile as he continued. "I was referring to what you said before you ran out. Ryan—"

"Look, Nicky," I interjected, unwilling to discuss my little slip of the tongue. "Forget it, okay? I'm not going to walk into the sun. I have a job to do, and I'll do it. We need to concentrate on the rogue and completing your mission. Everything else can wait."

I stepped around him as his hand fell on the crook of my elbow. "You can talk to me, you know. I mean, I'm not sure either of us will fit in the cupboard under the stairs anymore, but I can try and squeeze in if it makes you feel better."

The image of Nickolai squeezing himself into our childhood cubbyhole dragged a howl of laughter from me. Atticus and Jack glanced over at us as I shook my head.

"I'm not sure you could survive the embarrassment, Nicky. Imagine the guard having to knock down a wall to yank your ass free. On seconds thought, try it—I'd pay good money to see that."

Nickolai growled, but there was laughter in his eyes as he gently pushed me away. Grinning more than I expected to, I flopped down on a chair next to Atticus and Jack, kicked off my shoes, and set my feet on the table in front of me.

"Anything else, Ryan? You notice anything else about the rogue that could be useful?"

I nodded my head as I drank from my bottle again. "You know that show, *Chicago P.D.*? The rogue sounded like Voight from it, just with an accent—you know, gravelly, like he'd suffered an injury to his voice and it hadn't healed properly."

Atticus and Jack shared a look.

I sat up straighter in my chair. "What? Do you know who he is?"

Jack rubbed the back of his neck, glancing up at Nickolai.

They were clearly keeping something from me even though I was the one who'd found out about the rogue. I couldn't believe they were looking for Nickolai's permission to fill me in. Rage began to bubble up inside my chest, and I felt my skin heat as I got to my feet and shook my head.

"You know what, Jack? Don't tell me. I'll find out by myself. I give it two nights before he seeks me out again. Keep your secrets." Turning to Nickolai, I added, "Since you have two strong, capable members of the Royal Guard to watch you, I'm taking the bed."

Surging forward, I slammed the bedroom door behind me before anyone could speak.

I paced the length of the room, too mad to lie down. I didn't think I was angry at them, really—more the fact if I had a penis, I'd be more included.

The rogue's words sounded in my mind. *"It is not the nature of male vampires to leave such a prize to venture out by herself."*

Was that all I was, a prize to be won? Was Katerina humoring me with a position in the Royal Guard in the hopes I'd get bored, suddenly overwhelmed with the need to become a mother, and the crown would get what they wanted in the end?

With a sigh, I glanced over at Nickolai's bed. It had

been made with military precision, not a crease out of place. My body ached at how comfy it looked, and I couldn't wait to sleep my brains out.

Stripping off my leggings, I shucked off my jacket and tossed it to the side, unclasping my sai belt and setting it down on the bedside table. I liked to keep them close to me, as if having them nearby would summon the ghost of my mother, as if she were with me every single time I wielded her weapons.

Yanking back the covers, I slipped into the bed and smothered a groan. After six weeks of sleeping—or rather, *not* sleeping—in an air vent, lying down on this bed felt as if I were lying on a cloud of cotton candy. I reached over to the nightstand in search of a book, cursing as I realized I'd left mine with Krista.

There was no way in hell was I walking back into the living room, so I laid my head back and stared at the ceiling for what felt like forever. Considering how weary my body was, I was almost impressed how well sleep continued to evade me. I growled, punching the mattress as a knock sounded on the door a second before it opened.

Nickolai slipped inside, waving my worn book in the air. He must have gotten it back for me from Krista. "I know you can't sleep unless you've at least read a few pages," he said, holding out the book to me.

How did he know that about me? How did he seem to know a lot of things about me when I'd gone to extreme lengths to distance myself from those I cared for?

My lips remained shut as I sat up in bed, our fingers grazing as he handed me the book. He glanced around the room, looking the least comfortable I'd seen him in a long time.

"What?"

"I'm wondering how to ask you if I can stay here tonight without you thinking I'm being forward."

"I know it might be a foreign concept to most of the males of our species, but how about you just be straightforward and stop skirting around the truth? Eve only knows, maybe I'd be reasonable if you treated me as an equal."

A muscle ticked in Nickolai's jaw as he rolled his eyes. "The reason Jack didn't say anything is because you do not have clearance to know. You are not Royal Guard just yet. The secrets we keep are for the safety of the entire court, not just something we do to piss you off."

Now it was my turn to roll my eyes. "Puh-lease. I'm not that conceited. I cannot do my job effectively if I only know half the facts. In fact, knowing half the facts will likely get either you or I killed. I don't care about secrets and lies, Nicky. I just want to do my job."

Sitting down on the edge of his own bed, Nickolai scrubbed a hand down his face. "Not even I have clearance to tell you," he said, "but we will. I already sent a request to my mother for it. We should be able to brief you soon."

"Okay."

Nickolai smirked. "Okay? That's all I get?"

"I can't argue your reasoning."

Nickolai's mouth dropped open.

"Shut your mouth," I said with another eye roll. "You'll catch flies."

Opening my book, I began to read, though I couldn't concentrate on the words even though I read them maybe a dozen times. Nickolai remained quiet, sitting there at the end of the bed.

"Okay, Romanov, spit it out," I snapped. "You're getting on my nerves and interrupting my reading time. Why are you hiding in here with me?"

Nickolai glanced down at the floor, then cleared his throat before he replied, his words low and hushed. "I'm giving them some alone time. It's rare they get to spend the whole day together, so I said I'd sleep in here with you."

Confused, I set the book down. "Why would Jack and Atticus need alone time? I mean, they're guardsmen—they spend all night with each other. Why would they need to spend the day toge—"

My words broke off as it finally dawned on me, my eyes widening as my mouth formed an O. Atticus and Jack? Damn... how had I never noticed? But hey, that wasn't my main concern.

While same-sex relationships were not something the crown forbid, it was frowned upon since our species was dwindling. How had they managed to keep it a secret for so long? And why was Nickolai telling me now?

"How long have you known?" I asked.

"Awhile. I've been training some with Jack lately, and Atticus was hanging around. The way they were with each other, it was too familiar to just be comrades in arms. I never said anything until Atticus told me himself, drunk one night after a fight with Jack. There are only four alive who know their secret."

Shaking my head, I chewed on my bottom lip as I mulled this over. "You shouldn't have told me," I said finally.

"Jack ordered me to," he replied. "He said it was harder to sit next to Atticus and not touch him than it would be to have you know their secret."

Jack had been my father's closest friend—even more so than Anatoly. Jack had stood beside me as we gave my parents a warrior's funeral. Jack had kept his eye on me when everyone else had given up. Did I care if he was in a relationship with Atticus? Hell no!

I grinned at Nickolai. "I mean, when you think about it, I guess it's kinda hot. They're both rather handsome—not my shot of vodka, but I can still admire it."

Nickolai rolled his eyes, and any tension in his shoulders seemed to evaporate. Getting to his feet, he grabbed a pillow off the bed and tossed it on the ground. As he went to lie down on the floor, I surprised us both by asking what he was doing.

"Going to sleep, Ryan. What does it look like I'm doing?"

Ever the mature and sophisticated one, I stuck out my tongue at him as I scooted over in the bed. "Get in before I change my mind. And keep your hands to yourself."

He stared until I growled.

"Give me a second," he said. "I'm trying to decide if it's worth the pain of listening to you snore all night."

I threw a pillow at him before turning my attention back to my book. Nickolai laughed, lying on the bed fully clothed, his arms behind his head. We said nothing, lying in silence until the words began to blur on the page and my eyes grew heavy.

I vaguely felt Nickolai pluck the book from my hands and tuck the covers up to my chin. I let loose a sigh as I smiled, allowing myself to drift off to sleep and feel safe for the first time since I was seven.

Chapter 11

I slept better than I had in a long time but woke to find Nickolai gone; the only reminder we'd shared the space was the dwindling heat on his side of the bed. I stretched out my limbs, casting aside the duvet and pulling on my leggings before I walked out of the bedroom barefoot.

Night had crept in quietly, descending around us while I'd slept the day away. When the clock struck seven, I realized I'd slept longer than I'd planned. The apartment was quiet, with only Nickolai remaining, his eyes scanning a textbook as he balanced a notebook on his knee and jotted down notes.

"Jack and Atticus left to update Idris on our progress," he said, barely looking up from his notetaking. "Jack asked me to invite you to coffee on Friday night if you wanted to talk on neutral ground. He was adamant I let you sleep."

"I'll text him."

"I told Mother we would not be home for Samhain. Told her there were too many things going on around campus for me to disappear."

Coming into the sitting area, I sank down into the chair. "Why do I feel a *but* coming? You don't have a happy tone."

Nickolai sat back in his seat and set the notebook aside. Watching me with tentative eyes, he said, "Kristoph is going to stop by for a visit. He suggested we all go for dinner on Saturday evening."

I arched a brow. "The three of us?"

"The four of us."

I snorted, chortling as I shook my head. "If either of you expect me to sit down opposite Natalia and not stab her with a fork, then you're both nuts."

"I have to go. As my nominated bodyguard, you have to be there. If you want to sit off to the side and not speak to us, I understand. It just seems a shame for you to miss out on eating at Murphy's because of Natalia."

By day, Murphy's was a quintessential Irish pub, but when darkness descended, the back room became a vampire restaurant whose menu vampires travelled across the world to sample. The wait list for a table—assuming one could afford to dine there—was several months long. The night chef was a vampire, and the food... Well, the food was to die for.

"You fight dirty."

Nickolai grinned.

I clucked my tongue at him. "It will be your fault if I end up stabbing her."

"At least we'll all be entertained."

We fell into silence, Nickolai turning back to his books as I went to the kitchen to make myself some breakfast. I brewed some coffee and poured it into two mugs, setting one down in front of Nickolai before returning to butter my toast and eat it as I stood looking out the window.

I left Nickolai to his own devices as I showered and changed, having grabbed my bag of clothes out of the living room. I spent a little time brushing the knots out of my hair, then plucked out a can of hairspray, something I hadn't done in weeks as I'd tried to remain stealthy. I didn't have to hide now, so I shook out the can and sprayed the tips of my hair with a light, frosted blue.

While the color was drying, I left my hair down and went back outside. Nickolai was tapping away on his phone but stopped when he heard me approach. He blinked at the sight of my hair but didn't mention it.

"The guys want me to go play a game of soccer with them. We won't have classes until next week, so I said I'd go."

"Okay."

"I would suggest you stay here and get some rest, but I know that's not going to happen."

I replied with a nonchalant shrug.

We readied ourselves to head out after Nickolai changed into shorts and a tee, each grabbing a water bottle from the fridge even though we both knew a human soccer game was barely a warmup. I slipped my jacket on once I'd secured my sai, making sure I was equipped to face the rogue should he appear.

"Nickolai," I said as I waited by the door, waiting until the crown prince gave me his full attention before I spoke once again. "If the rogue does attack, you need to act as if you're human. You need to pretend to be afraid. You can't rush off like Superman and try to save the day.

If you want to keep up the pretense, then you need to be completely human."

Nickolai bounced on his feet. "I consider myself more Batman than Superman. Does that make you Catwoman or Supergirl?"

"If the next words out of your mouth are about you thinking of me in a catsuit, I'll knock your fangs into your stomach for you."

A slow grin spread across Nickolai's face. "I wasn't before, but I am now."

Letting loose an exasperated sigh, I pressed the button and ordered the elevator downward without waiting for Nickolai, the vampire slipping in at the last possible minute.

Once outside the apartment complex, we crossed the quad quickly. The amount of security around the college had increased significantly, but even a dozen of these men would be no match for a dangerous, bloodthirsty rogue.

Making our way to the field where we'd first encountered the rogue, I stayed hidden in the alleyway while Nickolai stepped into view. His friends called out to him, already kicking a ball around, but Nickolai hesitated, staring over his shoulder at me even as I waved him forward.

Coming back into the alleyway, he tried to steer me out, but I dug my heels in and refused to move.

"Come and watch us play."

"No thanks."

"Are you ashamed to be seen with me?"

Snorting, I shook my head. "No. I just have no intention of being the subject of gossip and speculation. I get that enough at home."

"You've never let it bother you before, Ryan."

"Contrary to popular opinion," I said, folding my arms across my chest, "I'm not made of stone. I might not be easily offended, but I am easily annoyed."

Nickolai's eyes went from mine to his friends. "I'd never let them insult you."

"You're not going to just let me stay here in the shadows, are you?"

It was Nickolai's turn to shake his head, flashing me an irritating grin as he nudged me out of the alley and into view. I was aware of the boys all watching us with amusement and interest as Nickolai and I walked onto the field together. Nickolai playfully nudged my shoulder with his as we walked along, and I glared at him.

He cast me a mischievous grin as he walked with an annoying swagger to meet up with his friends. The boys clapped him on the back, grinning like idiots.

"Nicky!" I yelled after him as I came to a stop by the edge of the pitch and sat down on the grass. "Remember what the doctor said. Try and avoid contact with others until the test results come back. We don't know if that rash is contagious."

Nickolai flushed a bright shade of red as his buddies began mocking him. He glared at me, his expression threatening retribution, but I simply wiggled my fingers in the air and smiled.

The minute they started to play, I zoned out. Stretching out my legs, I rested my back against the rail surrounding the field, reaching around to be sure I could still reach my weapons if things went sideways suddenly.

I closed my eyes and exhaled like my dad had shown

me, shaking the dust and cobwebs out of my mind as I focused on my surroundings. I could hear the thud of the boys' feet on the field, could pinpoint Nickolai's location by the slight difference in his gait. I felt the grass blades brush against my fingers, moved by the same silent breeze caressing my cheek as it came in from the south. Rain was incoming; I could taste it on my lips.

Even though my eyes were closed, I could see the world around me just as well—maybe better—using my other senses. So well, in fact, I knew the soccer ball was hurtling toward me even before Nickolai called out a warning. Snapping my hands up, I caught it without so much as a flinch and smugly opened my eyes to a chorus of "*Whoa!*"

One of the guys jogged up to me, smiling widely as I handed him the ball. "Don't suppose you'd fancy being our goalie, would you? With saves like that, we might actually win."

"Sorry, you'd totally have an unfair advantage. Plus, I'd hate to bruise so many male egos."

He chuckled, then jogged back to the game.

"That was awesome. I'd have totally ended up with a broken nose."

I glanced over my shoulder to see Krista standing behind me. I gave her a small smile, unsure of what to do next. After what seemed like forever, I motioned to the ground next to me and tried to smile as if I weren't planning her grisly demise.

Krista's California smile lit up the night as she flopped down next to me, holding out a bag of sweets. I dipped my hand in, amusing myself by snagging a set of vampire teeth and popping them into my mouth. I chewed and swallowed as Krista watched the game unfold in front of us.

"What happened to you the other night? You just up and left." Krista sounded upset.

I hadn't intended to hurt her feelings; I hadn't considered her after the fact at all.

"They wouldn't let me back in afterward," I said, scrambling for an explanation. "Nickolai had to come out, and then we went back to the apartment. I think the murder took place close to Nickolai's apartment, so that's quite scary."

Krista eyed me with suspicion and I readied myself to make up some more lies. Her eyes drifted down to my blue ends. "That's kinda cool," she said, changing the subject. "Did you do them yourself?"

Taking the ends between my fingers, I gave a little bow of my head. "Just from a spray can. I have to do it every couple of days to keep the color up. I could do yours, too, if you want."

Krista grinned excitedly. "That would be awesome!"

The game in front of us was beginning to wind down, so we both got to our feet, brushing the grass off us as we prepared to leave.

"I have to go call Conrad," Krista said, "but you fancy meeting up Friday or Saturday?"

I knew I'd be too riled up about the disastrous dinner on Saturday to play pretend all night, but I also had plans to meet with Jack on Friday.

"Uh, I have to meet my uncle Friday for a catch-up, but I should be free after. Can I text you when I'm free?"

"Absolutely."

We exchanged numbers. As Krista put her phone

126

away, she asked, "Are you going to the party Sunday night? There's no class on Monday because of the holiday, remember."

"What party?" I asked as Nickolai came up beside me, giving Krista a warm smile.

"The guys are throwing a casual-dress party Sunday night," he replied. "I told them we'd go."

"Absolutely not. We are not going to a stupid party."

Krista edged away, not wanting to get caught in our little spat. She waved a hand as she walked off, saying she'd see me on Friday. I waved in confirmation, then turned to face Nickolai, hands on my hips, lips pressed together, eyes narrowed.

"After Saturday I thought we could both do with some fun," he said.

"It might be fun for you, Nicky, but not for me. I'd rather pull my eyes out with chopsticks than go to a party."

"We'll talk about this later," Nickolai growled, and the predator in me snarled, my lips curling as Nickolai turned back to his friends and made a quip about how he liked his women feisty.

Laughter rang in my ears as I spun quickly and stalked off, not waiting for Nickolai to finish mocking me to his friends. I was so angry I made it all the way back to the apartment before I remembered I was supposed to be guarding Nickolai. Cursing inwardly, I rolled my shoulders and headed back the way I'd come, stopping when Nickolai came into view a few yards from the door.

With him safely within sight, I turned back and walked into the foyer, heading to the private elevator.

"Miss! Wait!"

One of the security guards came rushing out of a side room with a dazzling bouquet of white roses in his hands. Breathing hard as he ground to a halt in front of me, sweat beaded on his forehead as he handed them to me.

It was only then I saw the roses were frosted with blue—the same blue I'd colored the ends of my hair this evening.

Nickolai strode into the foyer and came straight toward us, grabbing the roses and demanding the guard tell us who'd left the flowers. I listened as the guard explained they'd been dropped off by the flower-shop delivery service about an hour ago, just after we'd left. Considering I'd only dyed my hair earlier tonight, it was clear the rogue was watching us closely.

Nickolai plucked a card from within the bouquet, his anger intensifying as he crumpled the card and tossed it aside, turning to question the poor, terrified guard once more.

Crouching down, I picked up the discarded note, smoothing it out so I could read it.

The roses pale in comparison to you. I like the blue. See you soon.

See you soon. A promise rather than a threat.

My plan to have the rogue focus his attention on me had worked—too well, if I was being honest. Now I was a bona fide celebrity, free stalker included.

As Nickolai continued to interrogate the guard, I snagged the flowers from him and headed up to apartment, holding my foot in the door until Nickolai finally came after me. The door closed, locking me in a tiny box with a testosterone- and anger-fueled vampire who was struggling to control his temper.

It would have been smart not to bait the bear, but who said I was smart? I knew Nickolai better than I knew myself, and sometimes he just needed to be yanked free of his anger.

Dropping my nose to the blooms, I inhaled their scent and gave a small sigh. "I never thought of myself as a flowers kinda girl, but these are gorgeous. They'd be even nicer if not given to me by a murdering sociopath. Still... gotta give him points for being original."

When the elevator doors opened, Nickolai stalked out, heading straight for his bedroom and slamming the door behind him. I set the flowers down on the counter and walked over to the window, pulling back the sliding door to let the night air in and hopefully let whatever the hell was wrong with Nickolai out.

"I don't know why you're mad at me, Nicky," I yelled through the door. "I didn't send myself the goddamn roses."

The door flew open, slamming so hard against the wall it rattled the open glass, and Nickolai stalked out, pulling a clean T-shirt on over his torso. I had to stop myself from admiring his physique.

"I'm mad at you for putting yourself in this position, for being so obnoxiously oblivious to yourself that you have now snared the attentions of one of the most dangerous rogues ever known."

Folding my arms across my chest, I struggled to remain calm, lifting my brows at him. "That was my plan. While he's trying to get his hands on me, he's less likely to go on a human-killing spree. And in case you've forgotten, My Liege, it's my job to put myself in these positions. It's what I was born to do."

"You'll end up getting yourself killed," Nickolai hissed, his hands clenched into fists.

"If that is my destiny, then so be it. You have no right to be angry with me for doing my job, or for something that may or may not happen."

Rage boiled in those heartthrob eyes of his, flashing a shade of red as he stepped up to me, leaning down so our noses almost touched. He breathed out as he snarled, "Hypocrite."

"Excuse you?" I snarled back at him, snapping my teeth as I clipped the words.

"You heard me. I called you a hypocrite. You cast me aside when you needed me the most because you were afraid of what might happen. You're angry all the goddamn time because you're utterly terrified of what the future might bring. So, hell yeah—you're a bloody hypocrite if you ask me."

Lifting my hands to his chest, I shoved him away from me, putting some distance between us. I didn't know if I wanted to kill him or kiss him... hopefully neither. Pointing my finger at him, my voice was as ice cold as my nickname as I said, "You wanna know why I'm angry all the time? You wanna know what twists my stomach and sends me seething with rage?"

"Yes!" Nickolai snarled.

"I'm angry at my parents for choosing the crown over me. For dying to protect your parents, not me. I'm so goddamn furious that, when they died, I was hiding in a cupboard, protecting your royal ass, when I could have been out there, helping them."

I took a menacing step toward Nickolai, watching

his anger dissipate as mine began to simmer and boil. Leaning in close, I lowered my voice to a whisper. "But more than that, I'm so fucking vexed for feeling angry at you, your mother, your entire family. My parents swore to die for the crown, and they did. I lost my entire world because of your family, and I *hate* myself for thinking of it like that."

"Ryan."

I ignored him. "I hate myself for thinking like this, for thinking like a little girl who lost everything, but there you go. I'm angry all the time because I can't help but blame the very people I'm now sworn to protect for losing my parents."

I gave Nickolai a sad smile. "Ain't life just a bitch?"

Chapter 12

Nickolai and I had not spoken in days.

We had fallen into a rather uncomfortable silence, neither of us venturing outside. That, however, did not deter the rogue from sending me gifts, which only seemed to aggravate Nickolai even more. Roses had only been the beginning—after that came chocolates, diamond and pearl jewelry, even a luxurious set of lingerie Nickolai tore to pieces in front of the window in case the rogue was watching.

To tell the truth, I was starting to worry about how intensely the rogue had fixated on me; however, I pretended like I didn't care and simply ignored all the pointed glares in my direction.

Friday finally rolled around although not as fast as I'd have liked, simply because I didn't want to leave Nickolai unguarded. As much as I wanted out of this goddamn apartment, I also wasn't looking forward to my little chat with Jack. It would no doubt be awkward as hell; then again, I was living in a pool of awkward right now.

I barely slept during the day; an abundance of nervous energy coupled with cabin fever made me restless. Usually, on days when I needed to unleash some tension, I'd train until I was exhausted. Unfortunately, spending time guarding His Royal Highness had left me unable to indulge myself. So here I was, stuck in the penthouse of a human apartment complex, lying on the ground with my legs planted against the wall, methodically pulling myself up and holding until the muscles in my stomach screamed in protest, then repeating.

I heard Nickolai stir inside his bedroom, then felt the heat of his gaze as he strode out and stood there, staring for what felt like ages before he let out a sigh and went into the kitchen. Ignoring the crown prince, I continued my workout, wondering how I could tell Nickolai he needed to stay indoors while I went to meet Jack.

Oh, *and* Krista.

I'd almost forgotten we'd arranged to meet after I caught up with Jack, but the human girl had texted me, reminding me of our plans. Last night, having received the text, I spent an awful amount of time staring at the message and trying to come up with a reasonable excuse to cancel on her, but... I found I hadn't wanted to.

I actually liked Krista. She wasn't like the females of my species, and that was awesome. She genuinely seemed like she wanted to spend time with me with no ulterior motive.

As I continued working out, I thought back to my early teens, when Nattie and her band of airhead friends had preyed on my loneliness, shattering any semblance of trust I'd had in people.

I glanced up from my book to see the Heathers standing

133

around me. My guard rising, I lowered my book, eyeing them with suspicion as Nattie flashed me a megawatt grin and the rest of her flock followed suit.

"Hi, Ryan."

"Nattie."

My response was clipped, my tone unfriendly enough it should have sent her scurrying back to the comfort of her privileged life. Yet she still stood there, her sallow skin and caramel hair both smooth and flawless. I picked at the frayed knees of my jeans, dropping my eyes to my book.

"We were wondering if you would like to come and hang out with us for a while?"

"Not really."

I heard Farrah snigger, the sound cut short after a glare from Nattie, no doubt.

Nattie explained they were sneaking in to watch the guys at a display for the queen, and my eyes shot up in surprise because I'd been told the training had been cancelled due to the trainers being off campus for the day. I got to my feet, anger coursing through my veins as I stomped away from the Heathers, mindful they were scurrying after me.

I continued my angry strides through the castle, growing even more enraged as I heard the clash of swords coming from the gymnasium. They'd excluded me once again. It infuriated me that my fellow trainees refused to spar with me as they felt I was not much of an opponent. They claimed it was a waste of time to train with a girl, and that had left me even more isolated. Until Atticus had stepped in front of me and offered to spar.

I shoved open the gymnasium doors, a snarl on my face, but halted suddenly, frozen to the spot as I realized a trick had been played on me—one that could lead to punishment.

It was not forbidden, per se, to see the queen without her crown or in civilian clothes, but considering Katerina was standing in the center of the gym in leggings and a workout vest top, her hair a mess and sweat on her skin, I knew this was something I should not be bearing witness to.

I hadn't been spotted yet by the queen or the teen with his back to me, but as I tried to retreat from the gym, hands shoved me forward from behind and slammed the door shut with a loud crack that announced my entrance.

Both royals spun in my direction, sending me curtsying on shaky knees as I muttered my apologies. I backed away and twisted the door handle, finding it locked to prevent a hasty retreat. So, I just stood there, eyes down, waiting for a telling-off that never came.

"Ah, Ryan, just what I need!" the queen exclaimed, beckoning me over. She asked me to show her how to hold her sword like a female would, declaring her son not to be a particularly good teacher as he was all brute strength and force.

I dared a glance at Nickolai, who was grinning at his mother, unperturbed by her words, and an awful ache rose in my chest. This was how I'd envisioned my mother and I— hell, even my father and I—interacting.

Quietly, I studied how Katerina was holding her sword. It was just like my mother had taught me, yet her grip was tight and her movement restricted. I held my hand out for her sword, which she handed to me with a smile. It was heavy, far too heavy for such a delicate woman to hold. It would get her killed.

"My Liege, if I may, this sword is too heavy for you to wield. It will make your movements sluggish and predictable. Perhaps the smith can take a few layers off the blade and hilt, or you could ask for a new blade to be forged. You will be able to strike even more effectively with a blade tailored to your measurements."

The queen gave me a brilliant smile. "That's exactly what Nico said, but I didn't believe him. It is hard for him to spar with me, as I am his mother. Would you be willing to spend some time with me, Ryan? Just like your mother once did?"

And there it was again, the comparison to my mother—a person I'd never be as good as. I was a pale imitation of the one whom they'd have preferred to live.

The ache in my chest speared into my heart as I shook my head. "I'd rather not, Majesty."

Guilt flushed my skin as the queen blinked in surprise, hurt bringing tears to her eyes, but I just couldn't take it. I couldn't breathe. I felt dizzy, nauseous, and trapped.

Nickolai took a step toward me, those cerulean eyes of his watching me like I was a wounded animal. Perhaps I was.

I shook my head, my eyes searching for an escape route. Before anyone could stop me, I was scaling the wall and swinging my legs over the balcony above, squeezing through an open window and disappearing into the night.

I'd not returned to the compound for seven days. The entire Royal Guard had searched the countryside looking for me. In the end, Jack had found me in a village in West Cork—the village my father had been born in—in the house where he'd been raised. I was half-starved, exhausted, and caught in a black hole of depression. Carrying me to the waiting SUV, Jack let me rest my head on his knee as I slept the whole way back.

No one mentioned my interaction with the queen again.

The soft ping of the elevator made me halt my exercise and get to my feet. The doors opened slowly, and Atticus strolled in. I could see why Jack fancied him. Soft brown eyes with hair the same color, Atticus had those atypical good looks you expected from the males of our species. He reminded me of Justin Timberlake circa his "SexyBack" days.

I must have been staring longer than I realized, because both Atticus and Nickolai were looking at me—one with a worried smile, the other with curious eyes—when I came to.

Needing to alleviate any tension Atticus might've felt, I pursed my lips and ran my eyes over him critically. "I mean, I get it. If I were interested in males, I'd say yes. I can totally see why Jack would be interested in a JT-lookalike boy toy."

Atticus burst out laughing and strode across the room to engulf me in a hug. I could tell from his body language he'd relaxed enough to be himself again, and it surprised me that my opinion mattered to him.

Releasing me, I heard Nickolai clear his throat, and I stepped away from Atticus.

"So, you don't like males?" Nickolai asked, his tone unreadable.

I smiled at him, slowly and deliberately. "Oh," I said with a shrug, "I like men. I'm just not interested in a relationship. Although if Tom Hardy or Jeremy Renner came calling, I'd not say no. Then again, Brie Larson is all kinds of hot, too. Options open and all that."

Atticus was laughing hard now, doubled over at the perplexed look on Nickolai's face. Having strapped on my sai, I grabbed my jacket and strode toward the elevator, stopping briefly to pat Nickolai on the cheek.

"Don't think about it too hard or you'll hurt yourself."

Nickolai snarled, snapping his teeth at me, and I rolled my eyes, ignoring the look on his face.

"What time will you be home?" he asked brusquely.

Home... as if he and I lived here together rather than I was babysitting his ass.

Peering over my shoulder, I asked Atticus if he'd mind staying with our liege until I returned as I was meeting a friend after coffee with Jack.

Nickolai's eyes clashed with mine as a jumble of words fell from his lips, asking who the friend was, where I was going, and was the friend male or female.

Ignoring Nickolai, I hurried to the elevator and pressed the button to call it, tapping my foot impatiently as I waited. A growl rumbled through the apartment, and Nickolai hissed my name in a tone that had me wanting to tremble. All my vampire urges wanted me to bend and break at My Liege's tone, yet I was Ryan Callan and I did not bend or break.

As the doors opened, I slipped inside, setting my foot in the entrance to stop the doors from closing. Lifting my eyes, I held Nickolai's gaze and smirked. "This is what you wanted, right? For me to make friends? And now you're acting like all the other males who want to put me in a nice box that makes sense to them. Shove that box up your ass, My Liege, and make up your goddamn mind."

Pulling my foot away, I gave him a perfect curtsy as the doors closed just in time to save me. They did not, however, save me from the very impressive sound and sight of Nickolai's fist crunching the metal of the doors. Apparently, I'd hit a sore point.

When the elevator doors opened, I stepped into the foyer and made my way to the small residence bar. Thick oak doors with the word "Private" embossed in gold barred the way, but I could sense Jack already inside, his heartbeat a steady but slightly faster thrum of energy than usual, as if he were nervous about seeing me.

I eased the door open, and Jack looked up from his phone as I approached, getting to his feet and slipping his hands into his pockets, rocking back and forth on his heels. I studied him as I neared, watching as he inhaled a breath, a brief flash of fear in his eyes.

But this was Jack; he was the closest thing I had to family. How could he think I cared who he was in love with?

Because everyone around you judges you for everything you stand for. He's judged for everything he is just like you.

I closed the distance between us, wrapping my arms around his waist and resting my head against his chest as he let go of a shuddering breath. We stood like that for an age before Jack released me and motioned for me to sit down.

We didn't start talking until we'd ordered and received our coffees. Once the waiter disappeared, we had the room to ourselves.

Jack sighed. "I'm sorry if you feel we lied to you, kiddo. Our species aren't known for their tolerance of those who aren't up to code. You know better than I do."

I gave Jack a small smile. "I don't care. I just want you to be happy, Jack. My dad wouldn't have cared, either."

The grin tugging at Jack's lips made me smile even more so. "He knew... Dad knew you were gay."

"Course he did. Not much ever got past Tristan Callan."

No, there wasn't.

"I was afraid, kiddo. Afraid you'd hate me. I mean, Atticus is a good bit younger than I am."

With a shrug, I replied, "Does that even matter? Vampires don't age once we hit maturity. You both look the same age. I don't see what the problem is, but I'm different from the rest of the court. I understand why you felt the need to hide it, but please, never feel you have to hide from me, Jack."

Jack scrubbed a hand down his face. "You are exactly how they would have wanted you to be, kiddo. Tristan and Imogen would be so proud of you."

Emotion thickened in my throat, and I blinked back some rebel tears threatening to slip free when Jack's phone pinged and a smile awakened his features. How everyone couldn't see Jack was in love with Atticus is something I'd never understand, but, then again, I'd been oblivious, too, so who was I to comment?

"Tell your boy toy he can come join us if he leaves his royal pain in the ass upstairs."

Jack chuckled, shaking his head. "You should give Nickolai a break. He carries the weight of the world on his shoulders."

I lifted my coffee, taking a sip before retorting with a snort, "He's going to be king—it's kinda his job."

Jack typed a response to Atticus and set down his phone, turning his attention back to me. "Just ease up on him, Ryan. All he wants is what's best for his people, and that includes you. You're walking a dangerous line with the rogue, and he thinks you have a death wish. We all do."

Setting my mug down on the table, I rested my elbows on my knees. "Like I told you all, I made a promise to my dad I'd keep going, and I am. I never promised to live—I promised to stay alive, and I'm keeping that promise. Do not judge me on how I choose to live my life, Jack. Extend me the same courtesy and respect I have given you."

Jack opened his mouth to speak, obviously surprised by the seriousness in my tone, but clamped his mouth shut as Atticus came inside with Nickolai hot on his heels. I drained my coffee, standing as Jack and Atticus embraced, giving each other a quick peck on the lips before they turned sheepishly in my direction.

"I mean, that's all kinds of hot—if Jack wasn't the closest thing to an uncle."

The couple chuckled as Nickolai rolled his eyes, stepping into my field of view to try and get my attention. I sidestepped him, yanking my phone from my pocket and responding to the text from Krista that said she was outside.

I texted her to come inside, explaining I was just saying goodbye to my uncle. Slipping my phone back into my pocket, I made to leave, but Nickolai blocked my way.

I snarled at him. "In the wise words of the great Ludacris, 'Move, bitch. Get out the way.'"

Jack gasped at my complete lack of respect, but Nickolai let a slow smile tug at his lips, calm and collected now after his growl and punch mode about half an hour ago.

He made to respond when the door creaked open and Krista strode in, halting with a sharp intake of breath as she was mesmerized by the men in the room. I rolled my eyes so hard they almost rolled right out of my head.

Jack and Atticus immediately dropped their hands and widened the distance between themselves; however, I was having none of it.

"Hey Krista, this is my uncle Jack and his partner Atticus. Unfortunately, you already know Nicky."

Shocked, Krista stepped forward, shaking hands with both Jack and Atticus, then nodding to Nickolai as I edged toward the door behind her.

"So, ladies. What are the plans for this evening?" Jack asked with a smile and that Irish lilt of his, which had no doubt melted many a heart.

"Oh, I'm hoping to take Ryan shopping for an outfit for the party on Sunday night. If I can talk her into going, that is."

"She's going."

I glared at Nickolai. "*She* can speak, and she is *not* going."

"Afraid you might have some fun and ruin that ice-queen persona of yours, Frosty?"

Jack took an aggressive step toward Nickolai, but I held up my hand to halt him. I was surprised to feel hurt by his words, by the nickname I hated, but instead of showing my feelings, I let a slow, dangerous smile creep onto my lips.

"I'm not afraid to have a little fun, Nicky. But the last time you promised me some fun, well... let's just say Missy Elliot was right; nobody wants a one-minute man."

Grabbing Krista by the arm, I all but dragged her out the door and into the night air as I gave Jack and Atticus a wave and blew Nickolai a kiss over my shoulder.

From the murderous glance he threw at me, I was beginning to wonder if I really *did* have a death wish.

Chapter 13

KRISTA MADE IT OUTSIDE THE DOOR BEFORE SHE WHIRLED on me with the biggest grin on her face. "Holy hotness, Batman!"

I could only shrug when she asked if I knew any not-so-perfectly gorgeous men, and she laughed like I was teasing her, like we are already the best of friends and she found me hilarious.

Linking her arm through mine, I let her lead the way as she rambled on about her life, filling me in on her boyfriend back home, her parents, and how she wanted all the trappings of the stereotypical American life: the career, the husband, the white picket fence, and the two kids. I listened intently, nodding and smiling at the appropriate times. Suddenly, I felt so nervous; Krista was like a little ray of sunshine in a petite package, and I wanted her to like me.

And I hated myself a little for it.

We crossed the quad, walking across the bridge I'd stood on a few nights ago with the rogue. I glanced around, waiting for him to spring out of the shadows and grab me or Krista. My entire body tensed, and Krista sensed the change in me.

"Oh my," she said, peering up at me. "I've been rambling on and on about myself, but I want to know all about you, Ryan Callan."

Again, I shrugged, which seemed to be my default action nowadays. "There's really not much to tell."

"I very much doubt that. You are this gorgeous woman who appeared on campus with a hunky I-don't-know-what-the-hell-you-guys-are. No one knows a thing about you. You're a mystery, Ryan, and I love a good old-fashioned mystery."

Shoving my hands into the pockets of my jacket, I shook my head. "I'm just an old friend of Nicky's who decided to hang around and see what college is like. We grew up... different. Our families used to be close, and all of us diplomat kids lived and were schooled with one another. That's it. No big mystery."

"Are your families still close? I mean, what happened there?"

"My parents were murdered."

Krista jerked to a halt, and I had to do the same to stop from colliding with her. The tears in her eyes made me want to bolt, but I just stood there, rooted to the spot.

"Oh Ryan, I'm so sorry that happened to you. How old were you?"

"Seven... I was seven."

Krista tilted her head, ready to listen, and I was surprised to find myself wanting to burden her with the sad, sad tale that was my life. I wanted to tell someone who could only know half the truth, who didn't know my parents, who didn't really know me and could never really know me. I wanted a friend. I wanted... I just wanted.

"It was... there was a terror attack on the embassy we were staying at in Russia. They came in and killed a few of the staff and guards. My parents were attachés to Nickolai's parents and died protecting them."

"That is terrible, Ryan. Did they ever catch the people responsible?"

I shook my head, because it was the truth. Some of the perpetrators had been killed that day, but no matter how many investigations had been done, the members of the rebel faction had never been found. To this day, they still posed a threat to the crown. But one day, I would spill their blood and have my revenge.

"Did your uncle raise you then? Or did Nickolai's family take you in?"

"I raised myself." My words came out harsh, but my life had been harsh. And brutal.

"Did you at least have friends to support you?"

I couldn't rake over the past anymore; I wanted Krista to be my friend because she liked me, not because she felt sorry for me. I couldn't handle one more goddamn person feeling sorry for me.

"Look Krista, I don't wanna be rude, but my childhood wasn't great. I was bullied and singled out for the most part, so I isolated myself... which is why I'm not good with people. I didn't have friends growing up, so I don't know how to do this. The Heathers made my life a living hell even though I was already living through my worst nightmare.

"If you feel obligated to be my friend because you feel sorry for me, please don't. I'd rather not waste each other's time. I may sound like a Grade A bitch, but one thing you can always expect from me is to be straightforward."

Krista stared for a few heartbeats before she spoke. "The Heathers?"

"That's what the mean girls call their version of a girl gang."

Her brow furrowed. "Are they all named Heather?"

"Not a single one."

Krista frowned as she rubbed her forehead. "Well, that's all kinds of stupid."

I chuckled. It was, as Krista so elegantly put it, all kinds of stupid. I expected her to walk away from me, but Krista linked her arm though mine and continued forward. We said nothing to each other for a while as we made our way through the city streets, the town bustling at this time of evening as the work week let out and humans let their hair down.

Walking through the crowds, I could scent the smell of alcohol, sweat, and other bodily fluids on all these bodies, wrinkling my nose at the overwhelming stench. Krista steered me away from the popular nightspots and into a more upmarket, cobbled-street area. She came to a stop outside a shop that looked closed and knocked three times on the door.

A few seconds later, the door opened and a woman ushered Krista inside with me following after her and closing the door behind us. The lights were dim, a red glare from some lamps casting shadows against the black-painted walls. Krista and the woman did that air-kiss thing women tended to do before Krista introduced me.

I studied the strange woman as if she were prey. When she held her hand out and met my steely gaze, I caught a glimpse of a red apple tattooed on her wrist. That made me pay real close attention to the woman who was grinning with a knowing smile.

With hair the color of coal hanging down the front of her dark dress, someone with less-keen eyesight would not have been able to tell where the woman ended and the dress began. It was a long and flowing garment, and I noted her feet were bare but her neck was covered up to the chin, presumably hiding signs of having been fed from at the neck.

This woman realized I'd recognized the tattoo, knew I understood her to be a Child of Eve, and clearly knew *what* I was even if she did not know *who* I was. She inclined her head in acknowledgement even as my heart began to hammer a steady beat in my chest. I wondered whether I'd be able to kill Krista if this woman told her what I was.

"Hello, I'm Rose. It's nice to meet you. Krista tells me you need a dress for a party. Come, let me show you some dresses that would look devastating on you."

Rose pulled aside a curtain and slipped into the back as I glanced at Krista with a brow raised.

"I know Rose can be a bit... extra, but she has the best clothes in Cork if you want to make an impression."

"I'm not looking to make an impression. I don't want to go to this stupid party. And what do you mean by extra?"

Krista grinned, pushing some of her California sunshine-blonde hair from her face and lifting her eyes to the sky as she did. "I mean, Rose thinks she's connected to the supernatural. She's part of a group that worships vampires. I mean, she might be batshit crazy, but damn—her clothes are worth it. Come on, let's go shopping."

I'd rather have been stabbing something than trying to navigate this awkward situation as Krista disappeared behind the curtain, leaving me no choice but to follow her.

Slipping through, I was amazed to see the shop seemed to stretch on for days, with rows and rows of dresses and other items filling what looked like miles of clothes racks. I browsed through the racks, lifting out a cropped, military-style jacket with patches sewn onto it. It was totally something I'd wear, and I imagined Nattie's face as I walked into Murphy's wearing it. With a grin, I threw the jacket over my arm as Krista called me forward.

Rose had handed Krista a fuchsia skirt and white, strappy top and was ushering my companion into the dressing room to try the outfit on. The fitting rooms were far off down the rows of clothing, and once Krista was out of earshot, Rose turned and smiled like I was a deity. I frowned, but she simply continued to smile at me. Taking the jacket, I held and nodding in approval, she pointed to a rail full of dresses for me to choose from.

"Your secret is safe with me. It is my pleasure to serve you."

If I could have groaned aloud, I would have, but these humans were vital to the survival of our race. As I'd never seen Rose before, I assumed she was one of the Children of Eve who fed off-campus vampires like Jack.

Rose handed me a lilac dress that had me scowling even as she told me how it matched the lavender of my eyes. said eyes scanned the clothes and found a ripped pair of black jeans, faded as if they'd been well-worn. Rose shook her head and pointed at another dress on the rail. It was a sleeved bodycon dress that would have hugged my curves but done little to conceal a weapon or give me freedom of movement.

When I said nothing, she held the dress in front of me and grinned. "What about this green one? It really does amazing things for your eyes."

Hoping to scare her a little—anything to take away the worshiping gaze in her eyes—I turned around and flashed my weapons at her. "I don't need to look pretty while I'm slicing people in half, you know."

"You don't *need* to," Rose retorted, returning the green dress to the rail, "but that doesn't mean you *can't*."

The next one Rose handed me was made of black lace with a slit from the knee-length hem halfway up the leg. I could still totally move my legs in it. The dress was one-shouldered with a capped sleeve, the material stretchy. I was ashamed to say I liked it, and Rose looked like she'd won an Oscar or something by the way she looked at me.

"Now, you'll have to go braless, but there are subtle cups in the dress lining to keep everything in place. Why don't you throw it on and see how it feels?"

I started to refuse, but Rose's eyes pleaded with me to do as she asked. Sighing, I took the dress to the fitting room. I carefully shed my clothes, stripped off my sai, and hid them and their sheath under my leather jacket as I unclasped my bra and slipped on the dress. The side zipper was easy to close, and I waited a few breaths before turning to glance at myself in the mirror.

The woman staring back was not me, even though I knew it was. My reflection looked sleek and sophisticated—both desirable and lethal, all in the same image. I wanted so much to be her.

I pulled my hair from its ponytail and fluffed it out, the ice-blonde a stark contrast against the dress. I ran my hands down over my body, wondering for a second what Nickolai would think of the dress before I scolded myself and unzipped it.

Dressing again quickly, I pulled my hair back off my face and exited the fitting room, nearly running into Krista as I did. She beamed at me, delighted with her own purchase as she bounced up and down, demanding I go back in and show her what it looked like.

Tears threatened to spill from my eyes at the thought of seeing myself in the mirror again, facing the girl in the glass who was didn't appear broken, and Krista's face instantly fell. Swallowing hard, she took the dress from my hands and called Rose over, explaining the dress wasn't what we were looking for. Rose glanced at me, then leaned toward Krista and whispered something.

I wasn't sure what had provoked such a response from me, or maybe I just didn't want to admit it to myself. The girl in the mirror had been the kind of girl who'd had a happy childhood, free of loss and grief. I could never be that girl—not since the fabric of my being had been woven out of loss. Sometimes I found it hard to remember what it felt like to be happy.

Rose proceeded to pack up the dress anyway. I frowned, first arguing I didn't want it, then fumbling in my back pocket for my card holder when she ignored my protests. When I held out my card to pay, Rose waved me off. I narrowed my gaze in suspicion, and she told me the dress had already been paid for, then theatrically held her finger to her lips.

After handing me the packaged dress, Rose turned back to Krista, chatting about shoes and the best way to wear her hair with the new outfit. That was when I felt eyes on me. My gaze wandered to the window at the back of Rose's shop—a long, frosted window revealing the silhouette of a man standing outside.

I couldn't see who it was, but I knew it was the rogue.

Darting out to the front of the shop, I shouted at Krista to stay with Rose until I came back and to lock the door. Rose hushed any protests from Krista as I raced out the door and paused, waiting until I heard the lock click behind me before using my vampire speed to race to the darkened alley behind Rose's shop.

He had not run. He was still standing by the window, his hood up, but I could see the glint of his fangs in the moonlight. I inched into the mouth of the alley, and the rogue took a step back.

"Anyone would think you were scared of me."

"Not scared, darling. Just cautious."

I let loose an annoyed sigh. "Listen, you *should* be scared. It would be smart to be scared. Vampires are always underestimating me, and it doesn't go well for them. So how 'bout we stop all these cat-and-mouse games, and you get on your knees so I can take your head back to my queen."

The other vampire smiled, blood dripping from his fangs. "I would never underestimate you. Only a fool would. Now I have another present for you. Let's see if I chose right."

The rogue vanished into the shadows like magic, which wasn't possible, and I heard the whistle of air passing. My sai already unsheathed, I quickly spun and sliced through the air. The tip of my blade nicked flesh, and the tangy scent of copper filled the air. I wrinkled my nose and growled, bracing myself for attack.

The second rogue in front of me was no older than I was, his eyes red with bloodlust as he charged me. The idiot came at me with brute strength, hoping to catch me off guard. But I was trained for this. I lived for this. This was when I most felt alive.

As the rogue lunged again, I dropped to my knees on the concrete and bent backward so he just ran straight over me. Crossing my arms over my chest, I sliced out my arms and pinned my sai into the backs of his knees. Tearing my weapons free, I jumped to my feet as the rogue howled, somehow managing to fall onto his back.

I braced a knee on his chest and pressed the tip of my right sai into the lovely, vulnerable part of his carotid. He snarled, snapping his bloodstained teeth and bucking wildly against me. He almost threw me off, but I slammed my other sai into his chest and watched as the light went out in his eyes.

In books, movies, and TV, vampires usually turned to ash when they died. At times like this, that would have been incredibly convenient. Unfortunately, that wasn't the case, and the dead rogue just stayed dead, even as I yanked my sai free.

I was suddenly conscious of the fact the rogue—the other one—was still nearby. Sure enough, I glanced over my shoulder and saw him watching me from the rooftop before once again disappearing in a swirl of mist like a movie vampire.

Now came the hard part. I couldn't clean up this mess *and* keep Krista from finding out my secret. My hands were covered in the second rogue's blood, and spatters of it marked my face. How would I explain this to her and have her believe me? I didn't know if I had the stomach to try and compel her—especially when it might not work.

Sheathing my sai, I dragged the dead rogue by the feet to a nearby dumpster, lifted the lid, and tossed him in. He couldn't stay there, but if I disappeared on Krista again it would be the end of our friendship.

Do it, my mind shouted. *It will be easier this way. You can't get hurt if you don't have anyone to be hurt by.*

I wanted to do as the voice in my head told me to, wanted to take the easy road. However, for the first time in my life, I didn't want to run away in case I got hurt. I wanted to face it head on and say a massive "eff you" to the consequences.

Pulling my phone from my pocket, I dialed one of four numbers I had saved and waited as it rang twice before a husky voice answered the phone.

"If I've interrupted sexy time, Jack, then I'm really sorry. But I've got a dead rogue in a dumpster and a very human companion I need to get back to. Any chance of a hand?"

I giggled when I heard Jack swear on the other end of the line, and then he asked where I was and if I was hurt. I told him I wasn't and asked him to bring me some wipes to clean the blood off my skin—and to leave Nickolai at home. I heard him pause, cover the mouthpiece, and then swear again as Nickolai declared in the background that he was going.

Shouting an address into the phone, I hung up, texting Krista to say I'd be back soon and I'd just run into someone I knew. It wasn't a lie, really. I had.

I hopped up onto the lid of the dumpster, swinging my legs as I waited for Jack to arrive as if sitting on the dump site of a dead body was the most natural thing in the world.

Was it wrong it had been the most fun I'd had in ages?

Probably.

Chapter 14

I WAS STILL SWINGING MY LEGS ON THE DUMPSTER WHEN Jack arrived, thankfully alone, in a beat-up Nissan about ten minutes later. Getting out of the car, I could tell the older guard was tired. It wasn't how I was used to seeing Jack, and I was a little taken aback by it. So, I did what I always did when I was uncomfortable and made a joke out of it.

"Come on, old man, get a move on. We're wasting night-time here."

Jack flipped me off as he approached, and as he took in my bloodstained face and hands, he ran a critical eye over my person to make sure I was unharmed. Rolling my eyes, I clicked my tongue even though I wasn't annoyed. If anyone else had tried it, I would've been pissed, but not Jack.

Pushing off the edge of the dumpster, I landed on my feet and inclined my head toward the bin with a grin. "Dead dude's in there. Soz."

"You don't look one bit sorry, kiddo," he replied with a grimace as he tossed me a pack of wipes.

I began the tedious motions of cleaning the blood from my skin, knowing I wouldn't feel truly clean until I was under the stream of a blistering-hot shower.

Jack retrieved the body, opened the trunk of the car, and dropped the rogue inside. Closing it with a bang, he leaned against the car and folded his arms across his chest, a stern expression on his face.

Oh, so Jack was gonna play bad cop tonight. Got it. *Face, look ever so chastised.*

"I'm not going to apologize," I said before he started in on me. "I took the chance to get a better look at him, and I did. I think I've got his attention now."

"The psycho's following you around now, kiddo. He's trying to romance you, which means he either wants to kill you or fuck you. Either way, that's not good."

I shrugged at Jack's blunt words; he didn't see it how I saw it. If "romancing" me meant he stopped killing humans to follow my boring ass around all night, then I'd take it. After a while of watching me do unremarkable stuff like babysit Nickolai, dodge social events, and engage in awkward conversation with humans, the rogue would probably walk into the sun himself for some excitement.

Jack shook his head. "Just like your goddamn mother. She was always willing to throw herself in front of a bullet so someone else wouldn't get hurt."

And... there it was again—the comparison to the ghost of my mother. When would I hear "That's just like you, Ryan"? When would my name be spoken without someone only thinking of me as the daughter of Tristan and Imogen Callan?

Rubbing my hands clean on my leggings, I chewed

on my bottom lip. "I gotta go back to my human friend and try to explain why I ran off like a crazy person. By the way, did you pay for my dress?"

Jack's mouth dropped open. "You wore a *dress*? Kiddo, I gotta see that."

I threw my hands in the air and stormed off, telling Jack to go back to his boy toy and leave me alone. By the time I reached the front of the building, Jack was still laughing so hard that I flipped him off before walking around the corner and knocking at the door just like Krista had when we'd first arrived.

Rose herself opened the door, and I slipped inside. I could hear Krista chatting away on the phone toward the back of the shop as Rose asked if I was all right. I assured her I was, stilling when she rested her hand on my arm and asked me what my full name was.

"Why does it matter?" I asked, suddenly even more wary of the woman than before.

"Please—humor me, old woman that I am."

Old woman? Rose had to have been in her forties—not even old by human standards. She'd clearly been part of the Children of Eve for a long time, though, based on how faded her tattoo was, and I wasn't sure I could handle watching another person realize whose bloodline I came from.

"My surname is Callan. Ryan Callan."

Rose blinked, the only sign she recognized the name, and then handed me a large bag of clothing. Holding up a finger, she rooted around beneath the register, then handed me a sturdy yet discreet thigh holster that would hold a small dagger.

I stared at her, perplexed, as she added it to the bag

I was already holding.

"Any daughter of Imogen Callan," she said simply, "is a warrior in her heart."

I thanked her again, struggling to breathe through yet another gut punch as yet another person compared me to my mother, when Krista came out, her face flushed as if she'd been arguing on the phone. I asked if she was okay, and she told me she was fine, then lobbed the question back at me. I nodded, and we bade farewell to Rose, promising to come back soon as we headed off into the night.

It was still considered early evening in vampire time, but Krista was yawning and rubbing her eyes, the chatty girl unusually quiet as we walked back the way we came. I told Krista I'd walk her home and she laughed, saying chivalry wasn't dead after all.

At the entrance to the student complex, Krista gave me a quick hug, asking if I was okay to get home by myself and insisting I text her when I got in safe.

I waited until the girl was inside before turning and sauntering through campus. I wished I'd remembered to bring my headphones along, wanting to disrupt the blanket of silence enveloping me. It made me twitchy, this silence, even if I was at home in it.

Reaching the apartment building I shared with Nickolai, I smiled at the Nissan parked outside. That meant the other two vampires were still here, and I wouldn't have to deal with Nickolai alone.

I wasn't quite ready to head upstairs just yet, even if I did want to wash the night off me. Before I knew it, I found myself standing at the bar, ordering a Jack and Coke and handing my ID to the bartender to prove I was over eighteen. I wasn't, but when he glanced at me skeptically, I was ready to drag him over the bar and gently "persuade" him I was legal to drink—in Ireland, anyway—when a whistle sounded behind me.

The bartender nodded and handed me my drink, talking the word of the whistler over mine.

Dropping my head, I collected my drink, told the bartender to put it on the apartment's tab, and walked to the source of the whistle. Flopping down in the chair opposite him, I raised my glass and took a sip before setting the tumbler down on the table in front of me.

His eyes wandered to the bag I was not setting down on the ground, and I suddenly knew that Nickolai had been the one to pay for my clothes. But I wasn't gonna thank him for it. No point in making it easy for him.

Nickolai cleared his throat. "I said I'd give them some time on their own. If they left, Atticus would've had to go back to the compound. It's unfair they have to hide like this."

"Something for you to change once you become king, My Liege."

Nickolai looked like I'd slapped him, and I wasn't sure whether it was calling him 'king' or 'My Liege' that had done it. He glared at me; his eyes suddenly heavy as he let out a tired sigh.

"Do you think, just for a night, we can drop the titles, drop the pretense, and just pretend we're two normal people having a drink?"

I didn't answer him, simply sipped on my drink as I glanced out the window. Dawn was still an hour or two away, so I wondered how long we would have to sit here, pretending we were just a boy and a girl having a drink.

We would never just be that, and Nickolai was being foolish if he thought we could.

"Jack said you took out the rogue without breaking a sweat. Said it was clean and expertly done—no unnecessary wounds. He was quite proud of you, as was Atticus."

I let loose a snort as I drained my drink and held it up for a refill. "You know, Nicky, this is why you're single. You want to pretend we're normal, yet here you are, complimenting me on my murdering skills. Most girls aren't like me."

"I'm not interested in most girls," he snapped. "That's the goddamn problem."

My heart began to race and I laughed, a short bark of sound, trying to brush off his words. "No wonder Nattie moved on to Kris. I mean, dude, seriously—if you told her that, no wonder she bounced."

As the waiter arrived with another drink for me, Nickolai ordered another for himself, but his eyes never left mine. Things were starting to get weird. Maybe Nicky was just hungry and horny, but we weren't going down this road. It would only end in chaos. Good, sweaty chaos, but chaos nonetheless.

Things had changed from when we were inseparable kids, our destiny carved out from the day I first came kicking and screaming into the world. Then, the world had fucked me over, and becoming a member of the Royal Guard was all I wanted—even if that meant closing off my heart in order to do so.

Fate was a fickle mistress, and we were merely pieces on her chessboard.

I drained my drink and stood, Nickolai's eyes never leaving me as I gathered my stuff and just left him sitting there.

Don't look back. Don't look back. Don't look back. Don't look back. Don't look back—

Goddammit, I looked back, and the heat in Nickolai's gaze did funny things to my insides. I cursed myself and shook my head, ducking out the door and heading upstairs before I could go back and do something stupid.

The elevator doors pinged softly as I reached the apartment, letting my eyes adjust to the dark as I crossed the floor. Opening the bedroom door, I glanced back, smiling at the figures embraced on the couch.

"You all good, kiddo?"

"Five by five, Uncle Jack. Don't worry about me." I stood there longer than I'd intended to, the ache in my chest shooting daggers as I focused on the way Jack embraced Atticus. "I'm all right, I swear," I reiterated. "Just be happy, okay?"

Jack called my name softly as I slipped inside and closed the bedroom door behind me. Setting my shopping bag on the floor by the wardrobe, I stripped off my clothes, grabbed a towel, and jumped into the shower, the blissful heat of the water burning my skin in an agonizing but addicting way.

When my skin was acceptably wrinkled, I halted the flow of the water and wrapped the towel around me, wiping steam from the mirror to stare at my reflection. Parting my hair down the center, I braided each side, leaving the braids hanging down my neck. Bracing myself, I opened the door and strode out of the bathroom, colliding directly with Nickolai and almost losing my towel in the process.

Nickolai's hands gripped my bare shoulders, and the

heat of his touch burned more than the scalding water. We stood like that for a flustering moment, and even though I wanted to keep his hands on me, I scolded myself and gently pried myself from his grasp.

Blowing out a breath, Nickolai went to stand by the window, his back to me as I quickly dressed in shorts and a tee, telling Nickolai he could turn around if he wanted.

He did so very slowly, deliberately, and suddenly I realized how exhausted I was. I just wanted to lie down and sleep the day away before I had to deal with Nattie and all the BS that came with her.

Tomorrow, I'd have to sit across from the queen bitch herself and try to hold my tongue. For hours. I wasn't sure it was possible, but I doubted Nickolai would let me skip it. I tried to appease myself with thoughts of food. And dessert... I should just think of dessert.

Without saying a word, I walked toward Nickolai, ignoring the way his nostrils flared as I lifted the duvet and slipped under the covers. Snuggling into the bed, I sighed as Nickolai stormed into the shower.

I heard him let loose a blue streak and wondered if he was having a cold shower. The thought made me giggle, shifting my body into a more relaxed pose as I closed my eyes and drifted off to sleep.

I ran as fast as my legs would carry me, avoiding the soldiers who tried to grab hold of me before I could reach my destination, trying to spare me the pain of what I was about to see. But I wouldn't have believed what they'd told me unless I saw it for myself.

Nicky called my name as I raced through the corridors, weaving and ducking until the smell of blood was so strong, I knew exactly where my parents were lying.

I skidded to a halt, almost slipping in the pooled blood already staining the oak floor, my bare feet struggling to find grip. My eyes darted from left to right until I spied a shock of ice-blonde hair.

Surging forward, I slipped, falling into a pool of blood and getting back to my feet even as I wanted to throw up. All that mattered was getting to my parents. As soon as I reached them, I dropped back to my knees, reaching out to touch my mother's face and pull back her blood-soaked hair.

Her once-vibrant eyes stared back at me, empty and void of life, and I screamed as I sank back on my haunches. My mother's hand was outstretched, reaching for my father who lay mere inches from her, their hands almost touching.

"Momma, Papa... please wake up. You gotta wake up. I promise I'll be good if you just wake up!"

They did not stir, the evidence of their demise leaking from so many wounds I was unable to tell which was my mother's blood and which was my father's. Crawling between their bodies, I lay my head in the small space where their fingers almost touched, placing myself in their outstretched hands.

Tears streamed down my face as I curled into them, wishing for the death that had claimed my world from me, waiting for it to send me to them, but the blow never came.

I was silent as vampires worked around me, cleaning up the mess and removing the dead to lie in repose before their funerals.

The moment someone touched my parents, I lashed out with my mother's sai, snarling like a feral thing. No one would separate me from them. No one.

"Ry, come on," Nickolai said softly. "They need to be taken away. We need to get them cleaned."

I hissed at Nickolai as he reached out to touch me, not caring that the queen had come in, tears matching my own streaming down her face. I ignored them all, trying desperately to get closer to my parents.

Suddenly, I was airborne, hoisted into arms that bound me tightly as I snarled and struggled like a wildcat, scratching at living flesh as I called for my mother and father, screaming at the top of my lungs as if somehow my screams could wake the dead.

Screams dragged me from slumber, and it took me more than a minute to realize the screams were coming from me. I thrashed in the bed, lashing out until strong hands wrapped around my wrists to stop me. My screams grew hoarse, and I hiccupped, my body wracked as I sobbed, the pain in my chest so tight I couldn't breathe. I didn't realize Jack and Atticus had come in at the sound of my screams until I started to mutter in Irish and heard Jack swear.

Embarrassed I was having an emotional breakdown, I started rambling at how sorry I was, but nobody knew what the hell I was muttering about until I lifted my head and looked at Jack.

"I'm sorry I scratched you," I said in a small voice. "I didn't mean to hurt you."

Jack stared in bewilderment until it dawned on him what I meant. Reaching up, he touched the scar on his face where I had once clawed at him for daring to take me from my slain parents—my dad's best friend the only one with courage enough to do what was needed and pry me from that horrible scene.

"It's okay, kiddo. You're okay. You're gonna be okay."

I burst into tears again, burying my face in Nickolai's chest as I screamed and beat my fists against him. I heard Nickolai order them from the room, and I was grateful they listened.

Nickolai held me close, murmuring into my hair as I tried and failed to cry the images of my parents from my mind. So, instead of prying myself from his arms and locking myself in the bathroom, I gave in and let Nickolai hold me.

He held me until my tears ran dry and I could no longer keep my eyes open. Terrified I'd be trapped in that nightmare again if I fell asleep, I tried to push Nickolai away, yet he refused to let me go.

"Let me hold you, Ry. Just for tonight."

It would've been so easy to wrap my legs around his waist and, for a few, blissful minutes, forget the memories of monsters and villains, of dead parents and the shattered fairy-tales of a girl who would never have her happy ending. But in the morning, I wouldn't be able to look him or myself in the eye.

I let out a shuddering breath as exhaustion overwhelmed me and clung to Nickolai, letting him wrap his arms around me and then, as he pressed his lips to the top of my head, I succumbed to the darkness.

Chapter 15

I woke with the sun still high in the sky, a sliver of Irish winter daylight slipping inside the curtains as I carefully opened my eyes, mindful I was tangled up with a very male vampire. For about ten minutes I was terrified to move, mortified at the mental breakdown they'd all seen earlier that day.

My body was half on, half off Nickolai's, my left leg curled around his right leg, my hands splayed across his chest, clutching at his T-shirt. His hand was weaved through strands of my hair. Thankfully, he was still fast asleep, and I spent an awfully long time wondering how I could untangle myself from him and avoid awkward questions.

I smothered a laugh, remembering an old *Friends* episode where Ross told Chandler to hug and roll so he didn't have to be uncomfortable sleeping with Janice. For some reason, all I could picture was Nickolai falling off the bed, and I was almost done in.

Slowly, like I was backing away from a sleeping tiger, I gently pulled back my leg, letting go of his tee as I did. Then, once my hands were free, I worked slowly to untangle my hair form his fingers. His chest rumbled as I did, and I froze for just a second before I was up and out of the bed faster than a sprinter off the block.

I grabbed a fistful of clothes and my music player, hoping I wouldn't interrupt anything intimate between Jack and Atticus as I exited the bedroom. Jack was sprawled on his stomach, one hand on the ground, but Atticus was awake and making coffee.

He flashed me a sad smile and I dropped my head, chewing on my bottom lip as I felt heat flushing my cheeks in embarrassment. I'd let them see I was broken. I'd let them see I struggled. I let them all see I wasn't the frosty, cold-hearted bitch everyone thought me to be, and I despised myself for it.

I needed to cut something. I needed to outrun my pain. I needed time to rein myself in.

"You know there's a gym in the basement, right? Windows are privacy-tinted, so you should be guarded from the sun. Her Majesty thought to send you some of your clothing, too, as you are to attend college after Samhain break."

My mouth hung open as I wondered what monstrosity of clothes Katerina would have sent me. I imagined pink and frills. I almost vomited.

To my surprise, the queen had packed some of my favorite articles of clothing. I pulled a pair of shorts and a vest top from the pile, yanking free a sports bra and motioning for Atticus to turn around because there wasn't a hope in hell I was going back into that bedroom.

Atticus chuckled softly, asking if I remembered he was gay, to which he got a middle finger and a scathing glare until he did indeed turn around.

I stripped and dressed quickly, asking Atticus for directions before I made to leave and tensing when he called my name. I didn't turn, couldn't face those puppy dog eyes without crumbling again, the nightmare of last night still replaying in my mind.

"Maybe it would help to talk to someone," he suggested. "Maybe if you told someone what was going on in your head, then people would understand you a little better."

I snorted. "It's not my job to help people understand me. I don't care. Besides, my mind is so dark even Stephen King would be terrified by what's in there."

Before Atticus could say another word, I popped in my headphones and fled the apartment. Crossing the foyer carefully, staying in the shadows so I wouldn't get burned by the sun, I found the stairs to the gym and descended. A small door at the end of the stairs opened, and a handsome man stopped to hold the door open for me.

I thanked him, ignoring his appreciative glance as I turned the volume up and pressed Shuffle on my music player. I grinned as Five's "If Ya Getting Down" blared in my ears. Anyone who looked would think I was a broody rock chick, and I was—mostly—but there was no denying that nineties pop songs were awesome. I just wouldn't broadcast that to everyone, or it might ruin my ice-queen image.

The gym was small but thankfully empty, comprised of three treadmills, a weight bench, a row machine, and a salmon ladder. The walls were covered in posters with empowerment quotes and sweaty men in various poses. Rolling my eyes, I glanced at my feet and realized I'd forgotten shoes in my rush to get out of the apartment. Never mind; the pain of running on the treadmill with no shoes would help take my mind off my internal conflict—like bleeding my feet raw would somehow compensate for the rawness I felt inside.

Backstreet Boys' "Everybody" began to play as I fired up the treadmill, and I upped my pace to match the music. I wanted to let go and run as fast as I possibly could, but I didn't know when my lone workout with be interrupted.

My feet burned as I ran from my pain, my muscles screaming and begging me to stop. I ran for the entire forty-eight minutes of poptastic tunes on my player and then stopped, hopping off the treadmill and swearing as my feet fucking burned beneath me. I'd barely broken a sweat, so when I glanced over at the salmon bars, I said what the hell.

The salmon bars were how vampires were judged during displays of strength—both of body and mind. This set wasn't as high as the set at the home gym—it only went up a few feet, whereas our bars reached nearly twenty—but they'd do.

Turning on another playlist, this time YONAKA's "Waves" thrummed in my ear as I rubbed my hands together, bent at the knees, and leapt up to grab the first bar. Rocking my legs back and forth, I moved the bar to next rung and continued on and on until I reached the top. It didn't take long, and then I swung my legs back until I released my hands and did a kinda front roll, landing on my aching feet with feline grace.

Stupidly grinning to myself, I flinched when I heard

a clapping sound and yanked my earbuds out. Some guy who looked vaguely familiar was staring open-mouthed at me, clapping, with a look of shock and awe on his face.

Cursing myself for being so reckless and showing off, I gave him a brief smile before heading for the door.

"Hey, you're Nico's friend, right?"

I turned back to get a better look at the guy and remembered he was the one who'd asked me if I wanted to play goalie for Nickolai's soccer team. I nodded and continued for the door, but he leaned against it, barring my way.

"I'm Braydon. Braydon Smyth."

"Ryan."

Braydon grinned and pointed to the salmon bars. "That was some impressive ninja shit right there."

With a shrug I replied, "I guess I was a little obsessed with Arrow a few years ago."

Braydon grinned even wider. "A girl who knows her comic heroes? Be still my heart."

Was this guy seriously flirting with me? He looked like the kinda person who had someone locked in his basement. His smile was so sweet my teeth ached from looking at him.

"Are you coming to the party tomorrow night?" he asked. "It should be fun."

I shook my head, my eyes cutting from him to the door and back again, as if the movement of my eyes would clue this guy in, I wanted out of both this gym and this conversation.

"Or... Does Nico prefer to keep his woman all to himself? I get it."

"I am not Nickolai's woman," I all but snarled, careful to keep my temper in check despite wanting to shove this SOB out of the way.

"Then I'll see you tomorrow night—save me a dance."

He opened the door for me, holding it open so I had to duck under his arm to exit. I was sure this pretty boy was used to girls fawning all over him, but I was surrounded by drop-dead gorgeous vampires daily and felt nothing. This dude had no chance.

I took the stairs two at a time, only realizing my feet were bleeding as I glanced down and saw bloody footprints trailing behind me. Oh well.

The sun had set as the doors to the elevator opened and I stepped into the hall, all three men awake, their noses flaring as they caught a whiff of my blood. They all started speaking at once, growling, snarling, and asking why I was bleeding.

Lifting a hand to stop them, I tilted my head slightly. "In the wise words of Taylor Swift, 'Y'all need to calm down.' No one hurt me; I merely went running with no shoes on. Jeez. Anyone would swear I was a delicate flower who hadn't taken down a rogue all by her feminine self last night."

I averted my gaze from Nickolai, who was looking as if he expected me to crack. Ignoring his eyes, I grabbed the first aid kit from under the counter, hoisted myself onto the kitchen counter, and proceeded to clean the cuts and blisters on the underside of my feet.

I hissed at the sting of the disinfectant, contorting my foot to get a better look, when a hand cupped my foot.

"Let me look at it."

"It's grand."

"Ryan."

"My Liege?"

His grip on my foot tightened as he leaned in. "Don't," he said in a low voice.

I snatched back my foot, not daring to lift my gaze for fear he'd see I was not okay, that I was on a razor's edge and couldn't deal with him right now.

"Don't what?" I asked angrily. "Call you by the title you deserve? I mean, whatever, but I don't think many vampires will be impressed with false modesty."

A strong hand gripped my chin and jerked my gaze sideways so quickly Jack called out in protest from the other room. Nickolai's eyes were full of heat, of anger and pain. I released the growl that had been building in my chest, but he was still my liege and I was honor bound to serve him.

"Take off your mask when you speak to me."

I gritted my teeth but managed to remain quiet as anger seethed inside me. I wanted to hurt him, wanted to wound him so irreparably he finally let go of his childhood friend and saw me for the shattered individual I'd become. He was fighting a losing battle, and I had to be the one to strike the final blow. I was so goddamn tired of games and crowns and politics. I was fed up of the pain and sorrow in my chest. I was pissed off at having everyone judge me. I was over being what everyone wanted me to be.

Switching gears, I fluttered my eyelashes and tilted my chin slightly, exposing my neck to him. "It is my pleasure to serve you."

I ignored the shocked intake of breath from the peanut gallery as Nickolai dropped his hold on my chin as if I'd burned him. His face paled, his hands clenched by his sides as I slid off the counter and bowed low as bile snaked its way up my throat.

Grabbing the duffel the queen had sent for me, I stalked past the two males in the living room so appalled by my words they seemed frozen in place, as if I'd done the unthinkable by reciting the phrase the Children of Eve used when they gave us lifeblood.

I'd used the phrase to emphasize I considered myself less than him. And didn't I? Didn't we all? Nickolai and I could never be equals, and the sooner he realized that, the better.

I showered quickly, freshening up for a dinner that would be awkward as hell after what just happened, but I was spoiling for a fight and Nattie would be a perfect target for my anger.

Dressed in gray jeans, my Chucks, and a *Buffy the Vampire Slayer* tee, I pulled out the military jacket and slipped into it. It was little loose, but I needed space to keep my weapons hidden. Shucking off the jacket, I was slipping on my holster when I heard the murmur of voices outside and, unable to stop myself, moved closer to the door to listen.

"You can't just go all macho male vampire on her, Nickolai," Jack said. "Ryan doesn't take well to authority."

"She has no problem taking orders from either of you," Nickolai growled back.

Jack gave a soft chuckle. "You've met Ryan before, right? She might follow an order from me or Atticus, but it kills her to do it even when she knows it's for the best. We earned that by not treating her as anything but the badass she is."

If I could have kissed Jack in that moment, I would have.

"I just don't know how to help her."

My heart sank at the sadness in his tone, but I swallowed hard and steeled my resolve.

"Listen Nickolai, Ryan is Ryan. You have to accept that if you want to have any kind of relationship with her. She's got such a good heart, does that firecracker of a girl, but she's had her heart broken. A lot."

I closed my eyes and leaned my head against the door frame, wondering how Jack understood my heart had been crushed to smithereens, and when the pieces were put back together, they didn't go back quite the same. Every name thrown at me, every moment of my life that would've seemed insignificant to them, chipped away at the fragile organ that was my heart until I'd become a shell of myself, a beating heart surrounded by an abundance of trust issues.

I placed my hand on the handle, ready to stride out of the room when Nickolai cleared his throat and began to speak.

"I understand—I really do. Ryan has a smart mouth, but she's honest as they come. She's sarcastic, but she's a heart of pure gold. She's also stubborn as hell but loyal as fuck. She can be a little crazy, but sometimes—like when we were kids—you just gotta smile and let her have her way."

I couldn't stand here and listen to them any longer. Swinging open the door, all three vampires came to attention as I stalked out of the room wearing the mask Nickolai hated so much.

"My Liege, Prince Kristoph is expecting us at eight sharp. If you do not wish to be late, I suggest you get dressed."

If Nickolai bristled at my tone I didn't see it. The crown prince donned a mask of his own as he rose and strode past me without so much as a glance, closing the door behind him and taking the tension with him as he went.

I was so relieved I almost collapsed against the wall and probably would have if it would not have betrayed a weakness.

"Are you sure you don't want to take the night off, Ryan? Jack or I could go with Nickolai to meet Prince Kristoph."

I raised a brow at Atticus. "And miss out on a free dinner at Murphy's? Are you psychotic? The dessert is the only thing worth spending the night across the table from Nattie for."

"Be careful, Ryan. Natalia Smyrnoi is dangerous."

I laughed, flashing Atticus a fangy grin. "So am I."

Both men shook their heads just as Atticus' phone chimed. He frowned and glanced at Jack, and my heart sank as I realized Atticus was being summoned back to the compound. Atticus reached out and cupped Jack's cheek, pressing his lips to the other man's as I glanced away to give them some privacy.

After they said a quick goodbye, Atticus hollered a farewell to Nickolai and then embraced me in a hug.

"Give the kid a break, Ryan," he whispered. "He means well."

Before I could come up with a snappy retort, Atticus was gone. Jack sank down on the couch and scrubbed his face with his hands. Against my better judgement, I walked over and sat down beside him, resting my head against his shoulder.

"How did you guys end up together?" I asked quietly.

Jack wrapped an arm around me before he replied, his own tone low but filled with emotion. "We were visiting the North American vampires, but I'd had feelings for him for a while. I didn't think much of it; the chances of him feeling the same attraction were slim. It was snowing, and we'd been drinking beer and blood. I slipped in the fucking snow, and Atticus caught me before I landed on my ass."

I smiled, keeping my mouth shut as Jack continued. "We were standing in the snow, and I watched as Atticus examined me like he was seeing me for the first time. And then he kissed me. We haven't looked back since."

"You should write that down and pitch it to Hallmark—a vampire Christmas love story." I giggled. "I'd watch it."

Jack nudged me with his shoulder, but he had the biggest grin. "I never thought I'd fall in love with someone who could know everything about me. I haven't felt happiness like this in a long time, Ryan. I want that for you."

I didn't want to burst Jack's little bubble, but happiness like that wasn't gonna happen for me. All I could hope for was to find some semblance of peace once I found out who was responsible for the death of my parents.

As Jack squeezed me tighter, I spared a glance up and saw Nickolai watching me with a strange look on his face.

Chapter 16

I gave a slight incline of my head and pressed a quick kiss to Jack's cheek. The vampire glared suspiciously, knowing full well I wasn't really free with my affection.

"What was that for, kiddo?"

"Just cause," I replied with a little lift of my shoulders.

I got to my feet and dragged my ass across the apartment to call for the elevator, watching as Nickolai shook hands with Jack. I ran my eyes over Nickolai, dressed in dark denim jeans, a button-down shirt, and a baseball jacket thrown over top. His hair was wild as if he'd forgotten to slick it back like usual, and the longer strands dipped into his eyes.

As if he felt me watching him, he turned his head toward me and I snapped my head away, but not before I caught a glimpse of his cerulean eyes and cursed myself.

Once the elevator appeared, I sank into the farthest corner possible, and Nickolai, thankfully, went to the opposite corner. We spoke not a word the entire trip down, through the foyer, and outside on the curb, waiting for our car to arrive.

"We need to talk about last night."

His voice broke through the stillness of the night, and I sighed. "We really don't."

A sleek black Mercedes S Class pulled up, and Nickolai reached around me to open the door. I scowled at him, muttering I could open my own goddamn door. He, however, said nothing, just indicated for me to get in, so I did.

Sliding across the plush leather, I folded my arms across my chest and slouched in my seat as Nickolai got in beside me. Suddenly, there wasn't any air in the car and I wanted out of this metal can ASAP. I rolled down the window, breathing in the night air and ignoring my companion as we drove off through the city. Sirens wailed nearby, the smell of smoke in the air as fire engines sped past us.

After an eternity, we arrived at our destination. I felt in my gut like I'd leapt out of the frying pan and into the fire, but I didn't wait for Nickolai to get out and open the door for me, choosing to rush toward the evening's festivities at my own pace.

I tapped my foot impatiently as Nickolai stepped out of the car, a gaggle of nearby girls whistling as he smiled at them. I rolled my eyes and opened the restaurant door, automatically scanning the place for any threats while keeping an eye on Nickolai at the same time.

A waitress gave me a massive smile, asking what name was on the reservation. Her eyes widened when I said "Romanov, table of four." Grabbing four menus from under the counter, she informed me that we were the first to arrive. I nodded, and the girl hesitated when I stayed put at the counter, waiting until Nickolai was ready to be seated.

He came up behind me, and a hand fell to the small of my back as he directed me after the waitress. I tried not to react to his touch. After all, I had a job to do.

The waitress stopped by a table in the center of the room, and I shook my head. I couldn't keep my eye on all the entrances and exits from there. Scanning the room, I spied a table in the corner, up on a small dais where, if I sat with my back to the wall, I could see the entire restaurant. I pointed to it, and the girl looked to Nickolai for confirmation. He must have nodded to her, but I'd already surged forward, yanking out the corner chair with a scrape before Nickolai could try anything like pulling it out for me.

He sat down next to me, his own back to the wall, and accepted menus from the waitress, ordering a beer for himself and a Jack and Coke for me.

"Water's fine for me," I interjected.

"She'll take the Jack and Coke," Nickolai reiterated.

The waitress flinched but nodded, rushing off as fast as her human feet would take her.

"Have a drink, Ry. Everyone's entitled to a night off."

"Forgive me, My Liege, but with two members of the royal family out in the open, I cannot let my guard down."

Nickolai leaned back in his chair, resting a foot on his knee. "Kris will have two guards with him who will keep watch."

"Then why am I here?"

"As my date, of course."

"Is that an order, My Liege?" I murmured, slightly

louder than I'd intended.

Nickolai growled. "Give me a fucking break, Ryan. For one night, just give me a fucking break."

It was on the tip of my tongue answer his snark with a comment of my own, but I swallowed it down as the door to the restaurant opened and Nattie stepped inside with Kristoph following after her.

When you saw Natalia for the first time, it was hard not to see she was a great beauty. A mass of caramel curls framed her face, her chiseled features cut like diamonds, her figure slim but with curves a Playboy centerfold would be jealous of, Nattie was considered the most beautiful vampire in the Sanguine court. Tonight, she wore a tailored pair of navy pants with a matching jacket buttoned over a cream-colored blouse that probably cost more than my entire wardrobe. Diamonds in her ears and around her neck, with a rock the size of a mountain on her finger, I suddenly felt self-conscious in my jeans and Chucks. Her eyes sparkled as they landed on Nickolai, the sparkle dying out when they landed on me.

I watched as Kris leaned in, whispering something that made her plaster on a fake-ass smile. Kristoph had the same face as his brother, though it was sharper and more angled, his dark hair, eyes, and thin frame just like his father's.

He regarded me with a warm smile that almost made me forget he was a year younger than me, intelligence written in his eyes as he escorted Nattie to our table, her designer heels audible as she crossed the wooden floor, their guard moving to the bar area.

Nickolai rose, kissing Nattie on both cheeks as Kris waited to embrace his brother. I was happy to see they were still close; the brothers' lives were headed in two different directions, and that could have torn them apart. Wars had been waged for much less than a dispute over a crown.

"Ryan."

Nattie purred my name with such fake sweetness I was certain I'd have to see a dentist from the toothache it was giving me.

"Natalia," I replied coolly.

"Ryan Callan, get over here and give me a hug," Kris said.

I smiled warmly, doing as he asked as he winked at me, his eyes full of mischief. We exchanged pleasantries as we sat, and I looked up to discover Nattie smirking at me. I arched a brow, but Nickolai cleared his throat and Nattie pursed her lips and fluttered her eyes at Nickolai.

Bitch, please. You're so fake even China would deny they made you.

A young waiter, an apple tattoo visible on his wrist, appeared with our drinks, handing me a water and the Jack and Coke. Kris ordered some fancy bottle of wine and then asked his brother how he was getting on.

They lapsed into comfortable chitchat, and I let my eyes roam the restaurant. The bar was a quintessential Irish bar, the kind that kept tourists flocking from near and to sample a pint of the black stuff or a bowl of traditional Irish stew. I remembered coming here once or twice with my mom and dad, Jack playing traditional songs and my dad singing along as the Irish lads celebrated St. Paddy's Day and sang songs about wars they'd fought in.

I could picture them now, belting out tunes and

banging tables at the appropriate times while my mother shook her head, her smile so brilliant it lit up the darkened corners.

"Ryan."

I blinked as Nickolai called my name gently, asking me if I was ready to order. I nodded meekly, blocking out the memories and leaning back in my chair as I pretended to study the menu. When the waiter returned, I almost fell off my chair when Nattie ordered a salad. I mean, who came to a restaurant like Murphy's and ordered a salad? It wasn't like the silly girl could put on weight.

Both Nickolai and Kris ordered the steak, rare, and as I opened my mouth to place my order, Nickolai spoke over me.

"I know it's not on the menu, but I called earlier and asked if Chef would mind cooking something off-menu. He knows what to make for her."

My mouth clamped shut with a loud smack, and I dropped my gaze, wondering what the hell I was in for. The wine arrived as I slugged my Jack and Coke, trying to ignore Nattie, but the girl just wouldn't stop staring at me.

"What?" I finally snapped.

She sighed as if I'd disturbed her and glanced at Kristoph, who gave a sharp shake of his head.

"You promised to be civil, Nattie."

"Don't chastise me, Kristoph. I'm not a child."

Lifting my glass to my lips, I chortled a little, and Nickolai nudged me with his knee. "Must be incredibly challenging, Nattie, dating someone who isn't even legally able to drink the wine in front of him. Would you call Kris your boy toy, or does he call you his sugar mama when you're alone?"

Kris almost choked on his wine, exploding with laughter as Nattie looked horrified at my words. Nickolai growled a warning as our food began to arrive. The waiter set the salad down first, then the steaks, the blood dripping from the meat, making my stomach rumble loudly.

"Oh, by Eve! Have you no sense of decorum? Are you feral?"

I snarled and snapped my teeth at Nattie, reveling when she shrank back in her chair. When the waiter returned, my mouth watered as he set a dish down in front of me. Duck—a meat nowhere on the menu—cut into sections on a bed of creamy potatoes and runner beans, and drizzled in a blood-orange glaze.

It was my favorite meal ever.

I peered at Nickolai, puzzled, but he was concentrating on his steak. Grabbing my fork, I stabbed a piece of meat, lifting it to my mouth. Sweet Eve, the taste of it! The sauce was laced with blood, and I almost moaned my approval, my toes curling as I made quick work of the dish, savoring every mouthful, not caring Nattie was studying us both and forgetting about her lame-ass salad.

We ate mostly in silence, with Nickolai and Kristoph making random conversation as Nattie continued to glare at me. Despite my full belly keeping me pretty content, I was over her BS.

"Take a picture, it will last longer," I said.

Nattie thrummed a well-manicured nail on the table. "Well, considering your family history, photos really *do* last longer."

Nickolai dropped his fork on the plate with a clang, growling low in his throat, while Kris looked appalled at his girlfriend.

Thoughts of my parents were always raw; however, I had a lifetime of experience hiding my feelings from Nattie and her band of mean girls. I smiled, giving Nattie the smile I reserved for those I was about to beat bloody, and Nattie retreated further into her chair.

"Sweetie," I said, maintaining the smile, "leave the sarcasm and insults to the pros. You're gonna hurt yourself."

"I do not see why everyone is so fond of you. You have the social skills of a wild animal."

"Nattie, you know you have the right to remain silent, right? Cause everything you say will probably be stupid anyway."

"How dare you!" Nattie exclaimed, her face turning red, but I wasn't done yet.

Turning to Kris, I grinned, taking a sip of my drink before calmly musing aloud. "Hey Kris, when you whisper sweet nothings in Nattie's ear, do they echo back to you from all the empty space in her head?"

Nattie smacked Kristoph on the arm. "Are you going to let her speak to me like that?"

"To be fair, darling, you did start this," Kris replied as he drank his wine, unimpressed by Nattie's antics.

I tilted my head, letting an expression of wonder fall on my face.

"What?" It was Nattie's turn to snap at me, and I flashed my fangs at her.

"If I threw a stick, you'd leave, right?"

Kristoph spat out his expensive wine, coughing as

Nickolai tensed next to me, his hand landing on my thigh and squeezing as if to say, "Enough."

But I wasn't fucking done yet, and neither was Nattie.

"Do you know who I am? How dare you speak to me like that? I am a high lady of this court, and I will be respected as such. As the prince's consort, I demand to be treated in the manner which is expected. You are nothing but the pet project of the queen, who feels sorry for you. Nobody cares about you, Ryan. You are insignificant."

My fingers itched for my sai, and Nickolai's grip on my leg tightened in case I launched across the table and stabbed her with her salad fork... or worse. Instead, I leaned back in my chair, drained my drink and called for another as I jerked my head up.

"Good story, Nattie, but in what chapter do you shut the fuck up?"

Nattie rose from her chair with a start, Kris blowing out a breath as he dabbed the corners of his mouth with his napkin, reaching for Nattie as she brushed him off and stormed off, almost falling off the dais in her stilettoes.

I burst out laughing, lifting my glass to salute her when she glared. Kristoph cocked a brow, like I was suddenly rather interesting, and I toasted him as well. "Prince's consort? You have my deepest condolences."

"Forgive me, Ryan. She was way out of order."

I shook my head. "Not your fault, Kris. She's not your responsibility. Next time you come visit, though, leave the raging bitch behind."

"I might just do that." Kristoph sighed before turning his attention to Nickolai. "I'll speak with you later,

Nico."

Nickolai nodded at his brother, his face stern as Kristoph left the restaurant in a flurry of movement, and I became suddenly very aware Nickolai's hand was still on my thigh.

"I still get dessert, right? Please tell me I still get dessert."

Nickolai rolled his eyes as he summoned the waiter and asked for a slice of cheesecake now and one to-go for later. My leg began to bounce in nervous energy; I'd enjoyed that far too much, and not even Nickolai's hand cupping my leg could stop it.

The cheesecake arrived, and I dragged the plate toward me for a split second before Nickolai pulled it back.

"Hey," I said, "get your own cake. I deserve this after being nice to Nattie."

Nickolai arched a brow, taking a mouthful of my dessert.

I shrugged. "Well, I made it through the dinner without hitting her with a chair. I'd say my people skills are improving."

Nickolai didn't respond, just continued to eat my bloody cheesecake until I punched him in the shoulder. "Don't be mean."

"You want some?"

"You know I do. Gimmie!"

"Open your mouth."

I didn't understand what he intended to do until he raised the fork and was heading toward me with it. I frowned, reaching for the fork. "Ryan can feed herself, thank you very much."

"Then Ryan gets no cake," Nickolai teased, eating

the bite himself.

How rude!

Sighing, I motioned for him to give me some cake, opening my mouth obediently and clamping it shut on the bite he proffered. A moan escaped from me as I tasted the sweet morsel, closing my eyes and letting the fork slide through my lips before swallowing the bite.

A scent filled the air, and I snapped my eyes open, finding Nickolai's eyes focused on my mouth. He set the fork down and reached out with his thumb, gently brushing some crumbs from my lips. He then placed his thumb in his mouth and sucked, his eyes never leaving mine for a second.

This was not how I'd assumed the night would go, and I wasn't about to drop all of my walls because Nickolai had remembered my favorite dinner and fed me a bite of my favorite dessert. We couldn't go down this road. Not ever.

As if sensing my thoughts, Nickolai lifted another mouthful to my lips, and I opened up for him, my heart threatening to punch free of my chest. I couldn't breathe; his scent was all around me, from his hand on my leg to his thumb grazing my lips as he continued to feed me cake. It wasn't long until all I wanted was to get right in his lap and see if his lips were as soft as his thumb felt.

Jerking backward, I leapt out of my seat and shook my head. "You have to stop. You have to leave me alone."

"And if I refuse?" he retorted with a smug smile on his face.

"This is my life, Nicky. My goddamn *life*. Whatever fairy-tale you have in your head, it can't happen. Whatever you think is going on here *isn't*."

"Liar." He rose and prowled toward me, setting his arms on either side of my head as he leaned his forehead against mine. "Liar."

I nearly had a heart attack. His lips were inches from mine, and I could smell the beer and blood on his breath. My body wanted him so badly it was screaming, but my mind yelled to at me to run.

So, I fucking ran. I ducked under his arms and bolted from the restaurant into the night, even as my training screamed at me for leaving Nickolai unguarded. But the cold night air did nothing to temper the furnace that burned me from the inside out.

Chapter 17

Like a coward, I stayed out until the sun's rays threated to pierce through the early morning cloud cover. I had watched from afar as Nickolai got into the Mercedes, making sure he was driven home safely before I walked the city streets by myself. I was, however, on high alert as the rogue had a nasty habit of popping up when I was all alone. It was only then I remembered none of the vampires had filled me in on the rogue's identity.

Slipping into the apartment as quietly as I possibly could, I saw the plastic container with the second slice of cheesecake on the counter, a yellow Post-it Note stuck on it. As I peered down at the note, I frowned at the single word screaming in the quiet.

Liar was scrawled in Nickolai's elegant handwriting.

I pushed the cake aside, taking off my jacket and flopping down on the couch. Covering my eyes with my forearm, I chastised myself for letting Nickolai chip away at my resistance. I should've stayed in the goddamn vent.

Was I so weak I turned to mush after a piece of cake?

Ryan, darling, before you can learn to wield a sword,

you must learn to fight with the weapons you were born with.

My mother's voice ran through my mind as if she were next to me, and I closed my eyes, and remembering how she'd sat me on her lap, telling me that a woman needed to fight with her words and her person first. She was the first person to inform me that males of our species would underestimate us because we looked beautiful and fragile.

My mother had never appeared fragile to me—she was the strongest person I knew, even over my dad. He had this way of making her seem softer than she was, but my parents were different vampires when they were around each other and me.

I smiled to myself as I plotted revenge against Nickolai, shooting off a text to Krista asking her to come to the party with me. She replied in an instant with a heck of a lot of emojis I couldn't translate. I told her to come by the apartment to get ready, and we could leave from here.

Evening arrived far too soon, though some of my bravado had dissipated during the day as I tossed and turned in bed. When the door to the bedroom opened and Nickolai strode out in nothing but a low-hanging pair of basketball shorts, I quickly decided revenge was a dessert best served cold.

"Evening," he said.

"Krista is coming over to get ready for the party, so you might as well head on over and help them set up."

"You're going?" Nickolai asked with a bemused expression on his face.

I shrugged. "YOLO."

I refused to move from the couch as Nickolai went

off to get dressed for his human party, rolling my eyes when he asked if I was planning on wearing anything fancy. There came the hum of the elevator around seven, and Krista stepped inside the apartment as Nickolai made to leave. She waved excitedly, wearing the outfit Rose had picked out for her. She looked like sunshine in a bottle, and when I was dressed, I'd look like the Grim Reaper.

"Bye, darling, I'll see you later," Nickolai called, grinning over his shoulder as I flipped him off.

"Bite me, asshole."

Nickolai winked at me, and I rolled my eyes because of course he would go there.

Krista watched us with amusement as I said hello and ran off to shower. Afterward, I towel-dried my hair and wrapped myself in one of Nickolai's tees, knowing he'd stroke out scenting his scent on my skin. I called to Krista, and she came in and worked some magic on my hair, curling it so that it bounced, light and effortless.

I took the dress out of the bag much to Krista's dismay—she gave me hell for leaving such a dress in a bag. Slipping it on anyway, I turned to face her, and Krista's jaw dropped to the ground. Suddenly, I felt self-conscious.

"I can change... you know, if it's too much."

"Oh, hell no! You look stunning. I wish I could pull off a dress like that. Wait, why are you putting your feet into sneakers?"

"I don't have any other shoes. It's my Chucks or barefoot."

Krista tapped her chin for a second or two, then grabbed my military jacket and slung it over my shoulders. "There. Now you look like Ryan."

Krista went into the kitchen to arrange a makeup station, and I slipped the lace sheath Rose had given me around my thigh and found a dagger small enough fit in it.

When ready, she made me sit on the counter as she dusted and brushed makeup on my face, applying a dark red lip that shouldn't have worked with my coloring but did.

By eight-thirty we were ready to go, and I was suddenly extremely nervous. We called a cab to take us to the frat house. On the drive, I listened as Krista told me that her boyfriend was coming to visit for Christmas and couldn't wait to meet me.

I smiled at my friend as she invited me to come to a show with her after the Christmas break, and I agreed— if I was still around, that was.

The cab pulled up outside a massive house that had obviously been converted into a living space for the athletes of St. Pat's. Music vibrated the ground beneath our feet as we walked up the path, the party obviously in full swing by the time we arrived. I hung back as Krista knocked on the door.

It swung open not a second later, and we were greeted by a smiling Braydon, plastic cup in hand.

"Ryan! You came! Damn, girl, you look good. Hey, Krista."

Krista greeted him and headed inside, and I followed after her as Braydon closed the door behind us. The smell of sweat and beer greeted me as I ran my eyes over the mass of bodies gyrating along to the music being played by a DJ over to the side. This main room was the size of a small nightclub, and I was sure this wasn't the first party they'd thrown.

I'd spent a lot of time watching TV shows and movies about college parties, and I was a little disappointed by how unremarkable it was in real life. Krista nudged me as I zoned out, dragging my attention back to Braydon, who was offering to take our coats.

Slipping out of my jacket, Braydon was practically drooling over me, making me squirm. Krista grabbed my arm and pulled me toward the alcohol, pouring two drinks from the keg and handing one plastic cup to me. We clinked our cups and I grinned, making our way toward the main party. When a classic NKOTB song came on, I bopped my head along with the music.

I drained my drink quickly, taking another offered by Braydon, who seemed to be clinging to us. But I guessed normal eighteen-year-old girls wouldn't drink like they were blokes. I sipped the beer Braydon had given me, frowning at the odd bitterness but drinking it nonetheless.

Krista nudged me again with a knowing grin lighting up her eyes, and I followed her line of sight to where Nickolai watched me like I was prey, his eyes almost comically bulging out of his head. I drained my second drink and set down my cup as the song changed to Ginuwine's "Pony," and I dragged Krista to the floor.

Closing my eyes, I moved my body in time with the music. Krista laughed at me, but I could feel her dancing beside me. We seemed to have gathered a crowd, and I opened my eyes to discover Brayden and the other boys from Nickolai's class sidling up to bump and grind with us.

I'd never felt free like this before, my body tingling as I felt familiar hands fall to my hips. As he swayed with the movement of my hips, I reached up and wrapped my hand around his neck. I dipped low a little, and Nickolai sucked in a breath.

"You're gonna be the death of me, Ryan. What in Eve's hell are you wearing? That dress is painted to your body."

His words were a husky whisper in my ear as the song ended and I reached for the second cup in Braydon's outstretched hand, chugged it down to whoops and applause.

"Careful, Ryan. Don't forget yourself."

I slipped free of Nickolai's grasp and stumbled a little, wrapping my arms around Braydon's neck for stability. "It's a party, Nicky. Try and look like you're having fun."

"Yeah, Nico. It's a party, and Ryan just wants to have fun."

Nickolai glared at his friend as Krista dragged me away from the testosterone and we danced our hearts out. For the first time in a long time, I was just Ryan. No one knew me, or judged me, or waited for me to make a mistake. I danced with men; I danced with women; I was having the time of my life. I felt more buzzed then I normally did, but to be fair, I was knocking back the drinks as fast a Braydon could hand them to me. At one point, I twirled myself around so fast I got dizzy and stumbled, but Nickolai was there to catch me.

Grinning, I snaked my arms around his neck. "Do you like my dress, Nicky? I wore it specially... specially for you. Thank you for buying it for me." I leaned into him, felt him respond to my touch, and sighed. "You look good, Nicky."

Nickolai froze, even as I continued swaying along to the music. "How much has she had to drink, Krista?"

"I'm not sure; I don't know why she's like this."

I dropped my arms from Nickolai's neck and pouted, my head beginning to pound. "Everyone wants Ryan to let loose, but when Ryan does, Nicky gets all grumpy. I can't win. Leave me alone, buzzkills. I don't need your negativizes."

I backed away from them, wondering why my legs felt all weird, pressing two fingers to my temple as the floor seemed to shift with each step I took.

Spotting Braydon coming toward me with another drink, I gave him a lopsided smile. "Braydon! Come dance with Ryan!"

Braydon chuckled as he winked at his friends over my head, but I didn't care. I grabbed him and wrapped his hands around my waist, then stuck out my tongue at Nickolai. I'd gone to all this effort for him, and he was acting like I was embarrassing him.

"Nico doesn't know what he's missing, Ryan. If you were my girl, I'd never let another man put his hands on you."

I took another sip of beer, and the room spun. I felt nausea creep up my throat, and I knew I was going to be sick. Stumbling away from Braydon, I managed to make it outside before I vomited into the bushes.

There was something wrong with me—really wrong with me.

I felt a cold hand on the back of my head as I was shoved against the wall of the house. For the life of me,

I couldn't so much as lift my hand to smack the person away.

"Dude, how much did you give her?"

"Enough she should be out cold. Or dead."

"Braydon?" I didn't realize I'd said his name out loud until I felt the press of his knee against my thigh. Suddenly, I was terrified.

"Braydon, at least take her around the side of the house. Too many people can see you out here, man. Nico will decapitate you if he finds out."

"Then it's lucky she won't remember a goddamn thing in the morning, isn't it? Now shut up and keep a lookout."

His hands were all over me, and I started crying. I wasn't this kind of girl, the girl who let things happen to her like this. This shouldn't be happening to me.

Braydon ran his tongue over the curve of my neck, and I shuddered with revulsion, begging my muscles to react as I ordered myself to fight. They just wouldn't comply.

I choked back a cry as I heard Braydon unbuckle his belt, and I wondered if the first time I had sex would be rape.

Braydon's weight against me was gone a second later, and I crumpled to the ground, unable to support myself. Suddenly Krista was next to me, bending down to take me in her arms, and I hid my face in shame and confusion. I could hear the sound of bone crunching nearby, and I tried to get to my feet, my muscles like jelly as Krista shouted Nickolai's name and I vomited all over my shoes.

"Nico, man, you'll kill him!" someone shouted.

"I don't care."

But I did. If Nickolai ripped his head clean off, we'd be exposed. I barely had the clarity to focus on that thought, but I put all my energy into it as I crawled forward, calling Nickolai's name. I vomited again, my body trembling, and I lay down on the cold concrete, utterly spent and wanting to die.

I must have drifted off because the next thing I knew, I was being carried away from the party, my head lolling against Nickolai's chest. Nausea rose again so suddenly I barely managed to tell Nickolai I was gonna be sick before I lurched forward and decorated the pavement.

I started to cry, and Nickolai hushed me.

The next time I woke, Nickolai was pacing the floor of the apartment, phone to his ear, growling. "Jack, they gave her enough ketamine to knock out a fucking elephant. She won't stop throwing up. Get here as quick as you can. Her pulse and heartrate are all over the place."

"I'm sorry," I rasped, my mouth as dry as sandpaper. "I only wanted to make you want me as much as you made me want you."

Nickolai dropped down in front of me, and I ducked my head in shame. "Hey, don't worry about that now, okay? I just want you to feel better."

"That's the problem," I slurred quietly. "You make me feel... you make me feel... And I don't like it. I want it to stop. Right now, mister." I lifted my gaze to Nickolai's and whispered, "You make me want things I know I can't have."

Promptly ruining the moment, I puked all over the floor, Nickolai's hands in my hair as he waited for me to stop vomiting. Vomiting turned into dry heaving, and

198

after an age of agony, the heaving finally stopped and my eyes were heavy again.

"I know you're sleepy, Ryan, but you've got to stay awake until Jack gets here. Don't close your eyes, dammit. Don't close your eyes on me."

I pried my eyes open with my fingers, and when he smiled at me, I could see the boy I had once known and the man he had become. I reached out and cupped his cheek, and he leaned into my touch.

"I don't know where I stand with you," he began, "and I don't know what I mean to you. All I know is every time I think about you, I want to be with you."

"Soppy git."

As the reality of what had almost happened crashed over me like a cold wave, I reached my capacity for staying calm. I could feel my face pressed against the coldness of the wall; I could feel Braydon's hands all over me.

I felt dirty, like his fingerprints were tattooed on my skin, and I tore at the dress, hysterical as I ripped the fabric off and swatted away Nickolai as I stepped out of the ruined garment. Falling to the floor, I crawled to the corner, hugging my knees to my chest, not caring I was naked.

Stupid... I was so stupid. I was so goddamn stupid.

Sobbing, I beat my fists against my temple, only stopping when I felt gentle hands on my wrists. I glanced up through blurry eyes as Jack let go of my wrists. He gently placed a T-shirt over my head, and I inhaled Nickolai's scent.

"You've been dosed really good, kiddo. But we got you."

I closed my eyes, and when I opened them again, my

dad was in front of me, his face full of concern and his eyes filled with pain. I reached out, touching my fingers to the stubble on his cheek. "Daddy?"

I blinked, and Jack's face came back into focus. I was so thrown I clamped a hand over my mouth before I up-chucked all over him.

Jack placed a bucket next to me, and I vomited into it, shivering as I rested my head on my knees and cried and cried and cried.

"I'm gonna kill him. I'm gonna skin him alive for what he tried to do."

"Take it down a notch, Nickolai. She feels bad enough without you getting into trouble for kicking a human scum's ass. Have her report it. If she wants to. Everything that happens from here on out is down to Ryan. She's the victim in all this, not you."

Victim. I was a victim. I didn't want to be. I wanted to go back to who I was before, to the confines and safety of my bedroom, sure of who I was and what I wanted. Now... now I was someone's victim.

What would my peers think of me that I could be felled by a boy and his drugged drink? I would be a laughingstock—even more than I already was.

I needed to leave. I needed to escape. I slowly got to my feet to walk away, but one foot almost immediately tripped over the other, spilling me into Nickolai's arms before I could crack my face on the floor. I wanted to shove against him, but instead I heard myself begging him to let me die.

Then Jack came over to me, pressed two fingers to the side of my neck, and I begged no more.

Chapter 18

When I came back to consciousness, I heard the sound of voices outside the bedroom, low enough I could only make out it was a male and female voice, suddenly terrified the queen had discovered my failure and had come to bring me home.

Glancing around, I saw I was propped up against a mountain of pillows, clean and dressed in another of Nickolai's T-shirts. I tried not to think about who had washed me while I was unconscious, wondering instead how I was going to play this.

"Then lucky she won't remember a goddamn thing in the morning, isn't it?"

But I remembered everything—flashes of the night playing over and over in my mind. I couldn't shake the feeling of Braydon's hands on my body, the way he'd sneered with my body pressed against the building, me powerless to stop him.

All this pain... for what? To prove a point to Nickolai? To prove some sort of point to myself?

Pulling back the covers, I swung my legs slowly out

of bed and stood, testing my strength before taking a gingerly step toward the door. The voices outside had died down; however, I could make out the sound of Nickolai's footfalls on the hardwood floor.

I gave myself a minute, hoping to get some relief from the drumming in my head before I twisted the handle of the door, opening it ever so slightly to sneak a peek outside. Nickolai stood with his back to me, his reflection in the window somber as he stared out into the night. Stubble caressed the curve of his mouth and chin, his shoulders were hunched, and his entire body looked as tense as mine did.

Maybe I shouldn't interrupt him... maybe he was angry with me for being so bloody stupid.

"All I know is every time I think about you, I want to be with you."

By Eve, the things he'd said to me... the things I'd said to him! I needed to dial it back, to rebuild the wall that was slowly crumbling between us and remind myself that, one day, he would be king of all vampires... and I would have to stand by and watch him find his queen.

I must have sucked in a breath, because Nickolai spun around so fast I felt dizzy—or maybe I was already dizzy.

"You're awake."

"Yeah."

We stared at each other for a moment, and I shifted uncomfortably, taking a step outside the bedroom to go in search of water. My mouth felt like I'd taken a trip to the Sahara.

The minute I took a step, Nickolai moved with me. I snarled, already feeling foolish without wanting to show more weakness in front of him. He ignored me, pointing at the couch as he went to get a bottle of water. Once he was sure I had made it safety to the couch, he handed the water to me.

"I heard voices."

Scratching his chin, Nickolai leaned back in the chair, resting a foot on the coffee table. "Krista came to check on you. You had a lot of people worried."

I didn't respond, simply uncapped the water and took a hesitant sip, remembering the sheer volume I'd managed to vomit up. Vampires rarely got sick, the most extreme cases of sickness happening during pregnancy. Sometimes, if we drank tainted blood, it could make us ill for a time, but I supposed ingesting a copious number of drugs would make any supernatural creature upchuck all over the carpet.

"I know you probably have regret—"

"I regret nothing," I snapped. I didn't know why I was snapping at him, but here I was making even more stupid decisions.

"Is that because you don't remember what you're supposed to regret?"

I chewed on my bottom lip, not wanting to answer that question because I would dig myself an even bigger hole if I admitted I remembered. I wanted to forget; I wished I didn't remember... I wished I could go back.

I must have spaced out for a moment, because I didn't realize Nickolai had moved to sit next to me until I felt his fingers graze the side of my neck. I jerked, recalling how Braydon had traced his tongue up the curve of my throat, and quickly got to my feet, my face in my hands as I tried to remain calm.

When I braved a glance at Nickolai, the prince looked aghast his touch had incited such a reaction from me. I wanted to tell him that it wasn't him, that it was a memory, but even though I suspected he knew, I wasn't telling the truth about remembering.

He had cared for me when I couldn't look after myself—I owed him even just a scrap.

"He... he..." I stumbled over the words and snarled at myself, frustrated I was letting this jackass win.

"Ry, stop... you don't have to explain."

"I do! I really fucking do," I barked. "He licked my neck, where you touched, and I remembered, okay? It wasn't you; it was me."

I dropped my head to stare at the ground, my face heating with embarrassment as Nickolai lifted my face to look at him. He held my gaze for about a minute, refusing to let me look away, using his dominance to make me comply.

"You have nothing to be ashamed of. I want to beat him to death. I want to make him suffer. Ask me to do it, and I will bring you his head in a box."

I opened my mouth to speak as the elevator opened and Jack stepped inside, relief on his face as he studied me. I kept my hands by my side as he embraced me.

"You okay, kiddo?"

"Yeah, I'm fine," I ground out, anger bubbling inside me. My body tensed; I felt as if I'd just proven I was less than the males of my species—that, I, Ryan Callan, had just given them all a reason to go back and change the laws to forbid women from joining the guard. I had failed my parents. I had failed myself.

As if to prove just how pathetic I was, tears flowed

from my eyes, earning me a look of pity from Nickolai and a look of horror from Jack. I hadn't cried in front of anyone since the day Jack pulled me away from the dead bodies of my parents—and last night didn't count because I wasn't exactly in my right mind.

Was I in my right mind now?

"Hey Nickolai, you mind giving me and Ryan a few minutes? I ordered some takeout and it should be here soon."

Nickolai glanced at me as if he were waiting for permission. I growled, turning to face the window, folding my arms across my chest. I didn't so much as exhale a breath until Nickolai was gone, leaving Jack and me alone.

"When do we leave?" I croaked, my throat still raw.

"Why, kiddo, where are we going?"

Slowly I turned to face the vampire, lifting my chin to glare at him. "No games, Jack. No bullshit. When am I being hauled off to face the queen for my indiscretion? I assume I failed my test. I won't become a member of the Royal Guard. I've let them down."

Jack didn't reply as he wandered into the kitchen and took two bottles of blood from the fridge. He tried handing one to me when he returned, but I didn't think I could stomach it. He then proceeded to sit down on a chair and asked me to do the same.

After a brief hesitation, I followed his lead and sat down, setting my full bottle down in front of me. Tucking my legs under me, I leaned my head against the back of the couch and waited for Jack to tell me how much I'd fucked up.

"Ryan, the queen knows nothing about what happened on Sunday. Nickolai hasn't said a thing to anyone but me, and I haven't even told Atticus because it's not my story to tell. The only reason I know what happened is because Nickolai freaked out and called me in. I've never seen the boy lose his cool like that. I think, if he hadn't had you to worry about, he'd have had a grand ole time ripping that asshole apart."

I blinked rapidly. "So, I'm not going back?"

"Not just yet anyway."

I reached for the bottle of blood, opened it, and took a small sip. Suddenly, hunger roared inside me, wanting me to sink my teeth into real flesh, feel the pulse of life on my lips as I drank. My stomach rumbled loudly.

Jack laughed. "I asked for a Child of Eve to pay a visit tomorrow. We need to get you some solid food first. I ordered some rice and veg, just to give you a baseline."

I scrunched up my face, and Jack's laugh deepened. "Don't knock it, kiddo. Back in the day, when Tristan and I used to go on some benders, I mean, we drank so much that last night would have looked like a normal night. We pushed the limits of our bodies when we were young and foolish."

Jack's face softened, even as my heart constricted, and I think for the first time I realized I was not the only one who missed my parents. Jack had been like a brother to my father; the queen a sister to my mother.

Was I wrong to be selfish in my grief?

"But Tristan never failed to awaken the next night," Jack continued, "a grin on his charming face and ready to tuck into a plate of rice and veg. He'd be fitting fit soon after."

Smiling faintly, I played with the ends of Nickolai's

tee. "What was he like, my dad, when he was my age?"

"You know the kind of man your da was."

"I know what kind of warrior he was. I know how he was the best dad in the world. Everyone tells me that I look so much like my mom it hurts. Am I like him at all?" I wanted to be like him so much I hated to admit it.

"Tristan could be serious with those who didn't know him—until he met your ma, that is. He wanted to be the best, but he had a wicked sense of humor. He made me a better vampire, and every goddamn day I see traits of him in you."

"Please don't lie to me, Jack. Not today."

Jack set his empty bottle down on the table. "I'd never lie to you, Ryan. You might be stubborn like your mother, but Tristan could be hella stubborn, too. He never gave an inch if he thought he was right. He loved you with a fierceness I'd never seen before. I knew your da better than anyone save your mother. You might have your mother's grace and beauty, but that steel in your spine that keeps you going? That's all Tristan, kiddo."

The whir of the elevator shattered the little bit of peace I'd found talking with Jack. He rose, even as I remained seated, coming over to drop a kiss on my forehead, lingering for a second or two before he smiled down at me.

"Tristan was the best vampire I've ever known. He gave me great advice once, and I'm gonna share it with you: If the path you travel demands you walk through hell, Ryan, then walk as if you own the place."

My father's words, said to me by the closest thing to family I had left, spoken in the same lilting tone, cracked a smile on my face. As Nickolai came in, I said to Jack tenderly, "He told me once, not long before he... well, I'd had a fight with some of the girls who told me I was stuck up and spoiled, training with the prince who couldn't even fight because he would be king. I punched Farrah and broke her nose. I thought my dad would be angry with me, but he sat me in his lap and said the same thing to me."

Nickolai ignored us as he went about fixing plates for each of us.

Jack patted me on the head. "Well, let me share one last bit of advice with you. Will you humor and old man and listen?"

I let loose a snort, rolling my eyes as Jack crouched down, leaning in to say the words discreetly, even though we both knew every single vampire in this apartment could hear.

"Please stop destroying what's left of your heart by constantly thinking about things that should have broken you."

Before I could even manage a response, Jack rose, bid farewell to Nickolai, and left the two of us alone, the weight of Jack's words heavy on my heart. I closed my eyes, my head still resting on the back of the couch as I felt the seat cushion shift, Nickolai sitting down beside me. After what had happened earlier, I expected him to sit as far away from me as possible, but I'd forgotten this was Nickolai, and he never gave up on anything.

Two weeks after my parents' funeral, Nickolai was hammering on my door trying to get me to come out. I hadn't spoken to anyone for almost two weeks, barricading myself inside with all of my parent's belongings, as if somehow, I could summon them back from Eve's garden.

"Ryan Skye Callan, open this door right now. As your liege,

I am ordering you to do so."

"Go away, My Liege," I yelled back, muttering a word in Russian that I had heard my Uncle Jack mutter many a time, before I could halt my words. I wasn't afraid I'd sworn at the prince—I did that a lot—but I'd spoken to him, encouraged him, and he would be relentless now.

The sound of a drill snapped me into action. I stormed over to cast the door open, revealing my best friend grinning on the other side. His blond hair curled under his ears, sticking out in a very unprincelike manor.

"Go away, Nicky."

His cerulean-colored eyes twinkled with mischief. "Not going to happen," he said, and proceeded to flop down on my bed, setting a bag of my favorite popcorn and a tub of ice-cream in front of him. When he pulled a spoon from his pocket, I sighed, closing the door behind me before joining him on the bed.

Flicking on the TV, Nickolai began to play a movie I loved, telling me if I ever told anyone he'd watched a romcom with me, then he'd cut my hair.

I laughed, a strange sound ringing in my ears.

I blinked my eyes open, casting the memory aside as Nickolai handed me a small plate of rice and veg. My appetite was shot, but Nickolai continued to watch me until I managed a mouthful. The flavors seemed to burst in my mouth, and the next thing I knew, I'd demolished the plateful, washing it down with a little blood.

I set my plate down and reached for the remote as I gave Nickolai a friendly smile, the poor vampire looking shocked when I asked, "Fancy watching a movie?"

Setting down his own plate, he balanced his feet on the edge of the coffee table. "Sure."

The massive TV on the wall was equipped with the

latest technology, embedded with every movie or TV show imaginable. In a short few years, the streaming platforms had changed drastically. Even in America, a protype had been launched where a chip inside one's ocular nerve meant you could access shows and stuff right to your mind.

Crazy right?

Smiling, feeling a little fragile and a little nostalgic as well, I found the movie we had watched that night, making a sudden, terrifying decision as the movie started. Sliding across the couch, I curled into Nickolai's side, resting my head in the crook of his arm. His body tensed, and I drew back immediately, mortified.

Nickolai wrapped his arm around my shoulders, pulling me back into him as he muttered, "I can't believe you're making me watch this again."

"Shh... let me ogle Shane West in peace. Just don't start crying like you did the first time around."

With a soft chortle, Nickolai dimmed the lights, and we simply sat there, watching the movie until the credits ran and my eyes burned from tiredness. Even though I knew sitting in the dark, cozied up to Nickolai, was not in either of our best interests, I couldn't help myself, feeling raw from everything that had happened. Every single emotion I'd suppressed was beginning to resurface, no longer content to hide.

"I knew this girl once," Nickolai began, his breath warm against my skin. "And she was the fiercest person I knew. On the outside, she had this tough exterior, but I saw through that. She might have been a badass, but she had this infectious energy."

"What happened to her?" I asked, my heart racing.

"Something terrible happened, and I lost her sort of. She was there but she wasn't."

After a moment, I asked, "Do you miss her?" my voice a ghost of a whisper.

Nickolai said nothing for a minute, then said, "All the goddamn time."

In four words, he broke my heart, even when I thought it couldn't be broken any more. I knew in if I tilted my head up, Nickolai would press his lips to mine, changing the entire nature of our friendship. My mind played over what Jack had said to me earlier, to not destroy what was left of my heart by thinking of all the things that should have broken me. But to lose Nickolai, if I let myself go there, would rip me heart to shreds even if he were still standing next to me. Once the crown was on his head, there could be no us.

And I wasn't about to let that happen to me.

Darting upright, I faced away from Nickolai, using the steel in my spine to blurt out, "I know you don't know where you stand with me, but I do care about you, Nickolai—more than I want to, if I'm honest. I can't hate you, no matter how hard I try. I didn't forget you or erase you when they died, I just can't bear to lose someone else. I won't survive it."

"I thought you said you didn't remember," Nickolai replied quietly.

I spun to face him, blinking as I realized my mistake.

Nickolai gave me a slow, deliberate smile as he mouthed, "Liar."

He laughed then, the sound of it like destruction and chaos.

Well, fuck.

Chapter 19

Braydon Smyth was dead.

I knew that for absolute certainty for two reasons:

One—Nickolai was watching the news report intently as I emerged from the bedroom, the look on his face a mask of indifference as the journalist squirmed, visibly ill as she described the grim murder. The former sports star had been gutted, mutilated, and staged outside his fraternity house.

Two—Braydon Smyth's head sat in a neatly wrapped giftbox on the kitchen counter. Blood soaked the bottom of the parcel, and terror was written all over the guy's face in the moment of his death.

Accompanying the head was a brief little love letter from our resident rogue, explaining that Braydon had died for daring to touch me, for daring, as he put it, to try and rip the wings off such a transcendent butterfly.

I'd be impressed at the poetry of it if the wide-eyed head of my attempted rapist weren't making a wonderful centerpiece on the counter.

Nickolai was angry. I could feel the waves of it flowing from his skin, although I wasn't sure if he was pissed that the rogue was still fixated on me or he hadn't been the one to gift me Braydon's head. It certainly wasn't that the slimeball was dead.

Ignoring Nickolai's fury, I lifted the lid off the box again and leaned in to get a good ole whiff of the dead guy. I swallowed back nausea as memories of his scent hit me, reminding myself he could hurt no one else. It was the greatest satisfaction I could have gotten. Closing my eyes, I breathed in again, catching the faint scent of cold and blood, the scent of the rogue. He wasn't afraid to let me know he was the one responsible, as if he were my white knight, riding in to save the day.

"He feels like he's protecting my honour. As if I'm his to protect."

"You are not his."

Oh, male vampire testosterone!

Rolling my eyes, I ignored Nickolai and continued my assessment. "I can't see if he drank from him. The jagged cuts around the base of the neck aren't clean, like he was frenzied. I'd have to get a better look at his body."

"What's your plan? Will you walk into the frat house and ask nicely if you can check to see how the git was gutted because his head is at your house?"

"No, Mr. Narkypants," I huffed, wondering how I could get a closer look at the destruction the rogue had done. "I'm gonna hide in the shadows and use my lovely vampire eyes to catch a glimpse of the body from a safe distance."

"And if you're seen? I mean, you have motive."

"So do you, dumbass!"

We glared at each other for a second before the intercom rang, reception advising Nickolai a detective was looking to speak to us. Nickolai advised the receptionist to let them up as I squeaked and grabbed the box containing Braydon's severed head, then dashed about looking for somewhere to stash it.

Eventually, I hid it at the bottom of Nickolai's wardrobe, striding out of the bedroom as the detective strode out of the elevator. She introduced herself as Margaret Collins, a detective working on Braydon Smyth's murder. Tall and thin, the woman had flame-red hair pulled back severely into a high ponytail. Her intense green eyes were filled with intelligence.

Nickolai invited her to sit, saying how shocked he was by what had happened, but he wasn't sure how he could be of much help.

The detective smiled slyly as I asked if she would like something to drink, politely declining. I sat dutifully beside Nickolai, my hands in my lap as Detective Collins began her questioning.

"It has come to our attention there was a bit of an incident at a party on Sunday night."

Neither of us said anything, so the detective continued. "Onlookers said Mr. Smyth and you had an altercation that resulted in a broken rib."

Nickolai leaned back in his seat. "Braydon dosed Ryan with ketamine and then tried to assault her. I was simply trying to prevent a crime from being committed. Ryan was extremely unwell afterward, so I brought her home to recover."

The woman's eagle eyes turned to me, and I returned her steely gaze. The predator in me wanted to snarl and flash my fangs even as it admired her obvious grit, but Nickolai's hand on my knee dragged me back to my senses.

The detective's gaze fell to where Nickolai's hand rested. "Did you report the crime to the police? Did you go to the hospital?"

I shook my head, clearing my throat as I said, "I come from an extremely strict community. If they found out I was at a party—or even drinking, for that matter—I'd be forced to leave. I was okay physically, so Nickolai looked after me here."

"I'm sure your family would want you to be safe."

I remained tight-lipped as the detective turned her attention back to Nickolai.

"Can you tell me where you were between midnight and two in the morning, Mr. Romanov?"

"He was here with me all night," I replied. "We had take-out and watched a movie. We didn't leave the apartment all evening."

"And can anyone vouch for your story?"

I was beginning to dislike her tone, and I guessed Nickolai was, too, because he stood.

"I'm sure the cameras in the lobby will be able to show that neither of us left the apartment at any point." Nickolai reached into his pocket and handed the woman a card. "Now, should you have any more questions, please refer them to my solicitor."

"Why would you need a solicitor if you have nothing to hide?" the detective queried.

"We have absolutely nothing to hide, detective. Your tone suggests you've already decided I'm guilty; however, I was quite clearly protecting my girlfriend's honor."

The detective pursed her lips and stood, turning for

the door, when she paused and glanced over her shoulder. "Don't leave town, Mr. Romanov. I'm sure we'll speak again very soon."

"No doubt, Detective Collins. Just remember one little thing: I am a diplomat's son and therefore afforded the same rights as they are."

"A boy is dead. I'd try not to look so smug about it, Mr. Romanov. It makes you look very guilty."

"A poisoner and rapist is dead through no fault of my own, Detective Collins, and my girlfriend is thankfully alive. I have every reason in the world to look smug."

As soon as the detective was gone, I smacked Nickolai hard on the arm. "You idiot! Talk about talking yourself into being guilty. They're going to be watching you like a hawk now."

"Yes," he said, grinning like he'd given me a gift. "And while they have eyes on the apartment, you will be able to slip out and get a look at the crime scene."

My eyes widened. "Genius! I could kiss you!"

His smile deepened, dimpling his cheeks. "Go on then," he replied, a hint of a dare in his tone.

Turning away from that awkwardness, I ran back to the bedroom, attaching my weapon holster to my back and slipping on my dark jacket, then bending down to lace my shoelaces tighter. Quickly, I braided my hair and tucked it inside my jacket, hiding the distinctive color from view.

When I emerged, Nickolai was waiting for me. "You *will* be careful," he said. It was an order, not a request.

I waved my hands at him. "Of course, My Liege."

"Ryan, I mean it," Nickolai growled.

I gave him a little salute, climbed up on the back of

the couch, and stretched up, removing the cover of the air vent. Handing it to Nickolai, I grabbed the edge of the vent and pulled myself up, feeling Nickolai's eyes on me as I crawled into the small space.

"Stop looking at my ass."

"It's a nice ass; I couldn't help myself."

Crouching low, I ignored the heat flushing my face and shimmied along the narrow vent until I reached the outer cover. Popping it open carefully, I swung it back and glanced down to make sure no one happened to be looking up.

Grabbing the ledge of the roof, I hauled myself out of the vent and clambered up until my legs were braced on either side of the slanted roof. On one side of the complex sat an unmarked saloon car, housing what were no doubt police keeping an eye out for Nickolai.

The wind gathered, the scent of rain in the air, but it was Ireland I lived in—the scent of green and rain was just how the old girl smelled. I smiled at how easy this was; all the years I'd spent with my feet on a balance beam, trying to keep my balance while wielding a practice sword was really coming in handy. Luckily enough, the buildings around me were awfully close together, so the jump from one building to the next was no more than a simple leap. I headed toward the blue-and-red flashing lights in the distance, assuming they'd direct me to the scene of the crime, which they did.

The staggering amount of police still there was shocking, highlighting the gravity of the murder. People were gathered as well, placing flowers on the lawn of the frat house—more male than female, though. Reporters called out questions, snapping pictures as they tried to get a closer look at the body blocked by a police screen.

Three murders around campus since we'd arrived. This was really putting a kink in Nickolai's whole bringing-vampires-and-humans-together-peacefully plan. I wondered if the rogue was near, watching the chaos below and keeping a watchful eye out for me, wondering if I was pleased by his actions. Was it wrong of me to be the smallest bit glad Braydon was dead?

I needed to get a closer look at the body. As I waited for an opening, I saw one of the crime-scene techs move the police screen slightly, snapping pictures of the headless body for the investigation.

Covering the short distance quickly, I landed on the roof of the frat house, dropping to my stomach and leaning over the edge to get a better view. The scent of blood and death was almost overpowering even from all the way up here.

Braydon's body, I noted, was positioned right where he'd held me up against the wall, his headless body horrifically posed, his arms bent in a fashion not possible without breaking the bones. His legs were bent in opposite directions, as if they'd been broken to torture Braydon before he was killed. Most of the boy's insides were sitting in his lap, and I was almost certain that another part of his anatomy was sitting in his lap, too, but I wasn't going to dwell on that.

Braydon had died in a vicious, violent fashion. I was beginning to understand the rogue's sense of honor, knowing full well I'd probably do the same to whomever was behind my parents' murders. We were vampires. Our lives were contingent on loyalty, sovereignty, blood, and vengeance. He may be a rogue now, but if he was trying to win my approval by killing the man who'd slighted me, then I was dead certain he'd once been a court vampire.

And now, more than ever, I needed to know who he was.

A voice in the crowd caught my attention, and my gaze wandered down to spy Krista among those asking questions. My friend, who would not let the fact she was queasy around violent crime halt her journalistic nature, was jotting down notes in her little pad as she peered through the crowd, trying to get a better look. After a few minutes, she ducked under the arms of a man holding a camera and slipped into the alley beside the house. Seconds later, a figure slipped out of the shadows and followed her.

My mind screamed as I scrambled to my feet and bolted across the rooftop, skidding to a stop just before I reached the edge. Krista was easy to spot as she walked across campus, her hair bouncing as she made her way back to her dorm, oblivious to the threat stalking her.

Krista's notebook slipped out of her hand as she walked, and the girl crouched down quickly to pick it up before the wind could whip it away. Focused on the notebook, she did not see the monster step out of the shadows behind her, his fangs bared and murder in his eyes.

I had a split second to make a choice: save my friend and risk exposing my kind, or stand by and watch her die?

That wasn't really a choice.

Reaching for my sai, I stepped off the building, the wind whipping my braid free as the ground rushed to meet me. A thrill went through me as I hit the ground in a roll, using the momentum to propel myself back onto my feet, ready for action.

The rogue was inches from Krista when I rushed him, slamming my shoulder into him and sending him flying into the side of the nearby wall so hard the brick crumbled slightly.

Krista screamed, stumbling away from the fray as best she could, but I ignored her, focusing solely on the rogue before me.

"Runaway now," I hissed, my fangs springing free, "before it's too late."

The rogue wrenched a steel pipe off the side of the building, and Krista's panicked gasps at the feat tore my gaze from the rogue for a split second. Glancing her way to make sure she was safe, I saw Krista's eyes bulge in fear, and she shouted for me to look out.

I ducked as the rogue swung the pipe, barely missing my head, and lunged forward, the tip of my outstretched sai only grazing the side of his torso as he moved at the last minute. I wasted no time in spinning to the side and stabbing down with my sai, trying to catch him square in the chest, but he anticipated my move, grabbing my shoulders and tossing me like a ragdoll. Adrenaline sang in my veins as I hit the ground, taking the blow and returning to my feet in a heartbeat. I'd taken much worse from my fellow trainees over the years.

The rogue made to go for Krista again, and I dove for him, leaping onto his back and sinking my fangs into his shoulder as I stabbed my sai mercilessly through his back. As he howled in pain, I repeated the action before dropping down and kicking him away from me. The wounds probably wouldn't kill him, but they'd hurt like hell for a while.

As the rogue ran his hands over the blood at his back, I seized the opportunity to take him by surprise. Shoving him to the ground, I drove my sai into the palms of his hands. The rogue screamed, a melody of pain and fury that sang to me as I leaned in, the rogue's blood dripping from my fangs onto his own face.

"Tell your master I got his present and was not pleased with it," I hissed. "I am not a princess who needs rescuing. I am the knight who rides in to save the day. The next time I see him, I will take his head, just like I promised. Now fuck off back to him and deliver my message like a good little minion." With that, I yanked my sai free, sheathing them as the rogue darted away down an alley.

I was still riding the high from the fight and stuck to the shadows as I approached Krista cautiously. I tried to get my fangs to retract before getting to close to her, but to no avail.

"Are you okay?" I asked softly.

"How long have you been a ninja?" Krista asked as she brushed dirt off her skirt, gaping in awe.

I waited for revulsion to set in, for her to run from me screaming, but she didn't. Then I wasn't sure what was worse—her running or not running.

"You should be safe now, but don't go walking around at night by yourself, okay? There are things out there you should be afraid of."

"Like you?" she muttered under her breath, her eyes never wandering from mine as she swallowed hard.

I snorted sadly. "Especially me," I replied, dropping my gaze as I continued. "Being my friend is dangerous, Krista."

"At least let me see your face when you try and break up with me."

This girl, this very human girl with no hint of fear in her voice, stepped forward as I came out of the shadows, moonlight revealing my face. As Krista came up to get a better look at me, I stood deathly still. She touched the area just over the curve of my lips, feeling the slight rise due to my fangs beneath.

"This is incredible. I mean, I always suspected, always wondered, but you're real. How are you real?"

"Well, Krista, when two people love each other very much—"

"Ryan, now is not the time to be a smartass with me. I've just discovered monsters are real!"

"I'm sorry," I said, wiping the blood from around my mouth. "Being a smartass just comes naturally to me." Krista stared as if she were looking at an animal in a zoo. Finally, I clicked my tongue on my fangs and sighed. "Monsters, whether human or not, were always real."

"I have so many questions! Oh. My. God. My best friend is a vampire!"

I dropped my head as Krista bombarded me with questions. The night was beginning to wane, but Krista, now over the shock of her almost-demise, not wanting to let up on her journalistic nature, begged me to tell her everything.

I hadn't ever wanted to involve Krista in the murky world I lived in. Her curiosity was not a welcome commodity in our race, and now I'd broken a covenant and told her I was a vampire, it would be on me to make sure she kept her mouth shut. I didn't want to think of what would happen if she spilled the beans on us.

So, I did the only thing I could do when faced with impending dawn and a human who'd discovered my secret identity—I took her back to the apartment to annoy Nickolai.

Chapter 20

IN FAIRNESS TO NICKOLAI, HE HANDLED KRISTA'S QUES-
tions like a pro, smiling and looking as relaxed as he
possibly could when being grilled by an overenthusiastic
journalist with a vampire fascination.

"So, you guys aren't dead?"

"Not at all. In fact, our heart rates are always slightly
elevated," Nickolai replied as he reclined in his chair, his
hands in his lap. He spared me a quick glance, arching a
brow at me.

Sitting on the floor by the window, I shrugged my
shoulders and continued to wiping blood from my sai.
This was what Nickolai had come to see—to decide
whether humans could handle knowing there was another world hidden in the shadows.

Krista leaned forward in her seat as she regarded
Nickolai, glancing over her shoulder before turning her
attention back to him. "This is awesome. I mean, I really should have known. You both are incredibly fast and
strong, and you don't go out in the sun. I've seen enough
episodes of *Vampire Diaries* to know all vampires are

supernaturally beautiful. Ryan's eyes, for one, and that hair—it's not normal."

Nickolai grinned at me, and I gave him the finger as Krista continued. "Not to mention Nickolai, here, looks like he stepped out of a Russian bridegroom catalogue."

Nickolai's grin faltered as I burst into a fit of laughter. The crown prince growled at me but stifled the sound a second later, remembering he didn't want to frighten our little human.

"Oh my God! I know what you guys are! I can't believe you're vampires!"

Having polished my sai, I get to my feet. "All right, Bella Swan, be cool."

Krista laughed as if I were the funniest thing in the world. Then she sobered, pointing to me with her finger. "How old are you? How old is he?"

Slipping my sai into their sheath, I set the weapons down on the kitchen counter. "I just turned seventeen. The crown prince over there is nineteen."

"Oh, come on. You mean to tell me that you really are only seventeen, and pretty boy over there is—I'm sorry, did you say 'crown prince'?"

Lifting a shoulder in noncommittal response, I suppressed a smile, keeping my face blank of emotion and forcing Krista to look to Nickolai for answers.

I gleefully watched as Krista, stumbling over her feet, tried to bow and curtsey to Nickolai at the same time. Perching myself on the counter, I sat quietly as Nickolai explained how the Romanov court of vampires came to be, how his mother ascended the throne, and how one day, so would he. The pride in his voice as he spoke was infectious, and my heart swelled with a sense

I hadn't felt in a long time. I wanted our race to survive, and I knew Nickolai would one day make a great king. And, like I was destined to do, I would keep him safe.

"Your mom is like Akasha from *Queen of the Damned*—just less psychotic and power hungry?" Krista asked.

Nickolai's brow furrowed, and I knew he'd never seen the movie. Clearing my throat, I inhaled a breath, my skin prickling as Nickolai peered over at me.

"Queen Katerina is more like a Disney princess. Think Snow White, without the birds and animals following her around. My mother once said Katerina could defuse the darkest of situations with only her smile. She did not have to speak, our queen, for her tranquility flowed into all around her, easing tensions in even the worst arguments."

"Your parents knew each other?" Krista queried, lifting her probably cold coffee to her lips before she carried on. "Before they were murdered?"

The air thinned as Nickolai raised a brow, obviously wondering why I'd so easily shared such secrets with the human girl when, most of the time, I couldn't talk about it to him. Sometimes, it was far easier to speak to someone who didn't know the tragic soap opera that was my life.

I arched my brows as if to say, *you were the one who wanted me to make friends!* To Krista, I replied, "My parents were the queen and king's personal guard, but they were also friends. They died protecting the royal family in a coup many years ago. It was a warrior's death to be proud of."

"And now you're Nickolai's guard?" Krista asked, a sheen of wetness in her eyes.

I shrugged. "Not yet. I'm still a novice. If I manage to keep Nickolai from being killed, then maybe I'll become a full member of the Royal Guard, but if that happens—"

"*When*, Ryan," Nickolai interjected. "Not if; when."

Rolling my eyes, I tried to ignore him, but inside my pulse was racing and I knew he could hear it. "*When* I do," I said, pointedly looking at Nickolai before turning back to Krista, "it will be My Liege's choice as to who he chooses as his personal guard."

Reaching behind me, I grabbed the pot of coffee and poured myself a cup, taking a sip and nearly choking on it as Krista exclaimed, "Oh my God, and here I thought vampires would be stuck in the Dark Ages, but you guys seem super progressive. I mean, you have a queen and Ryan is such a badass."

"Progressive?" I sputtered. "Vampires? Krista, court vampires are the most stuck-up, backward-thinking idiots you could meet!"

"Hey!"

Ignoring Nickolai, I ground out some hard truths about home that perhaps my future king needed to hear. "My mother was the first female member of the Royal Guard. Ever. I am only the second. I cannot hold my family seat on the royal council because my parents are dead and 'a family does not consist of only one person.' Until I take a mate, take his name, and give the council a child, I do not get a voice in my world. The only reason I got sent on this mission is because the queen feels sorry for me; and the king, well... If he had his way, I'd already be home, picking out floral arrangements for my arranged wedding."

I sucked in a breath as I finished my rant, slightly

mortified as Krista glared at Nickolai, my human friend's face twisted in horror. "You would *never* make her do that, would you? Force her to marry someone she didn't love? She's your friend, right?"

Nickolai tried to catch my eye, but I suddenly found the floor remarkably interesting.

"I would never force Ryan to do anything she didn't want to do. Ryan is my best friend, and nothing will change that."

Krista beamed like she'd solved a vampire diplomatic crisis, not hearing the layer of double meaning in his words. Did he think that becoming king would not change him? Because *of course* it would. It would change everything.

"I'm still reeling from the fact you guys are alive—have heartbeats and babies and everything. Do you drink blood from birth? Or is it only when you become teenagers? How do you get blood? Do you guys have magical powers? How can you even eat normal food?"

Nickolai let loose a howl of laughter, slapping his hand on his knee. I lifted my head, smiling at my friend.

"We have volunteers who donate blood to us, descendants from families who've known of our existence for centuries. We're taught how to feed from humans as children, kind of like weaning for human kids. Unfortunately, we have no magic powers apart from compulsion and a supernatural healing ability, and that doesn't really work anymore due to technology and people being less susceptible to suggestion. Did I forget anything?"

"You forgot the food question," Nickolai remarked with a sly smile. "Yes," he said, answering for me, "we eat human food and enjoy it. For example, Ryan likes cheesecake."

I lifted my head in exasperation, heat flushing my cheeks so much I didn't dare look to Nickolai. But Krista's next question had my head snapping back to glare at her.

"What's it like, feeding and being fed from? Will you feed from me?"

"Absolutely not!" I exclaimed, shaking my head.

"Why not? I'm offering, right? It's not like you're forcing me. I want to know what it's like."

"Ryan," Nickolai said softly.

I knew he was going to do it, but I still shook my head. I barely felt Nickolai move, and then he was in front of me, his hand on the slope of my chin as he gently raised my face to his.

"If we are to survive, we must find humans like Krista who are open to having us feed on them. Is that not what our mission here is? I will do it, though I'll take but a sip, just so she knows. It is a gift given freely."

"Krista isn't part of this," I said quickly. "She shouldn't be. If the rogue hadn't attacked her tonight, she would have never known about us. I can't help shake the feeling this is wrong."

"Ryan, I want to know," Krista protested, shifting her blonde hair from her shoulders as Nickolai let go of my chin and strode over to her.

Kneeling, he held out his hand, and Krista place her hand in his, shivering as he turned it over and ran a finger over her pulse.

She gasped, her eyes opening wide in shock as Nickolai's fangs elongated before her. It sent a shiver running down my spine. I wanted to look away, to flee the room and not bear witness to this, but I was mesmerized.

"Last chance to say no, Krista," Nickolai said calmly. "It will hurt, but just a little. Do you trust me?"

"Only because Ryan does."

Nickolai lifted her wrist to his mouth, and I clutched my own wrist to my chest as if I could feel the touch of his lips. I heard Krista's sharp intake of breath the moment Nickolai pierced her skin and witnessed her eyes grow heavy as Nickolai swallowed down her blood.

I'd witnessed feedings many a time, but I'd never been so attuned to one before, my skin tightening, my body heating, aching in places I didn't want to mention. It was as if Nickolai were feeding from me directly, and I craved more of it.

Nickolai pulled his lips back from Krista's wrist, ran his tongue over the puncture wounds, and cast a glance over to me—one that assured me I was not the only one affected by the feeding. He rose to his feet and took a step toward me, then hesitated, turning to study Krista.

Krista blinked, staring at her wrist for a second until the high had worn off. Then she glanced between me and Nickolai. "Not gonna lie, that was all *kinds* of hot. And I don't feel anything apart from a little sleepy now."

Wanting to break whatever connection Nickolai and I were sharing, I slipped off the counter, walked to the fridge, and grabbed a carton of OJ for Krista. By the time I'd returned and handed Krista the container, Nickolai had retracted his fangs and cleaned the blood from his lips. She sucked on the carton, draining the juice in seconds, and sat back in her chair. Nickolai reclaimed his seat, too, and I leaned against the farthest wall.

Krista sighed, and her lips pursed. "I understand you

guys are, like, posh vampires with courtly etiquette and all. But what's the thing killing everyone on campus?"

I chewed on my lip. "Rogues," I answered. "Vampires who think themselves superior to humans, godlike, with a divine right to take what they want from humans. They've renounced the rules of the crown and now kill and murder as they please. One seems to have a hard-on for me, so when Braydon, uh... you know... he decapitated the kid and sent me his head in a box."

Krista regarded me for a second and then nodded. "I get it. You're not exactly a flowers-and-chocolates kinda chick, so he sent you the head to woo you. It's creepy, but he definitely got your attention."

Nickolai smothered a chuckle as the elevator came to life with a whir and I stood.

"Are you expecting anyone?" I asked Nickolai, who shook his head.

The doors opened, and a smiling Kristoph stepped into the apartment. Dressed in a long peacoat, his hands were in the pockets of his pleated trousers, his shirt tucked into his pants and his shoes making an audible clack on the wooden floor. His dark hair was slicked back, and he looked far older than his years as he flashed Nickolai a smile.

"Now *he* looks like a vampire," Krista muttered.

Kristoph froze, tilting his head to watch Nickolai with eyes so like his father's. "What have we here, Nickolai?" he asked.

Nickolai strode over and gave his brother a hug, giving me time to circle around and grab my sai before casually leaning against the chair where Krista sat, my friend still oblivious to the danger her words had put her in.

"Krista is a friend. Stop being rude and come and introduce yourself."

Stepping back, Nickolai beckoned Krista forward, and I moved with her. Kristoph reached out a hand, taking Krista's in his as he did as Nickolai asked.

"Hello, Krista, my name is Kristoph, Nickolai's brother.

I saw Krista's spine straighten. "Oh my God, are you a vampire prince as well? Should I bow?"

Tensing, I coiled my fingers around the hilt of one of my sai as Kristoph gave her a smile reserved for the Kris I knew in private.

"I am not as important as Big Brother here—no need for any pretense. Here, I'm just Kris. And Ryan," he added, turning my way, "you can put away those weapons of yours—I'm not likely to snap her neck with you watching over her, am I?"

Grinning, I lifted my shoulders. "Not that you could stop me, Kris. But as My Liege asks it of me."

Kristoph whooped with laughter, slipping his hands back into his pockets as he rocked back and forth on his feet, and then the room settled into an uncomfortable silence. Nickolai finally broke it, asking his brother if he wanted anything to eat or drink.

"I'm all good, Nico... unless the lovely Krista is offering," he drawled, winking at Krista as my friend blushed a furious shade of red.

I punched Kris in the shoulder lightly. "Krista has enough on her plate after being attacked by a rogue on campus. She doesn't need another rabid animal after her. And besides, Kris—you're sixteen, and Krista has a boyfriend."

Kristoph quirked his brows. "Rabid animal?"

I let a slow, deliberate smile creep over my lips. "Sure. What else would you call your cougar of a girlfriend?"

Nickolai chuckled, even as Kristoph shook his head, a silly smile on his lips. I nudged Krista and shifted my eyes to the door, then announced to the boys I was going to see Krista across the quad before sunrise.

Kristoph took Krista's hand in his and lifted it to his lips as Krista ran her eyes over the younger of the vampire brothers.

"You are trouble," she mused, earning another wink from Kristoph. "You have Damon Salvatore-kind of vibes going on."

"Damon Salvatore has been quite the role model in my life. Alas, I can only aspire to be as quick witted and handsome."

Krista gave him a skeptical look as she reclaimed her hand. "Oh yeah, you're *definitely* trouble."

Leaving the brothers behind, we exited the apartment, Krista not saying a word until we'd made it out of the apartment and crossed the quad.

"That was..."

She broke off, unable find words to express the information overload she'd received over the last few hours. I could see how tired she was, and as Krista yawned, I felt sorry she'd been brought into this. Her life would never be the same.

"I'm sorry you had to find out like this, Krista. I'm so sorry for pulling you into the drama of my life."

Stepping inside the doorway of her building, Krista pivoted toward me, a silly smile tugging her lips upward. "Are you kidding me? This is awesome! I mean, if

Nickolai does ever decide to go public, I can be the one to release it! I knew there was something special about you, Ryan Callan. Even if you weren't some Ninja Turtle vampire badass."

Krista hugged me then, and I returned her gesture, letting myself feel loved for a blissful moment before stepping away from her.

"Don't go wandering around at night, Krista. Promise me. Nickolai said classes are cancelled for another two weeks because of Braydon. If you need to go out, you call me, okay?"

Krista saluted me, and then she was gone, vanishing inside as I breathed out a sigh of relief and quickly made my way back to the apartment.

The elevator doors opened on Nickolai gathering up some of his stuff. He stopped as I came in, Kristoph turning as they heard me arrive.

"The Sanguine Council has called a meeting to get an update on our rogue problem. Mother had requested you both come stay for the day. Mother wants Nickolai to join us for breakfast before the meeting. You too, Ryan."

Dinner with the royal family? Sitting across the way from Anatoly? Yeah, hard pass on that.

"The car is waiting below to take us home, Ryan. Grab what you need for a night or two, then we'll be coming back."

Nickolai's words were a whisper of a promise as I sighed to myself, knowing I had clothes and stuff at home I could use. Then, a thought crossed my mind and I strode to the fridge, taking out the cheesecake still left over from our night at Murphy's. Taking a fork from the drawer, I headed for the door as Kristoph came up behind me, his hand squeezing my shoulder as we headed down to the car.

"Life is never dull with you around, Ryan."

I said nothing in reply, simply let myself be guided to the car sitting outside with sun-protected windows. Atticus smiled as I slipped into the car, Kristoph sliding in next to me, leaving Nickolai to sit facing us when he arrived down to the car, his knee touching mine as I popped open the container and proceeded to eat my cheesecake, ignoring the fact Nickolai was staring at me.

Kristoph chuckled, shaking his head. "As I said. Life is never dull with Ryan around."

Chapter 21

WHEN YOU HAVE A RATHER DEADLY REACTION TO THE SUN, being able to witness the sunrise while encased in a moving metal vehicle is truly something special. Even now, as the sun was coyly shielded by an abundance of gray clouds, fine rays of sunlight were still visible, trying to break through.

My face almost pressed against the glass, I kept my eyes on the sun as she tried to emerge, feeling almost morose as the car descended into the underground parking garage reserved only for royalty. Nickolai and Kristoph had agreed to keep Krista's knowledge a secret for now as it would not help us catch the rogue.

Just before Atticus turned off the engine, my ears pricked at the news bulletin on the radio. I asked him to wait and then gasped, horrified as the reporter announced a mass killing at St. Patrick's. A group of media students filming on school grounds. A citywide curfew was to be introduced, and all students were advised to stay indoors after dark.

All of the dead had been drained of blood.

Atticus turned off the car, getting out and opening my door so I could slip out. I immediately headed for the comfort of my own room, not bothering to stop even as Nickolai called my name, saying he would see me for breakfast.

Taking the stairs two at a time, I strode into the foyer as the shutters came down and enveloped the house in darkness. Hoping to avoid any stragglers, I hurried up the winding staircase, halting on the next level as Scarlet Hamilton paced the hall floor, one hand resting on her stomach, the other pressed against her back. Sweat dripped from her forehead, and I approached her slowly to ask if she was okay, worried I might startle her.

The pregnant vampire gave me a pained smile, then grunted as a burst of pain hit, causing her knees to buckle. I lurched forward to catch her, and her hands gripped me with such intensity I feared the bones in my hand would shatter.

I glanced around, trying to find some sort of adult who can help poor Scarlet, but the halls were empty. When the woman let go of my hand, mumbling it hadn't been like this the last time, I made sure she was standing steadily before racing down the hall and banging hard on the door of her family suites.

A couple of minutes later, a sleepy Spencer opened the door wearing just a pair of boxers, rubbing his tired eyes. "Ryan?" he said, his voice thick with sleep.

"Hey, your mom's not doing so good. I think she might be in labor."

Spencer all but shoved me out of the way as he went to aid his mother, leaving me standing at his door as he escorted her inside, calling for his father. Scarlett turned her head and gave me a small smile as the door closed behind them with an audible click.

Shaking my head, I headed for my own rooms, opening the door into safety and comfort. Flopping down on the bed fully clothed, I breathed a sigh of relief, closing my eyes and drifting off to sleep.

I woke to the sound of banging on my door, my eyes springing open as I sat upright just as the door opened and an angry Nickolai stormed in. Folding my legs underneath myself, I let him ramble on about missing breakfast and how he was surprised at how quickly I'd reverted back to old habits once we were home.

Once the prince had blown all that hot air out of his ass, I tilted my head and began my response. "First, I was exhausted and didn't wake until you started beating down my door. Second, I had no intention of cozying up to your parents over breakfast—especially not your father, who hates me for some reason. And finally, the next time you barge into my room without invitation, I'll give you a nice haircut with one of my sai."

Folding his arms across his chest, Nickolai scowled. "We have a briefing in ten. Get some food and be on time."

I slid off the bed, running my fingers through my hair. "Yes, My Liege."

Nickolai growled as I brushed past him, then grabbed my arm and spun me back around. I faced him, snarling. "Let go of my arm, My Liege, or I will break your fingers."

"Stop."

"Stop what?"

"Stop with the 'my liege,'" he said, grinding the honorific out through clenched teeth. "Stop changing the rules on me."

I yanked my arm free. "I'm not changing any rules, Nickolai. This isn't a game. You come barging into my rooms like the entitled prince you are, and *I'm* changing the rules? Grow up, Your Highness, and get your ass down off that high horse. Close the door behind you on the way out—that is, if you remember how to do shit on your own."

I ran out the door and down the stairs, nearly reaching the end of the staircase before I heard my bedroom door close. Skidding to a stop at the bottom, I saw a smiling Jack waiting for me.

"Déjà vu much?"

Jack laughed at my comment, lifting his eyes to Nickolai as he descended the stairs.

"Vampires will talk, kiddo."

I huffed, coming down the last step. "Well, I just loudly handed him his ass on a plate, so let them talk. Come on, let's get this over with."

I filed into the meeting room with Jack, sitting in the exact spot I had when I'd first been asked to join the mission. Jack sat down next to me, pouring me a coffee as Nickolai came in, taking his seat at the head of the room without looking at me. Atticus, however, was doing a terrible job of avoiding looking at Jack.

If someone wrote a soap about vampires, we'd be ideal characters.

I'd just snagged an apple when the queen strode in and we all stood, her face warm and welcoming as she glanced in my direction. When the queen had taken her seat, we returned to ours. I bit into my apple before realizing the queen was focused on me.

"Ryan," she said, "we missed you at breakfast this

morning."

I swallowed the piece of apple before I answered her, conscious of all eyes in the room seemingly studying our interaction. "Forgive me, My Liege, I overslept. I haven't had much time for sleep in the last few months. Worry not, however; Nickolai has already voiced his displeasure at my laziness."

Katerina pursed her lips and cut her eyes to Nickolai before returning to her warm smile. "There is nothing to forgive. You have been working so hard; it is understandable you are tired. Maybe we can catch up before you and Nickolai head back to college."

"Of course."

I'd rather pluck my eyes out with chopsticks, but sure.

"My son, update us on your progress."

Nickolai reclined in his chair. "I have been able to integrate into college life, making friends easily and adapting to circumstances. As Ryan said before, the youth are our way to integrate with humans as they have more of a capacity to comprehend the supernatural."

"How long before you feel you can reveal yourself to a human to gauge their reaction?" Idris asked.

Nickolai scratched his forehead. "It is far too soon to predict that. Most of the friends I have gained are acquaintances, not close friends. Instead, it is Ryan who's made a friend we've considered telling, as she is trustworthy and already intrigued by the supernatural."

"It is not in Ryan's job description to make friends, My Liege. It is her job to give her life for yours."

Just like her parents.

I lifted my eyes to Idris and smiled, hearing the unspoken words in his tone. My mouth opened, ready to respond, but the queen beat me to it.

"Idris, Ryan has already done just that, as you are well aware. She has killed one rogue and injured another. We cannot throw stones around here when we've had her fighting with one arm tied behind her back."

Leaning back in my chair, I tried not to look smug as Idris's jaw ticked.

"Ryan has diverted the attention of the primary rogue from humans to herself. He has been sending her gifts, following and watching her. She has a right to know who the rogue is so she is better equipped to find a weakness."

The entire room of men turned to me, and I shifted uncomfortably under their scrutiny.

"Why would he be interested in her?" Boris sneered.

Where Natalia had inherited her pleasant disposition from was obvious.

"I'm a fucking delight, didn't you know?"

Jack barked out a laugh, Nickolai joining in with him. Even the queen chuckled softly, trying to hide a smile. Idris and Boris merely stared like I'd just told them I was leaving the court to become a stripper.

Rolling my eyes as the laughter died down, I leaned forward in my chair and rested my chin in my hands. "Because he thinks I am beautiful and wants to make me his rogue queen. And as long as he's focused on wooing me, he won't kill innocent strangers. He's already tried flowers and diamonds. Then he watched me fight and kill a blood lusted rogue. Finally, he sent me the head of a boy who'd upset me."

"And have you been encouraging his weird affection

toward you?" Boris asked.

"Sure," I answered, sarcasm dripping from every word. "Who wouldn't want a psychotic, human-murdering vampire hanging around, trying to prove he's better boyfriend material than a court vampire. I mean, looking at all your sons, I'm starting to think he might have a point."

There is a roar of growls and snarls as the council begin to yell and scream in outrage, their raised voices grating on my patience even before the queen called for order. They ignore her, pointing fingers in my direction as they rant and rave, and I finally lose my patience.

Yanking my sai free, I sent one sailing through the air, shattering an ornate Ming vase, spilling water over the table and silencing the room. Getting to my feet, I retrieved my weapon before speaking.

"This is why we are dying—this male chauvinistic outlook on our lives. Do you know what I learned about the rogue while you all were keeping his identity from me? This vampire was old court long before he was a rogue. His voice was damaged either when he was born or in an accident that never healed properly. He's from old Russia, and his accent gets thicker when he's excited. I've never seen his face, but from the way he holds himself, the way he's tried to sway me, he is handsome and knows it."

Pausing as I walked back to my seat, I remained standing, my hands resting on the back of my chair. "He knows females are treated as lesser vampires and knew I was not like the other girls at court. He *used* that to his advantage. He is smart. Careful. Calculated. He knew that murders, especially with the crown prince on campus, would cause chaos among our ranks. And he was right."

I'd saved the best for last, having kept the knowledge to myself for a long time. Flashing my fangs and giving these vampires my most sinister smile, I continue.

"To know who Nickolai is, he must have a contact at court, or one of his minions was a member of court, but to know us as intimately as he does, the rogue has to be related to one of the royal clans."

Boris snapped his head in Nickolai's direction, and Nickolai shook his head, holding his hands up. "I did not say a thing. Ryan is smart, Boris, and nosy as hell. She'll figure things out eventually if left to her own devices."

My grin deepened as I finally sank back down in my chair, triumphant.

The queen cleared her throat. "Ryan is right. We spend so much time trapped in a cycle of tradition we assume many things. Have you an idea to lure out the rogue, Ryan?"

"I do, My Liege. However, I will not be kept in the dark anymore. Either you tell me the identity of the rogue, or I will have no choice but to ask him myself."

"How dare you!" spluttered Boris, slamming his fists down on the table. "Do not think beyond your station, little girl, and speak to the queen in such a manner."

"At least I'm not throwing fits like a toddler, Boris. Based on your behavior, one might think you were related to this rogue."

As Boris's face turned purple, I knew I'd guessed correctly. My lips tugged upward into a smile. "Ah, Boris. This wouldn't happen to be the rogue brother you were supposed to have killed fifty years ago, would it?"

"He was supposed to be dead. I drove a dagger into his throat and left him in the snow for the sun. I didn't realize he was still alive until the attempt on the queen's life."

Blood rushed to my head, the monstrous rage in me exploding to the surface as I hissed out a breath and lunged for Boris, my sai in my hands before I knew it.

Jack snared me around the waist, and I drove my elbow backward, crunching Jack's nose. He yelped but kept hold of me, the coppery scent of blood filling the air as I tried in vain to get to Boris.

"You piss-poor excuse of a vampire. Couldn't even kill him right! If you'd only done your fucking job, we wouldn't have lost so many vampires. Those deaths are on *you*! I'll kill you; I'll fucking *kill* you!"

Boris, who now clung to the wall behind him and stunk of fear and guilt, looked to the queen for assistance when I managed to get free of Jack's grasp and stalked toward him. I was poised to strike, to rid the world of his stain, my sai already pointing at Boris's heart, when a familiar form moved to block me from my prey.

My hand froze as the tip of my weapon kissed the spot just under Nickolai's heart. I growled, pulling my arm back and moving to slip around him, but he grabbed my arm, holding me firmly.

"Stand down, Ryan," he commanded, pouring every ounce of authority he had into his tone.

"With all due respect, My Liege, go fuck yourself."

"Stand down, Guard Callan. That is an order."

I sheathed my sai at his words, pointing to Boris. "This isn't over."

Shoving past Nickolai, I walked to the far side of the

room, where I inhaled a deep breath and tried to find my calm.

"Perhaps," suggested the queen, "this would go more smoothly, Boris, if you excused yourself."

"Pardon me, My Liege, but should the trainee not excuse herself and her infantile behavior?"

The queen gave Boris her most brilliant smile. "Ryan is necessary to this mission, whereas you are not. And it seems my son has already promoted Ryan to a member of his guard, so she is a trainee no longer. Now, get out, Boris."

The queen's words hit me like a sledgehammer. I was a member of the Royal Guard? Nickolai had chosen me? That made me the youngest guard in history. Emotion caught in my throat as I managed to find my seat. Jack's hand dropped onto my shoulder, a comfort as I tried to steady my breathing. I wondered if my parents would be proud of me, then turned and offered Jack a small smile in apology as he cleaned the blood from his almost certainly broken nose. He gripped his nose and yanked it back into place with a crunch. I cringed.

The moment the door closed behind Boris; the room was immediately less tense. I listened to Idris as he fleshed out the details of who the rogue was. Maxim Smyrnoi, older brother to Boris, had turned rogue seventy years ago when, after the Guard caught him trying to flee with the love of his life, Mia—Natalia's mother—his parents had married her off to his younger brother. He'd joined the rebel factions, spreading anti-court and anti-royal propaganda, luring impressionable vampires to his way of thinking.

Boris had tracked him down and thought he'd killed

his brother, but Maxim's followers found and cared for him for days as his wounds healed. He remained hidden for decades, mounting support until they attempted an assassination in Russia... and the rest was history.

When Idris finished speaking, I realized the plan I'd already formulated would likely work even better, now that I understood his history. The room was drenched in silence as I lifted my gaze, all eyes watching me as the queen asked how I planned to lure Maxim out.

Leaning back in my chair, I folded my arms across my chest. "Maxim thinks he was wronged when Mia was given to Boris. We can play on that. He assumes I'll fall for his charms, so now I will—almost. I'll make him think he came so close to having a mate, but once again, it's being taken away from him."

The entire room acted as if I were speaking a foreign language, and, to them, I supposed I was. I share a look of understanding, however, with the queen, who nodded her approval despite her eyes filling with a little bit of terror as she glanced to Nickolai. She assumed I would use Nickolai to make Boris jealous, but that was never my intention. The crown prince had to stay safe at all costs.

Swallowing hard, I let my eyes roam over Nickolai and then shift to Atticus. "Let's make Maxim think that, like Mia, I've been given to someone else." Smiling, I looked at Atticus. "Fancy being my pretend boyfriend?"

Chapter 22

As I stood outside the apartment complex waiting for my date to arrive, I rolled my eyes, thinking about the absolute eruption that had happened after I'd asked Atticus to play my boyfriend. Nickolai had stood up so fast he knocked his chair over, and it hit the ground with such a loud bang the queen had jumped in her seat.

"Out!" Nickolai roared, and the room began to scatter.

Jack and Atticus froze as Nickolai growled at them to stay, and the queen arched her brow in amusement as I prayed to Eve that Nickolai would remain professional about things.

I mean, yeah, male vampires were possessive, but it wasn't like there was anything going on, really.

"Liar!" Nickolai's voice sounded huskily in my mind.

When the room was clear of all but Jack, Atticus, and the queen, Nickolai clenched and unclenched his fists. "It should be me."

"Why's that?" I retorted with a snort.

"Because."

"Whoa there, Shakespeare. Stop with all of the words."

I chuckled at my own joke even as Atticus turned a horrid shade of white, even for a vampire.

"You want this to be believable, right? You and Atticus have no chemistry."

"Neither do you and I." The words slipped from my lips before I could reign them in.

A snarl curled Nickolai's lips as he stalked forward, backing me against the wall as he leaned his face into the curve of my neck and inhaled, the sheer possessiveness in his stance sending a shiver along my spine.

I dropped my gaze, my face heating as Nickolai wrapped his hand around my throat and forced my eyes back to his.

Suddenly, I forgot we were not alone in the room. There was only Nickolai, and I was powerless to the way my body was reacting to him. It screamed to loosen the hold I had on myself, to indulge this aching need I had for him, and screw the consequences.

Nickolai released me and stepped away as suddenly as he'd approached, and I stumbled forward, blinking as I turned away from my embarrassment. How dare he do this to me in front of his mother, in front of my friends?

"I don't care."

"Excuse me?" Nickolai pivoted in my direction as I steeled my resolve. I wanted to hurt him, to wipe that smug smile off his face.

"I don't care how my body reacts to you. I'm touch-starved and lonely, but that doesn't mean we can convince Maxim that I'm being given to you as a prize. Atticus is the safer bet; we are the safer bet."

I said the words to convince myself more than anyone, even as Nickolai gave me a murderous look.

"I cannot stand by and watch you play house with Atticus. It will turn my stomach."

"Then don't watch. Stay up on that high horse and pretend I wasn't sick every time you cozied up to Nattie."

Nickolai blinked in surprise, and the queen cleared her throat.

"What my son should have said, Ryan, was how unrealistic it would be to have Atticus play the part of a boyfriend. Maxim is smart—smarter than most—and it would be easy for him to spot Atticus does not lean toward the female of our species."

A hushed, stunned silence followed the queen's words.

Inclining her head, she continued. "It matters not to me, gentlemen. I merely find it amazing what us women see when men disregard our intellects. Let us do them the courtesy, Ryan, of not disregarding theirs. Besides, who better than the crown prince to compete with for your hand? It will... how do you usually put it? Piss him off to no end?"

And that was how I ended up going on a date with Nickolai.

I made sure not to dress up too much, knowing the rogue would smell a rat if we overdid it, and left my hair loose, curling softly against my shoulders. Once ready, I stood outside, tapping my foot against the pavement as I waited.

We had hatched this plan under the assumption Maxim would be watching me, waiting to get me alone, but if his fascination with me had dwindled, then the rogue could slip away and we'd likely never catch him.

With my back to the entrance, I felt Nickolai appear before I saw him, my entire being more attuned to him than ever before. He wore a pair of basketball shorts and a loose red T-shirt stretched tight across his muscled chest. In his hands, he carried a picnic basket.

"Let's get this over with," I mumbled as I started forward, then freezing as Nickolai slipped his hand into mine and grinned down at me.

"Make it believable, Ryan. If you look constipated the entire time, Maxim will smell the trap a mile off."

Knowing he was right, I flashed him a smile, stretching on my toes to press a quick peck to his cheek that I swear had the prince purring. Hand in hand, we meandered through the quad, weaving through the throngs of people wandering campus, trying to get things done before curfew kicked in.

We deviated from the path, heading toward the bridge where I'd first encountered the rogue. I froze as it came into sight, my eyes wide at the array of fairy lights twined through the bridge's railings, a checked blanket already spread in the middle of the bridge.

I might've been a vampire, but I was a vampire who'd spent enough time watching Hallmark movies to be impressed with the setup. We hadn't left the apartment all day, so when I turned and eyed him with suspicion, he grinned. "Present from Jack and Atticus."

I rolled my eyes, and Nickolai slipped his hand from mine, shifting it to the small of my back and steering me toward the blanket. Lowering myself down, I stretched out my legs and placed my hands out behind me.

Nickolai kneeled beside me and set the basket down and pulled out champagne—straight from the royal stash! —chocolate-covered strawberries, and all kinds of delicious nibbles. I dove straight in, attempting to commandeer a strawberry when Nickolai swatted my hand, telling me to have patience.

He was enjoying this far too much.

The prince poured the champagne and handed me a glass. I took it, sipping slowly, unsure how my stomach would react considering the last time I'd had alcohol. Then again, having the person who'd wronged me dead as a dodo made sipping champagne easier.

Nickolai chatted away, telling me details about his mother's upcoming birthday party next week, the party that would be thrown to celebrate our liege's day of birth. I nodded and smiled at appropriate times, my answers sounding bored and tired as Nickolai growled to be more enthusiastic.

This was part of the plan, for me to look as if the last thing I wanted to do was deal with royal politics even if I was supposed to be in love with the prince. Dropping the royal talk, Nickolai lay down on the blanket, his tall frame stretching across the entire bridge.

My senses prickled, sending a shudder running through my body. Turning so I'd be looking down at Nickolai, I took one of the strawberries in my fingers and held the fruit to Nickolai's lips. He parted them slightly, the berry moving to just on the edges of his lips.

His eyes never wandering from mine, he bit down on the strawberry, flicking out his tongue to graze my fingers as he leaned up before sitting upright and took the rest of the fruit into his mouth. I grinned, putting my fingers in my mouth and sucking the flavor from them.

The heat in his eyes was enough to set the bridge on fire. We toyed with each other, joking and playing, feeding and drinking champagne until the curfew neared and our time was running short. Nickolai threw a piece of dried fruit at me, and I ducked, laughing softly as I downed my champagne, waiting for his next strike as I flicked a nut at him.

His arm snaked around my waist, pulling me astride him, my hands falling to his chest as he inched closer to me. My heartbeat kicked up an awful fuss as Nickolai tucked my hair behind my ear, leaning in so close his breath tickled my neck.

"I want so badly to kiss you. To claim you like I've wanted to do since you stormed back into my life. But when I do kiss you, *when* I claim you, it will be on our terms, not some rogue who has a hard-on for you."

One of my hands followed the path from his chest to his shoulder, cupping his face as I struggled to find a coherent word. "You seem very sure of yourself, Nicky."

"I am."

He tilted his head ever so slightly, the ghost of his lips on my neck, and this time, this time I didn't freeze or flinch because it was Nickolai and I trusted him.

Nickolai's phone vibrated, breaking the connection as I rolled off, looking extremely annoyed.

Nickolai groaned. "I have to take this."

"Of course you do."

"Hey, don't be like that, Ry. Please."

I turned my head away from him as Nickolai gave a very overexaggerated sigh and stormed off out of view. I drained another glass of champagne, and my body jerked to attention as I lowered the glass from my lips. Maxim had appeared at the end of the bridge, and I leapt to my feet and braced for an attack.

Maxim came into view as he lowered his hood, and I could see the resemblance he bore to his brother. But where Boris was sleek and regal, Maxim was wild strength, his shoulders broad, his face stern, his neck thick. He glanced in the direction in which Nickolai had disappeared, then back to me.

"If I had you pressed against my body, my little butterfly, I would not be called away by silly phone calls."

Taking a step toward him, I tilted my head as if interested in what he had to say. "Tell me, Max, tell me. How would it be different with you?"

The smile he gave me was breathtaking, and Maxim moved even closer, the need to hide his identity gone. "Clever, clever, girl. Tell me," Maxim rasped, "did my brother despair when you discovered his failures?"

I heard the hoarseness in his throat thicken as his eyes filled with hate for his brother.

"I'm not Boris's favourite person at the moment," I replied.

"No, I would think not."

We stared at each other for a moment, neither of us making any sudden movements. I stepped forward ever so slowly as Maxim regarded me.

"I know who you are as well, Ryan Callan—my beautiful butterfly created from the ashes of her parents' deaths."

"Did you kill them?" I spat.

Maxim smirked. "And what would you do, Ryan," he purred, holding his hands out as if he expected me to react, "if I told you it was, indeed, I who ripped your parents' heads from their bodies?"

His statement rocked me to my core. Maxim was a murderer, but he hadn't killed my parents—he probably didn't even know their names. My parents hadn't been decapitated; they'd died of multiple stab wounds.

Shaking my head, I gave Maxim a look of surprise. "Why lie, Maxim? Why take the blame for something you didn't do? Do you really wish to be villainized so much you take responsibility for others' deeds?"

"Clever Ryan—far more than her species gives her credit for. Beautiful, smart, and a warrior as well. The prince will never know your worth. Come with me now, and I will make you a queen among vampires."

I needed to switch gears, to throw Maxim off his game, hoping he'd get sloppy. His intelligent eyes flashed with lust as he studied me, and I knew exactly where to kick him to hurt him the most—his heart.

Channeling my best Nattie impression, I chuckled. "Oh, Max, I pity you really. Why would you think I would trade a real prince for the likes of you? I mean, Boris isn't exactly a catch, but Mia still chose him over you. Why is that? Did you have *problems*, Max?"

Maxim didn't catch my meaning under I dropped my eyes to his crotch and then lifted them back to his bloodred eyes once again with a shrug.

Maxim sneered, flashing his stained teeth as he lurched forward a step or two. "Come closer and see for yourself, butterfly. I will show you how much of a man I am."

Rolling my eyes, I dismissed him with a wave of my hand, feeling a presence behind me. I dropped to my stomach on instinct as a second rogue flew over me. Pivoting, I smashed a glass and drove the shards into his throat the moment I was on my feet again. The blood gurgled from him as the vampire tried to scream in agony, stopping almost immediately as I ripped the glass from his throat and plunged it into his chest.

I tossed the dead rogue to the side, stepping over his body as I rolled my shoulders. "If you want me, Max," I said, taunting the other vampire, "come and get me."

Maxim paused, highly amused by my bravado. "In which way, darling? Do not get me wrong—both ways involve rope, but I feel it is important to clarify my intentions before we continue."

There was a 99.9 percent certainty this would not end well for me.

The other 0.01 percent were the odds I would win.

Hell, sometimes even *I* got lucky.

"Oh, by Eve, *men*," I said in exasperation. "Can't we just kill each other without the sexual innuendo?"

Distracted by my snark, I took the opportunity to surge forward, my sai in my hands a heartbeat later as Maxim pulled a dagger from his waist. I leapt, bringing my weapons down, the clash of metal screaming through the air as we collided.

Maxim was strong, there was no denying it as his hand closed around my throat, squeezing so tightly I was sure he'd snap my neck like a twig. I attempted a move my girl Arya Stark had perfected, dropping one of my sai and then the other, letting the second fall into my now-free hand and shoving the sai through Maxim's ribs, trying to pierce his heart.

The vampire flung me away, my sai thankfully coming with me, and I rolled with the momentum of my body when I hit the ground, coughing at the soreness in my throat. Maxim let loose a roar of pure animal frustration, and I rose, darting forward and kicking up my other sai, then falling into an attack position.

Maxim pressed a hand to his ribs, growling at the

blood he felt as he staggered backward.

It was now or never; I had to kill him now.

Starting forward with a growl, my rumble cut off as the wind changed and a number of scents accosted me. My eyes darting to the forest, I saw red eyes shining through the trees, so bloody many I couldn't count them all.

Hundreds of rogue vampires, men and women—warriors, from the way they carried themselves—stepped out of the trees, various weapons in their hands that told me their ranks were many. We were more outnumbered than we'd imagined, and I knew this was not a war I could win by myself, no matter how skilled I was.

Maxim sneered as he retreated, the support he had marking him as truly a king amongst rogues. He tipped an imaginary hat to me as one of his vampires came forward and helped him away.

I snarled in frustration, even as Maxim turned back to me.

"I will see you again soon, Ryan Callan. And perhaps then you will see you were wrong to choose the Sanguine Crown over me."

"I doubt that, Max, but why wait? Let's finish this now... or are you afraid to have your ass handed to you by a girl?"

The rogue holding Maxim waved the field of rogues forward, but as they closed the distance, sending my heart ricocheting into the stratosphere, Maxim held up a hand to halt them.

"Think on my words, little butterfly. You are wasted bowing to a crown who would betray you. When we come face-to-face again, if you do not join me in creating my kingdom, one of us will die."

I snorted. "The only kingdom we'll create together, Maxim, will be six feet long and six feet deep. I'll make sure it's dug for you."

As one unit, the rogues retreated into the forest, and I ran a hand gingerly over the abrasions on my throat when they were gone. Sinking to the ground, I sheathed my sai and took a massive gulp from the champagne bottle. I barely noticed that Nickolai, along with Jack and Atticus, had returned, no doubt having witnessed my failure.

Glancing up, I offered Jack the bottle of champagne and cocking my brow. "Well, I think we're all fucked. They have an army. If they launched an assault right now, we'd all be dead."

I didn't bother to listen as the men made calls and updated the crown with regards to what happened. But I found myself thinking on Maxim's fake confession. Why had he claimed to have killed my parents when he must have known I'd know he was lying? Someone had to know exactly what happened that night, and I would find out.

Nickolai crouched down and asked me what was wrong. For a moment, I considered telling him, but I didn't. I kept it to myself. Instead, I let Nickolai help me to my feet and gave him a smile so fake, I felt sick at myself.

But what were a few lies between friends, right?

Chapter 23

THE NEXT FEW DAYS WERE A BLUR OF STRATEGY MEETINGS and frenzied calls to the vampires of other, smaller courts for aid. Should the rogues eviscerate the Romanov vampires, we reminded them, what would stop them from spreading across Europe and Africa?

As a lot of foreign dignitaries would be coming for the queen's birthday celebration, it was decided discussions would take place after the party. Nickolai and I remained on campus for the few days as classes resumed, and I finally got to have the college experience—pouring over textbooks and feeling alive during debates on religion and politics.

I spent a lot of time with Krista, too, laughing harder than I'd ever laughed, but in the back of my mind I was constantly thinking about my parents. I felt driven to discover the secrets behind their deaths and had planned to grill Jack, but he'd been suspiciously absent for the last few days.

Avoiding Nickolai was harder than finding Jack; the crown prince was everywhere I went, it seemed. Even when Krista and I went to a movie night at the restaurant where we'd had our first conversation, Nickolai was there with the remainder of his gang of guy friends.

When the on-screen vampire flashed his fangs I groaned, knowing all too well the clichés that would follow: the clap of thunder and flash of lightning as the vampire dipped his well-endowed companion low, exposing ample cleavage to the audience before sinking his fangs into her neck. Turning away from the absurdity, I caught Nickolai watching me from afar.

Before I could give into the desire to glance in his direction again, Krista nudged me, handing me some popcorn. I smiled at her, taking the popcorn as she turned back to the movie. We'd had so much fun together lately, and I was surprised at how much I'd let myself relax—even when my mind was a constant melee of questions.

Now, having said goodbye to Krista, I waited outside for the car that would take us home for the next few days—a long weekend of diplomatic pleasantries. Well, that's what the school thought, anyway.

Shifting my weight to my right side, I wondered if Maxim was recovered by now. The memory of his fingers on my throat was still enough to rankle me. I would train harder; next time, I'd be ready. Not even his army of rogues would stop me from ending him.

The car pulled up to the curb, and I ducked inside, not waiting for Nickolai. I enjoyed a brief respite before the door opened and he slid in, the air heating around us as I struggled to go back to how we'd been before. He'd tried to pry my thoughts from me, but I'd brushed off his concerns.

We made the journey in silence, and the moment we

arrived at the compound, I scampered away like I was being chased. Nickolai made to follow after me but was halted by his father as he welcomed his son home.

I secluded myself in my room for most of the night and then the following day, rising to dress in my formal guard uniform despite my worries that, since I hadn't killed Maxim, Nickolai would rescind my promotion to his guard. Sweeping my hair off my face, I braided it so it hung loosely down the front of my uniform, the ends free of color as I tried to be respectful of the queen's birthday.

The party was in full swing when I arrived, and I kept to the shadows as I slipped into the ballroom. A full-blown orchestra was seated where the thrones were normally located, the queen content to be whirled around by her youngest son. They played a slowed-down version of Alessia Cara's "Out of Love," and it was beautifully done.

My eyes roamed around the room, taking in the vampires from all around the globe, the contrast in skin tones and accents so tantalizing it made me smile. My smile dropped, however, as I considered if someone wanted to rid the world of all of its most influential vampires, then now would be the time to mount an assault.

Spying Jack dressed impeccably in a uniform that, apart from the badge attached to the lapel of his jacket, matched my own, I stepped out of the shadows and hot-footed it in his direction. Before I reached him, however, I was ambushed by the Heathers.

Each one of the girls looked like a model—dripping in jewels and dolled up to the nines. They circled me like a mangy pack of dogs, Nattie giving me her trademark sneer as she said my name in greeting.

"Ryan."

"Natalia." I didn't bother greeting the rest of the sheep as Nattie tried to bore holes in me with her laser-beam eyes.

After several heartbeats, I sighed, making to step outside their little circle. "Well, this has been anything but fun, ladies. I'll just leave now."

Nattie stepped in front of me again, blocking my way as she leaned in, the scent of her flowery perfume an insult to my nose. "You think he will choose you, right? You think just because he asked his mother to be allowed to choose his own bride, he'll pick you instead of one of us?"

"I have absolutely no idea what you're talking about." And I didn't. I was so clueless Cher Horowitz would have approved.

"Nickolai asked his mother to let him pick his queen, and she agreed. It's tradition for the reigning monarch to choose their child's spouse."

Taking a step back and almost colliding with Farah Nasir, I held up my hands. "Again, I haven't the foggiest as to what you're going on about. Ask Nickolai himself if you're so bothered, but get the hell out of my face."

"Nickolai might keep you as a consort, but you will *never* be *queen!*"

Her shriek came out shriller than she'd expected, and I laughed as her face reddened.

"And *you* will? Oh please, get a grip, Nattie. You're sleeping with his baby brother because he dissed-and-dismissed you. The difference between me and you is you reek of desperation and everyone can smell it."

261

Nattie lifted her palm to strike me, and my fingers snapped up to catch her before she connected with my face. "Try it, Nattie. Let's see who ends up bloody."

"Ladies, is there a problem?"

Kristoph's voice cut through the tension as Nattie tried to take back control of her hand. I maintained my grip on the first attempt, and again for fun on the second, letting her go on the third attempt and grinning as she staggered backward. I snapped my teeth at the other girls, and they stepped out of my way.

Kristoph grinned as I strode by, patting him on the cheek as I passed. "Don't forget to muzzle your pets, My Liege. Dangerous animals should always be broken in, you know."

The prince's laughter followed after me as I returned to my pursuit of Jack. Crossing the floor, I nodded to vampires who bowed their heads in my direction. I must have made it halfway across the dancefloor before a shadow bore down on me and I twisted to discover Nickolai blocking my way.

Handsome as always, his uniform clung to his toned body as if molded to him. His eyes twinkled in the dim light, his smile as bright as the sun. Placing a hand across his torso, he formally bowed to me, holding out his hand as he straightened.

"May I have this dance?"

"No, you bloody can't!" I exclaimed loudly.

Twitters of nervous laughter escaped the people around us, and I shot daggers at Nickolai for embarrassing me in front of everyone.

"How can you decline your crown prince?" he asked calmly.

I quirked my brows, a rebellious smile threatening to appear on my lips. "Is that an order, My Liege?"

"If it means you'll dance with me, yes, goddamn it, it's an order."

Nickolai didn't wait for me to respond, and the next thing I knew he'd lifted my arms to his shoulders and placed his hands on my waist. The music changed tune, and we disappeared into the crowd of bodies.

When no one surged forward to pry us apart, I rested my head against his chest, his heartbeat a comforting pulse against my ear. I ignored the pointed stares and murmured comments as we passed by, allowing him to sway his body against mine for the length of the song before I uncoiled my arms from around his neck and placed my hands to his chest.

"I'm not done yet," Nickolai purred as he spun me toward a darker corner of the room and my pulse, bloody hell, it raced.

I tried to move away from him, only to find my back against a pillar.

Nickolai crowded me, oblivious to those openly gawking at us. He lowered his head as if to kiss me, but I ducked at the last minute and Nickolai got nothing but air.

His chest rumbled as he spun to me. "I've been wanting to kiss you all damn day."

And by Eve, I wanted him to kiss me, too.

Instead, I said, "Why did you ask your mother to let you choose your queen?"

Nickolai jerked back in surprise, his eyes darting to his brother and Nattie, who watched us with vastly different expressions on their faces.

"My little brother enjoys pillow talk far too much," Nickolai groaned, trying to steer us back to our previous positions.

I quickly shook off his advances. "Nicky, you know we can't. I can never be queen."

"Laws are made to be broken, Ryan—especially by kings."

I threw my hands in the air. "You don't get it—I don't *want* to be queen."

"Is it that you don't want to be queen, or you don't want me?" Nickolai asked, bracing himself as if he expected me to reach out and remove his heart from his chest if I told him I didn't want to be his.

That was the problem, though. No matter how much I denied it, I wanted him, I just didn't want all the baggage that came with it.

My phone chose that moment to ring, Krista's name appearing on the screen as I pressed end, but the ringer sounded again as soon as I tried to slide it back into my pocket.

Pressing the green button, I quickly muttered, "Krista, not really a good time. Can I call you back?"

Laughter, cold and heartless, stopped me dead in my tracks as the voice rang down the phone. "Having a little spat with your prince, my butterfly?"

My heart dropped into my stomach as my eyes scanned the room. Someone was spying on me for Maxim.

"Well, you know what they say, Maxim—the make-up sex is nearly worth the argument."

At my words, Nickolai lifted his hand to cut off the music, and the entire room fell silent. As Jack and Atticus came over, I turned on the loudspeaker on my phone so everyone could hear what Maxim was saying.

"I believe you look radiant tonight, my love. Even fiercer than you were when you nearly stabbed me through the heart."

"Tell me where you are, Maxim, and you can see how fierce I am this time when I do not miss," I purred.

"You know where I am, darling," he chortled. "Krista is keeping me company."

"I swear by Eve," I yelled into the phone, my knees threatening to buckle as I heard a whimper in the background, "if you so much as lay a finger on her, you bastard, I will gut you like a fish!"

"All you have to do is say you'll be mine, Ryan. Say it, and I leave Krista as pretty as I found her."

"I'll do it. I'll go with you. Just let her go. *Please.*"

His laughter deepened, sending chills across my flesh. "If I thought you meant it, I would walk away this moment. But alas, I cannot trust you. Now you will know I am serious."

"Let me talk to her, Maxim. If you want me to trust you, then let me speak to her."

There was a moment of silence, and then Krista's voice came on the line.

"Ryan?"

"Krista—you stay alive, you hear me? I'm coming."

Krista was silent for a minute, and I was terrified she was already gone and everything I wanted to say would remain unsaid, just like with my parents. Then I heard a crack, and Krista yelped in pain.

"I think someone turned off his humanity switch."

I laughed as my heart blew apart into a thousand

pieces.

"Ryan?"

"Yes, my friend?" I replied, my voice so low I was surprised Krista had heard me.

"He wants me to tell you it's all your fault, but it's not. I don't regret being your friend—you have to know that."

"It *is* my fault, Krista. I dragged you into this."

"I wouldn't change a thing, Ryan. Please, tell Conrad I love him, okay?"

I swallowed hard, then promised her I would. "I'll make it in time, Krista. I'll make it. You stay brave for me, okay? Don't give him a fucking thing."

"Say goodbye to Ryan, Krista."

I screamed at Maxim so loudly I almost missed Krista telling me goodbye. Just before the phone call ended, Krista's last words hit me like a sledgehammer.

"Kick his ass for me, Ryan."

The line went dead, and I dropped my phone and bolted across the floor, Nickolai chasing after me. I waited for no car, simply using all the strength Eve gave me and praying to my ancestors I would get there in time. I outran the boys out of sheer anguish. I promised her I would get there in time.

But I was too late. I'd asked her to be brave, to hang on for me, but I didn't make it in time.

Pushing open the door to Krista's dorm, the scent of blood overwhelmed me, leading me on a trail to where I knew my friend lay dead. Shoulders squared, I entered her bedroom and cried out, horrified.

Krista's blonde hair was soaked in blood from a gash across her forehead. She lay on the bed, naked, with a diamond-encrusted dagger stabbed through her heart. Her eyes stared blankly at me, filled with the horror of what she'd endured. The dagger was overkill, merely there for dramatic effect. The various fang marks covering her entire body betrayed her true cause of death. The bastard had let every one of his lackies take a bite of her.

Swallowing down bile, my eyes fell to a folded piece of paper nestled between Krista's uncovered breasts.

Tentatively, I took the paper off her body, my eyes scanning it for a clue as to where Maxim had gone, but the scrawl on the paper simply said *A butterfly for my butterfly*.

I glanced back at Krista's torso, and the sight of her butterfly tattoo wrenched sobs from my body as I went to the bathroom to empty the contents of my stomach. When I was finished, I splashed water on my face and came back into the room.

Nickolai stood in the doorway of the bedroom, the horror in his eyes mirroring my own. I was drowning in grief and needed my anger to stay afloat. Striding over to Nickolai, I slapped him across the face so hard his head snapped round.

Jack tried to step in, to stop me from essentially committing treason, but Nickolai stopped him. I beat my fists against his chest until my strength left me.

"This is on you. You get that, right? I told you I didn't want friends, but you and your mother just couldn't let me be. I was safe. These emotions couldn't cripple me. But you dug your heels in and decided what was right for me. I despise you. Do you hear me, My Liege?"

Nickolai said nothing.

"Ryan," Jack said, stepping in, "I get you're upset,

267

kiddo, but the only one responsible for your friend's death is Maxim."

"No. Maxim may have ended it, but *he* told me to make friends. And now she's dead. Are you happy now? Are you fucking happy?"

Just like that, any tentative relationship we'd built over the last few months was gone; suddenly, we were strangers again.

I took my anger with me as I turned back to Krista. Using my fingers, I gently closed her eyes, pressing a quick kiss to her forehead. I crumpled the piece of paper in my hands and dropped it to the floor, clenching my jaw as I stormed past Jack.

Nickolai caught me by the elbow, and I jerked my arm from his grasp. "*You* don't get to touch me anymore. Don't speak to me; don't even breathe in my direction."

"Ryan, please... I'm—"

"If you say you're sorry, I will stab you. You and I are done, Nickolai."

Too exhausted to run back to the compound, I let myself be driven back, ignoring everyone as I climbed the stairs to my room. Once inside, I slid down the door and cried until my lungs burned and my cries turned into screams of agony against the press of my fists to my mouth.

I allowed myself time to grieve, and then I dried my eyes, packed some clothes, and gathered my weapons. Opening the safe that was on my dresser, I stashed a couple grand in my bag and then strapped my sai on.

Standing on my bed, I pushed the small window above me upward and hoisted myself onto the roof as rain began to pelt down on me.

I would kill every single person who'd dared to lay a finger on Krista.

I would get vengeance for her if it killed me.

I would hunt down every single rogue in Ireland if I had to. Blood would spill; they would fear me.

There was a new kind of rogue in town, and her name was Ryan Callan.

Epilogue

"She's gone."

"Good work."

The vampire at the other end of the phone sounded so proud it was hard not to let her heart swell at the sound of it.

"It's time for phase two, my dear. Time to use those feminine wiles of yours."

"I won't let you down, I promise."

The call ended, and she stashed the phone under the sink in her bathroom. Exiting the bathroom, she let her silk robe drop to the ground. The vampire in her bed gave her a lustful smile as he crooked his finger at her.

"Come to bed."

"As you command, My Liege."

Kristoph's husky laugh sent bile rising from her stomach as she crawled into bed, switching off her mind as Kristoph rolled on top of her and Natalia focused on what her prize would be at the end of all this.

A crown of her own.

Ryan's Personal Playlist:

- "Devotion" (ft. Cameron Hayes)—Dimension
- "Loner"—YUNGBLUD
- "Song About You"—Mike Posner
- "ME!" (feat. Brendon Urie of Panic! At The Disco)—Taylor Swift
- "Don't Hurt Like It Used To"—Grace Carter
- "Hold Me While You Wait"—Lewis Capaldi
- "Who Will Save You"—Katie Garfield
- "Love Me Anyway" (feat. Chris Stapleton)—P!nk
- "Punch Bag"—YONAKA
- "90 Days" (feat. Wrabel)—P!nk
- "Tell Me How"—Paramore
- "Feel Something"—Bea Miller
- "F.I.N.E."—Too Close to Touch
- "Will We Talk?"—Sam Fender
- "You Need To Calm Down"—Taylor Swift
- "All Day And Night"—Jax Jones & Martin Solveig Present Europa Jax Jones
- "Time"—NF
- "Death of Me"—PVRIS
- "Mad Love"—Mabel
- "You'll Never Find Me"—Korn
- "I Caught Myself"—*Twilight* Soundtrack Version

Paramore
- "Poison"—Freya Ridings
- "Time In A Bottle"—YUNGBLUD
- "What's It Like"—You Me At Six
- "Wishbone"—Freya Ridings
- "Love Is Fire"—Freya Ridings
- "One-Minute Man"—Missy Elliott
- "Move, Bitch"—Disturbing Tha Peace
- "Salute"—Little Mix
- "When the Lights Go Out"—Radio Edit Five
- "If Ya Gettin' Down"—Five
- "Pony"—Ginuwine

My Writing Playlist:

- Feral Love—Chelsea Wolfe
- Hurts 2B Human (feat. Khalid)—P!nk
- The World We Made—Ruelle
- Hollow Crown—Ellie Goulding
- Medicine—The Pale White
- Nunchuk—SAINT PHNX
- Flake—FIDLAR
- Crowbar—Frank Carter & The Rattlesnakes
- Adrenaline—Simple Creatures
- Turn on Me—The National
- Lose Our Heads—YONAKA
- God Was Never on Your Side—Motörhead
- That Dress—The Pale White

- Legendary—Skillet
- Don't Wait 'Til Tomorrow—YONAKA
- Sick Thoughts—Lewis Blissett
- Gun in Your Pocket—Sick Love
- Bad Guy—Billie Eilish
- Find the Water—The Coronas
- Burning Bridges—Bea Miller
- Rockstar—YONAKA
- Be Someone—CamelPhat
- Dance in the Dark—Au/Ra
- Further Than The Planes Fly—Eves Karydas
- Good Intentions—Too Close To Touch
- Antisocial—(with Travis Scott) Ed Sheeran
- She's Not There—YONAKA
- Waves—YONAKA
- In Dreams—Ben Howard
- You Need To Calm Down—Recorded At Abbey Road Studios, London YONAKA
- Hope for the Underrated Youth—YUNGBLUD

Acknowledgments

FIRST AND FOREMOST, I NEED TO THANK MY PARENTS, FOR always believing in me and pushing me to achieve my dreams. If I am resilient, it is because you guys taught me to never give up. I love you both so very much.

LJ AND TAYLOR—You two bring so much happiness into my life that being an auntie really is the best thing in the world. I love you both to infinity and beyond.

I have to thank the amazing ladies of Clean Teen Publishing, REBECCA, COURTNEY AND MARYA, for their continued belief in me as an author. We have experienced so much together that it can only make the bond stronger, and we worked hard and never stopped believing that, together, we could be unstoppable.

MELANIE NEWTON—By Eve, words cannot describe just how grateful I am to have you in my life! You kick my ass when I doubt myself, you listen when I need to vent, spark my creativity when I need it the most. I mean, Ryan and Chaos Theory would not be possible if it wasn't for your invaluable input. I mean, you vetoed half the names for the main character but I can totally forgive you for that...

MARYA—Thank you again for such an amazing cover and bringing Ryan to life in such a gorgeous imagery.

Special thanks to CHELSEA BRIMMER for taking such good care of Chaos Theory and making sure this book is ready for readers to sink their teeth into.

JAIME CROSS—My trusty beta reader...thank you for all you do!

KRISTA MEYERS GILL—Thank you for letting me use not only your name, but your personality to create such a great character. You may not have known that you were going into the book but you are, and book Krista is just as awesome as real-life Krista!

To my friends, MICHELLE, HELEN, ORLA AND SUSAN, thank you for keeping me sane and supporting me.

To MELANIE'S MUSERS—you guys are the best group of people ever! The love and support that you give not only me, but other authors is amazing and I heart you all for being such amazing human beings.

To GREG—thank you for the music recommendations, the shout outs and for the inevitable side eye from Mel when you say something inappropriate on the live shows every Sunday! Comedy gold!

And last, but certainly, not least, thank you to THE READERS, whether you have been with me since the start or have recently joined the family, I thank you for reading because I am not an author without you guys...Slainte, go raibh maith agaibh go léir.

About the Author

SUSAN HARRIS IS A WRITER FROM CORK, IRELAND AND when she's not torturing her readers with heart-wrenching plot twists or killer cliffhangers, she's probably getting some new book related ink, binging her latest tv or music obsession, or with her nose in a book.

She loves to hear from her fans, so be sure to visit SUSANHARRISAUTHOR.COM to find out where you can stalk her!